RELIC HUNTER

By

CC DeHavilland

Published by

Llyfrau Cambria Books, Wales, United Kingdom.

Cambria Books is a division of

Cambria Publishing.

Discover our other books at: www.cambriabooks.co.uk

"My life often seemed to me like a story that has no beginning and no end. I had the feeling that I was an historical fragment, an excerpt for which the preceding and succeeding text was missing. I could well imagine that I might have lived in former centuries and there encountered questions I was not yet able to answer; that I had been born again because I had not fulfilled the task given to me."

Carl Jung

CONTENTS

PROLOGUE

The halls of the old granite-built library smelt of old books, leather and polish. The slightest noise echoed through the corridors and enormous central void. For a brief moment, sitting at the oversized oak desk surrounded by the finest leather-bound reference books, watching people immersed in their own little worlds of research, made Jake feel almost like an accepted part of the establishment. He pulled his messenger bag closer to him and quietly hunted inside for a pen and buried his head into 'Herodotus's Histories.' It was only when the scornful and dismissive looks poured down on him that his bubble burst. He may have been a little sensitive, but the attitude was there. The young man hadn't been to university to study under one of the well renowned names in his chosen field. Neither did he have the luxury to be able to call himself an 'old boy' of some exclusive school. He had only got to where he was because of his passion, hard work, tenaciousness and sheer bloody mindedness. A handful of A levels at a sixth form college was the sum of his academic prowess. But this wasn't the yardstick to measure a man by, particularly not this one. A brain can be trained in many ways, and he certainly had a brilliant mind, he was just never given the opportunity to prove it. Nevertheless, it would never stop him doing what he adored — delving into the past and answering questions that had been hidden away for centuries. It was fair to say that 'the establishment' didn't think much of Jake Finch, but then again, he didn't think much of them.

Scribbling on a pad, Jake became aware of a presence standing over him. He looked up and saw a tall man cradling a couple of books and staring at him with disdain. Behind him, one of his lackeys, eager to impress.

'This is a place for scholars Finch, not an all-night cafe. When are you going stop infecting places like this?' The individual spat the words, obviously unimpressed with the young man.

Jake looked up and placed a book over the writing on his paper pad and closed a nearby reference book. 'Charming Muir — did they teach you that at Cambridge or Eton?'

'Oxford, actually. But I wouldn't expect you to know that. What is it now?' Muir strained and saw the book Finch had closed. 'Herodotus? What could be interesting you now, Greeks? Persians? You're after the Golden Fleece or is it Atlantis? That's A-T-L-A...' he said scornfully.

'Brilliant! What do you want Muir?'

'I thought I'd let you know that the dig in the Hebrides was a waste of time, just as I thought it would be. Your research is appalling, your practices are laughable, and it was ultimately three weeks of freezing my balls off on some windswept island for nothing.'

'If you were so sure it was going to be a waste of time, why did you exert so much effort stealing my work and deriding me yet again?'

'Well, as you ask, I conducted my own research — the way one is supposed to do. If there was a chance of finding the "Jade and Golden Buddha," then it would be appropriate that a proper archaeologist should find it and prove the theory that the Chinese travelled long sea-bound journeys, far before they were thought to have happened - and not some idiot on a Duke of Edinburgh's award scheme weekend,' Muir sneered.

'Well, as we're being honest with each other, I'll let you know something. While you were playing it by the book at my expense, I asked the farmer if he needed any help with his livestock with it being lambing season, and he was delighted.

2

That meant I was able to watch what you were doing and take a look around as well. Although you managed to pilfer most of my work, it wasn't everything and I did my own detecting and inspected the coastline. It occurred to me quite early on that you were digging in the wrong place.'

Muir placed his books on the table and leant in, closing in on Finch as he continued talking.

'The coastline was treacherous but, in my research, there were a few references to a whale. Now whales are sometimes spotted up and around there, but it is not a common sighting, so why bother talking so much about one. Then it occurred to me — what does a whale do? It has a blow hole so it expels air and water then breathes again. Anyway, I put two and two together and watched the coast and sure enough, on the high tides, a blow hole would erupt from out of the rocks, so I followed it. A quite perilous journey and it meant I got wet and cold, plus it took some balls on my behalf as I had to enter the water and allow myself to be sucked into the current of the blow hole.'

'Does this have some sort of point to it?' Muir sighed.

Finch smiled and ignored Muir's interruption. 'Well, I was dragged into a small, claustrophobic cave system, and discovered some artifacts in a corner, which proved the area had been used to store merchandise and indeed that travellers from distant shores have visited the island long before history tells us they did. My paper will show all my findings.'

Muir was visibly angered by Finch, 'Your paper!' Muir's voice was raised enough to draw attention to their conversation. A deliberate attempt to embarrass Finch. 'Your paper. Why would anyone in my profession waste their time on reading the scratchings of an amateur, uneducated child who can't get on a dig for love nor money. You are and always will be a laughingstock. So, do yourself and everyone else a favor and leave this to the people who have spent their lifetime studying and educating themselves in this field and hence know what they are doing. I'll even buy you a metal detector so you can play on the beach as a going away present. You're a joke Finch, a tiresome, pathetic joke and it is time to go!'

Finch was acutely aware that all eyes were on him, and he wished the earth would open and swallow him whole. The anger was rising, and his fist clenched. He wanted to vault the table and teach this arrogant sod a lesson. It was all he could do to quell his temper. But that wouldn't achieve anything, except merely prove that he was not to be taken seriously and was just a thug. Muir could tell that Finch was twitching and his initial bravado was leaving him. He was no match for Finch physically and although he had a vicious tongue, he was no fighter.

Finch ran his hand through his blond hair and packed up his belongings. He stood and stared intently at Muir with his piercing blue eyes. He was also aware that a lot of what Muir had said was true, and that cut deep.

'Don't worry Muir, it may seem a good idea now to knock you off your perch and onto your arrogant arse, but even I know that it wouldn't be the wisest course of action. Besides, my father always taught me that violence was never the answer. You're right, people will never take me as seriously as a man with your background and credentials. The great Raymond Muir, Eton, Oxford and distinguished fellow. So, I will need to up my game, get better and forge my own path. But what you won't do is stop me from carrying on and beat me down with your spiteful rhetoric. I will earn your respect and I will prove you wrong,' Finch said, brushing past Muir and heading for the exit. Then he stopped and swung around to Muir. 'I think you'll find that my paper will make a difference, particularly when I show them this.' With that, Finch removed a small green and gold carved Buddha from his bag and waved it at Muir.

Muir gasped as he saw the object and struggled to get any words out of his mouth.

Finch smiled, replaced the artefact in his pocket and winked at the attractive receptionist who was manning the desk. Finch would prove that he was no less of a scholar than Muir and any of the others.

This was just the start.

CHAPTER 1

20 years later.

The cool wind played with the loose sand and it danced over the surface of the desert like children skipping with the carefree abandonment of youth. The camels stirred and gave a muted rumbling roar and the flames from the log fire cracked and flared up into the starlit sky. The desert was a harsh foreboding environment but the prize for surviving it was the savage beauty it had to offer. It was bitter by night and relentlessly hot by day. Parched of water and abrasive. All the while, holding a mystique that had to be experienced at least once in a person's life to understand its attraction. The figure by the fire twitched. His eyeballs flitted uncontrollably while he dreamt yet another dream, so tangible that it could almost have been real.

***

1513. Branxton, Northumberland - England.

The cool air of the English summer morning had left a blanket of dew on every surface it caressed. There were men everywhere. Dirty, hungry, tired and cold. This Scottish army had amassed on the English border under the banner of James IV, keen to tell King Henry VIII that he was no potential overlord of Scotland. Although years of fighting had been ended by the Treaty of Perpetual Peace in 1502, the hatred was still tangible between the two patriotic neighbours, and it didn't take much to ignite the spark of war once again. Now, after much belligerent and truculent rhetoric from Henry, coupled with Scotland's 'Auld Alliance' with France, whom England were fighting already, meant that Scotland were ready to fight and were embedded on sassenach soil, keen to kill the English once again.

The atmosphere was tense but not fearful which, understandably, it should have been, for all war was a frightful business. Henry's army was vast, led by The Earl of Surrey and it consisted of 26,000 men, including artillery, archers, cavalry and infantry. They were all battle-hardened soldiers who were keen on clearing the Scots from their land. This was not a force that would have deterred the Scots though, for they amassed 30,000 men of their own, all filled with hatred and a desire to inflict as much damage and retribution upon the English as possible.

Gillie rose from his seat and stirred the pot of oats and barley to prevent it from catching and sat once more. His appearance was feral. His beard, unkempt hair and kilt gave him a barbaric and menacing look. As he sat watching the flames, a squat, solid man made his way toward Gillie's pot. As he passed, he slapped the crown of his head as if swatting an irritating horsefly. Gillie whipped round, his eyes ablaze at being accosted, only to calm immediately at the sight of his childhood friend and kinsman, Mowbraid.

'Here! I brought you some drink! This dammed weather seeps through to the very soul,' grumbled Mowbraid, throwing Gillie a bottle of mead he had liberated from the monks earlier. Gillie smiled.

'Ah! You're the man – Health!' he said, taking a fair slug from the bottle and instantly feeling the effects of the warm liquid permeating down his throat and around his body. 'What's happening?' asked Gillie.

Mowbraid sat beside him. 'Things are starting to move and the English are getting twitchy, not that there's any need. There's bloody thousands of the bastards.'

Gillie smiled, unscathed by the thought of hordes of Englishmen waiting to maim him. He took his pot off the fire and tried the concoction. It was good and the two men shared a warm meal before the day's proceedings. Suddenly, the call to arms came. A large, bullish man carrying a double-headed axe rallied around. 'Come on, you lazy bastards. Gets youse up to the line, and hurry on or you'll get the thick end of this up your arse!' The man indicated by shaking his axe at the soldiers.

All the men gathered their belongings and made haste to the line overlooking the English. The roars went up, first from the Scots and then the English. The noise was deafening but the calls were united against their foes and it sent a shiver up Gillie's spine. Before they knew it, the call was made and the Scots started to charge the line of The Earl's army.

Gillie was fit but the ground was heavy. He ran as fast as his legs could take him without a hint of fear in his heart: blood and adrenalin screaming through his veins. The English were getting closer and he picked his man. Sword in hand and targe in the other, he crashed headlong into an infantryman carrying the colours of Henry. Gillie was filled with battle frenzy. He had caught his enemy square in the throat with his shield, which stunned him and without a second thought, he whipped his sword round and opened up his face and neck with a single blow.

The throng was thick and there was barely room to move an arm. Blows rained in from all sides and it was as much luck as it was skill that Gillie wasn't sliced from another angle. As always, Mowbraid was at his side shrieking and laughing as he scythed his way through man after man. The blood ran fast and the smell of urine and faeces intermingled with warm blood was enough to make a man retch.

The fight was intense. Pushing forward, Gillie felt a sharp pain to his thigh. A blade had cut into his femoral muscle, though not enough to disable him. This just spurred him on even more and his blood-crazed eyes bore into the man who had just injured him. Then he heard a sound all men feared on the battlefield: the eerie hum of arrows in flight. Hundreds of them piercing the sky and impaling anything they hit. There wasn't time to cover up, just to pray that the arrows would miss their target and hit somewhere or someone else. Men from both sides screamed in agony as broad-heads and bodkins slammed into muscle, bone and soft tissue. The man next to Gillie tried to cry out, but it was a guttural growl as the arrow had sunk itself deep into his throat.

Gillie was in his element, completely focused on pushing through and killing anything in his path, but he was aware that his footing had changed. Instead of the slippery smear of blood, it was now sticky and tacky and then the smell gave it away. He was standing in a trail of tar laid by the English earlier. He instantly panicked and called to Mowbraid. 'Mo! Get back. We're standing in tar! They'll light us up like a torch. Get back!' Mowbraid looked down and realised that it was true, but the crush behind was too much. The only way out was forward through the English. But they had little time to worry, for the haunting noise of arrows punctuated the air once more, but this time they were alight. As soon as the flames hit the tar, it ignited with a roar, sucking the oxygen from the air and spawning thick black smoke into the sullen sky. All around Gillie and Mowbraid were thick, yellow angry flames spitting and grabbing hold of anyone close and inflicting its own personal misery on them. Gillie could feel the intense heat building all around him and the air was filled with the anguished cries of men burning alive. Gillie was scared and couldn't get out.

He whirled his sword around, trying to carve a way through the lines, which had now fractured significantly with the introduction of the fire, but the acrid smoke was suffocating and Gillie was losing strength. The panic was welling up inside and overpowering all his other emotions, and then everything started to fade and the darkness enveloped him.

CHAPTER 2

Jake woke with a start. It was dark and the fire was still alight. He rubbed his face with the palms of his hands and grabbed his water bottle from his backpack and took a swig. Sleep wasn't going to be an option now; just a bit of peace to collect his thoughts and some warmth offered from the flames was all he could expect. The small campfire was mesmerising and Jake found himself lost in the twisted dance the flames created. They were magical, but they were menacing. Lulling their audience into a trance, just waiting for the right time to pounce and devour whatever it was that dared to venture too close. Jake blinked hard and removed his gaze from the glow and thought about what the next day would bring, for he knew that he was close to uncovering the tomb of Satyros, which could in turn, if his studies were correct, lead him to the resting place of the so-called 'mythical' Library of Alexandria – in his view, the greatest of all the Wonders of the World and in no way a myth.

Jake didn't like labels but if he had to call himself something, it would be an historian and archaeologist. He was also a protector of days long gone, an adventurer, a man who craved a way to be able to touch the past and live the life of both the ordinary and extraordinary of yesteryear. Living in the present in this relentless modern world of excess and greed and frantic pressure, was a hell that Jake tried to escape and the past offered him the peace and excitement he needed. He was a man most definitely born into the wrong era. Growing up, his father died young of cancer, which meant that life was tough. He wasn't the type to go off the rails; in fact, he studied even harder, though his sixth form college never really offered the education he craved. He had dreams of studying at Oxford or Cambridge; he was certainly bright enough. But a lack of funds, coupled with poor opportunities, put pay to those lofty plans. Nevertheless, nothing was going to stop him from doing what he loved. In his spare time from working odd jobs, he would bury himself in books and languages, both ancient and modern. He was a sponge, absorbing every ounce of knowledge he could get. He would apply to get on digs and was occasionally successful, but he loathed the arrogant way the others treated him. He felt like the pot washer in amongst the commis and sous chefs. He hated that and learnt little as they were not willing to give him the time of day. So, he followed his own path and began to make his mark. He was still shunned from the established 'old school' circles as being a chancer and merely just 'playing the game.' He was no academic. No letters after his name to say that he knew what he was talking about. One man called his theories flimsy and whimsical and without substance. Plus, his general appearance made people wary and perhaps jealous. He was dark from his outdoor ventures, with a mop of blond hair. Tall with a good physique but had a regal quality that gave him a certain 'air', a quality the historical society despised, particularly as their wives rather fawned over him like one would over a cute puppy. He was charismatic without being smarmy and had striking blue eyes which gave him an ethereal look. He would say 'to hell with the establishment' and hated them collectively for their attitude, but deep down, he wanted to be accepted and welcomed as their equal. This wasn't to satisfy his ego but more to be thought of as their equal. He may not have any official credentials, but he had worked hard to get to where he was today and people hired him because he got the job done, but a little appreciation would have been nice.

Although born and raised in West Wales, his tanned looks and English accent always betrayed his Celtic roots. Roots he was fiercely proud of. Indeed, his little cottage made of Welsh flint overlooking Poppitt Beach outside of the town of Cardigan, was the only place he could really relax and unwind. It was his little piece of heaven in an unsettled, messy and often spiteful world, and he adored it.

As he sat on his roll mat on the sandy ground, he retrieved his old Moleskin notebook and thumbed through the leaves. He came to a page with its corner dog-eared and in bold letters was the phrase 'ANGELS WILL SHOW THE WAY!'

He sighed and stared up at the night sky which was ablaze with a billion stars. 'Angels huh? Well, if you are up there, you couldn't give me a hand now, could you?' Jake smiled whilst addressing the heavens. He was a Christian, but not a practising one. He never went to church, only read the Bible if it was part of an historic investigation, but he believed, and more so, wanted to believe. His problem, and one of the reasons he was sitting on the parched, cold ground in the middle of North Africa was, that he needed to KNOW! Believing was not good enough. He was happy to believe for a while, but he wanted to know the facts. The world for Jake Finch wasn't grey; it was black or white. He didn't like grey, which was tough in his line of work as history was awash with assumption and hypothesis and he didn't like it; he liked facts. A reason why he was so fastidious in his work. As for religion, he allowed himself a little leeway, owing to the fact that he didn't want to be proved wrong. He had seen much of the world, good and bad, but he knew that there were some strange things that couldn't be explained and he would have to accept that. One thing was for sure, and that was Finch was a good man.

Dawn broke and the sun rose slowly over the desert and with it, the first rays of warmth to dull the chill of the night. Finch had already risen and was fixing a cup of coffee for himself, a prerequisite for the day. Accompanying him was a workforce of ten or so Egyptian diggers. These guys were the usual 'rent-a-crew, used for excavating in the hot Egyptian desert and they knew the routine well. Also present was the representative of the Antiquities Department from the Cairo Museum, Femi El Masri. He was a rotund jolly man with a wisp like comb-over, who always gave the impression of being a bit of a push-over. But Femi was nothing of the kind, he had a mind as sharp as a blade, coupled with a rare wit and cunning outlook. His knowledge of antiquities was barely paralleled, but money was his Achilles heel and Finch had paid him handsomely to enable him to gain access to the tomb. The deal was that everything in the tomb was Cairo's and all credit would be Egypt's too; all Finch wanted was to sift through the 'grey matter' and get the answers he desired to find what he was really looking for. The Great Library. Of course, the powers that be in Cairo would have had a vested interest in Finch's results. If the Great Library of Alexandria did exist, it would belong to Egypt and they would seek to lay claim to it, wherever it may be. Finch was positive it did; he had researched too long and forfeited too much of his life to be proved wrong. Moreover, there was a voice from somewhere that pushed him forward. It gave him hope when he doubted himself. With Femi's, help, he could complete his work without hindrance and get out of Egypt quickly.

Finch didn't like Egypt. It was strange that an adventurous historian would have such an active dislike of a place with so much rich history, but he loathed it. It wasn't just the heat; it was the culture. Everything had a price and everything was for sale. No one was trustworthy. There was no honour or moral courage and he hated that. The only thing that kept him here was his goal and the love of the rare items of historical note that Egypt had in abundance. His wish was to find what he wanted and get back to Wales.

Femi rose with a broad grin, dressed as always in a dirty suit, tie and leather shoes. An odd mode of dress for the desert but it suited his being. Finch, on the other hand, was wearing his white T-shirt, cargo trousers and ex-army issue desert boots and as usual, his well-worn beige baseball cap with black wrap-around glasses balanced on the peak.

'Good morning, my friend, *Salam Aleikum*,' Femi said in his soft voice, 'and Inshallah today may be the day that we will break through and find whatever it is we are looking for.' This was accompanied by one of the many handshakes he liked to offer.

'Here's hoping,' Finch retorted, just a little grumpy after his lack of sleep. 'Would you like some coffee – it's hot and fresh?' he asked Femi, but he had already headed towards the other Egyptians for a glass of hot sweet tea. It was all the Egyptians drank and not to Finch's taste at all.

It was now just gone one in the afternoon and the desert sun at its zenith had been particularly spiteful. Work on the dig was progressing, albeit at a slow pace. There was a definite change of soil and sand colour and they were at the right depth to be there or thereabouts. Finch took a break from the digging. He liked to lead from the front and get his hands dirty and the Egyptians liked that. Besides which, he knew that the moment his back was turned the pace of the dig would reduce significantly. He got to the tent, pitched fifty metres from the site and took a huge swig of lukewarm water and poured a little on his hand and rubbed his face and neck with it. Sitting slumped in a chair in the corner was Femi. For a local, he didn't seem to handle the heat well at all. He was still in his suit and was out for the count. His head had fallen backwards with his mouth wide open and was producing the sort of sound one would expect to hear from a lion trying to eat a live wildebeest whole. With a damp handkerchief in one hand and the other resting on his ample stomach, which was protruding from the bottom of his shirt, he was a sight to behold. Finch chuckled to himself and was just about to take another swig when there was a great shout and furore from the dig site.

Finch dropped the bottle and ran down to where the noise was coming from. When he got back to the site, he could see that a small part of a wall had been unearthed. The Egyptian workers stood motionless, anticipating that a great find of ancient Egyptian wealth had been discovered and awaited their next instructions. Finch stared at the wall. Could this be what he was looking for? He lifted his cap and ran his hand through his wavy, blond matted hair. He could hear the panting of Femi running down the slope behind. He was flustered, having been woken so suddenly by the commotion, but there was no way he was going to miss overseeing the unearthing of the tomb.

After a while, Finch gave the instruction, 'Knock it through – gently! Let's see what's inside.' The wiry Egyptian by the wall pulled a cloth over his mouth and nose and took the sledgehammer in his hands and struck the wall with surprising power for a man of his stature. Instantly, the wall began to succumb. And it wasn't too long before a hole large enough for a substantial man to put his whole torso through had been formed.

'Enough!' Finch shouted and held his hand up to emphasize the point. He removed his powerful Maglite torch from the holster on his belt and made his way to the hole. He peered through and smiled to himself. Inside, the walls were fairly plain with a few hieroglyphics, and apart from a sarcophagus on a stone table, all that was in the room was an ordinary silver box no bigger than a small suitcase. *This is it!* Finch thought. *This is bloody it!* He took a moment to control his emotions, for it was vital that he kept them in check otherwise, suspicions would be aroused.

'Let me see! Let me see!' shouted Femi, grabbing the torch from Finch and pushing his way past him to squeeze through the

15

gap. He shone the beam of light on all four walls and stared at the puny offerings that were being offered to him after so much effort.

'I am sorry, my friend. It appears that luck is a cruel puppeteer,' Femi said, handing him back the torch.

'But this is it. This is what I have come here to find,' answered Finch.

Femi squinted, looking at him with suspicion. There was a pause, almost uncomfortably so. Then Femi erupted with enthusiasm. 'TEA! Come, let us have tea!' He turned Finch and guided him to the tent whilst barking instructions in Arabic to the workforce to stop and take tea themselves.

At the tent, Femi put the kettle on the gas stove and lit it. He prepared the cups for the revolting sweet tea and turned. He motioned for Finch to sit and whilst he did so, went to the door of the tent and took a good look around so that what he was about to say did not fall upon anyone else's ears.

Femi turned and sat opposite Finch. 'Mr. Finch. Jake. We are friends …Yes?' said Femi, not requiring an answer. Finch nodded. 'You are a most eminent historian and friend of Egypt and a light for many less worthy to follow. So why is it that a man like yourself can dig in the insane heat of an Egyptian desert and find a tomb which holds no treasures and is clearly belonging to a man of no repute. It must be one of the most stark and uninteresting finds that I have witnessed in my career. The question I must ask is why do you have the look of a man who has found a tomb akin to that of Tutankhamen? You hid your emotions well. Nonchalant…Yes? But I am a man who can see what there is not to be seen. You have found what you are looking for, after all, you said so yourself, Jake, and I want to know what that is. And please, before you speak, understand that I will know the truth that will pass your lips and a lie. If you lie

16

to me, Inshallah, you will never see inside of that tomb. It will be excavated by museum staff and you can read about it in my paper. Do you understand me?' Femi finished and sat back in his chair, clasping his hands and holding them to his chest.

The easy-going, quiet Egyptian had flashed a side of his character that Finch had suspected but was still nevertheless surprised by. A man he thought he could manipulate had just changed the rules of the game. Finch had to tell him the truth, but he knew also that Femi's love and passion of antiquity would be the key and that his being a part of what Finch was about to say would ensure his reputation for years to come. It was time to come clean. It was Finch's time to stand and 'check his arcs', to ensure there were no spying ears close to the tent. No one could hear what he was about to say. As he did so, Femi flinched ever so slightly, wondering what Finch was going to do. Finch ignored this and after inspecting the scene outside the tent, pulled his seat toward Femi, sat and leant forward.

'OK. You got me! But I thought you would,' Finch said, trying to flatter him. 'We are friends and so I will tell you exactly what I know, and you can believe it or not.' Femi sat up, eager to hear more. Finch waited for a moment, his blue eyes burning into Femi, making him feel uncomfortable. 'The tomb you have just seen is the tomb, I believe, of Satyros. He was a Greek architect who oversaw the building of the Mausoleum of Halicarnassus and friend of the Ptolemaic dynasty. In 323 – 283BC, more or less, Ptolemy I who was the first pharaoh in the dynasty of the Ptolemaic Pharaohs, presented what was one of the greatest wonders of the ancient world: the Great Library of Alexandria. You've obviously heard of this.'

Femi shifted in his seat at the ridiculous thought that a man of his standing would not have heard of such a place. 'Of course, everyone has heard of it. It was destroyed by a fire!'

Finch continued as if Femi hadn't interjected. 'Ptolemy was a lover of the arts, math, literature and everything he felt the Greeks had given to the world. He adored Alexander the Great and felt that the library was a tribute to him. But he was paranoid that this priceless collection could be stolen or destroyed by an invading force or by an accident which indeed it was in 48BC by Julius Caesar.' Finch got out his notebook and read:

'It is often said that the Romans were civilised, but their most famous general was responsible for the greatest act of vandalism during antiquity. Julius Caesar was attacking Alexandria in pursuit of his arch-rival Pompey when he found himself about to be cut off by the Egyptian fleet. Realising that this would leave him in a desperate predicament, he took decisive action and sent fire ships into the harbour. His plan was a success and the enemy fleet was quickly aflame. But the fire did not stop there and jumped onto the dockside which was laden with flammable materials ready for export. Next, it spread inland and before anyone could stop it, the Great Library itself was blazing brightly as 400,000 priceless scrolls were reduced to ashes. As for Caesar himself, he did not think it important enough to mention in his memoirs'. He finished reading and placed the book back in his pocket. 'Yes, it was destroyed and the world mourned its loss. But in his paranoia, Ptolemy had got an army of learned scribes to copy every single parchment that was housed in the Library. There were thousands upon thousands and it took years, but it was done. It was these copies that were burned.'

Femi leaned forward, his eyes like saucers, wide and in wonderment. 'Well, if the copies were burnt, that means… I mean what happened to… where are…?' His words were failing him in his enthusiasm and excitement. Jake held up his hand to slow him down, threw a cursory glance around again and continued.

18

'Every time a copy was made, it was placed where the original sat and the original parchment was removed. The copies were all marked with an ancient equivalent of an invisible marker which denoted that it was a copy and not the original itself. It was ingenious. The scribes were sworn to secrecy and were told that if they uttered a word of this, they would be mutilated along with their family and would be disgraced in the eyes of the gods. One scribe was apparently heard whispering the secret to his wife, so it was said, and was pegged out in the sun and, after watching his family endure the same fate as him, was then blinded, his tongue cut out, hot oil poured down his throat and then left for the animals to feast upon. The Wonder of the World wasn't just the Library itself; it was the fact that the biggest secret of the ancient world was actually kept! Anyway, there needed to be a new resting place for the Library, so Ptolemy got Satyros to build him a place in which to house this Library, away from invaders and natural disasters and where only a choice few knew of its whereabouts. He had heard that there was a man by the name of Eupalinos of Megara, a Greek engineer who built the Tunnel of Eupalinos on the island Samos in the 6th century BC, which was an amazing feat of engineering. Ptolemy liked this idea of tunnelling into rock and wanted Satyros to take this job on.'

'And he did so. He found a place and dedicated his life to building a subterranean Library of Alexandria to survive for millennia to come. Ptolemy was thrilled. It was finished just before his death and he had all the workers who had built it slain. Satyros had proved his worth, but unfortunately for him, Ptolemy had him put to the sword as well, as he didn't want anyone to know this secret. He buried Satyros in a modest tomb making everyone aware that he had nothing to give to prospective robbers. I believe that the tomb we have found belongs to Satyros and that in the box will be a few coins and bits and pieces but, more importantly, a clue to where the Library is today. For I believe that his son, who was privy to the

19

information, wrote an obituary, if you like, to his father after his death and placed it inside the box. This information will give me the whereabouts of the Great Library of Alexandria. That is why I look pleased on seeing such a mundane tomb in the middle of a forsaken desert.'

Jake finished and slumped back in his chair, with the look of a relieved man who had told his last confession. 'I need you to believe me. I need you to help me unravel the greatest find of the entire world. You can be the reason I find this. You!'

Femi sat, his mouth agape. 'Well, I have heard some nonsense in my life, but this…!' Finch's heart was in his mouth. 'But this,' he continued. 'If this is true and there is a chance it exists – and a little credit went my way – then it is a chance you must take!' Femi stood suddenly and pulled Finch up grasping him by the shoulders. 'If, my friend, this is true then I will do all I can to aid you in your quest. We spend our lives peering down a tiny hole trying to find and make sense of the past. If you find what you are looking for, you could smash a hole the size of Egypt and walk through the past answering questions that I have not even thought to ask yet!' By this time, Femi was shaking and salivating with excitement. The kettle on the gas was steaming ferociously and he moved it without thinking of the heat raging from the handle. He recoiled and the shock brought him out of his trance. 'Come quickly, we must see whether the greatest adventure of your life starts today or will dissolve away like the fine sands we stand upon. Come! Come! There is not a minute to lose!'

CHAPTER 3

The two men made their way towards the dig site and called two of the Egyptians who were sitting enjoying their tea break, completely unaware of the excitement that had just been generated in Finch's tent. When they got to the wall, Femi told them to widen the aperture into the tomb. Without much effort, a path was cleared and a large hole opened up in front of them. Finch took his torch out from its holster and stepped into the tomb. He hadn't got more than a few yards inside when he was accompanied by Femi. The air was stale and there was something incredibly melancholic about this bare room. For if it did hold the body of such a great man as Satyros, then it was a sad and ill-fitting end to someone with such a talent and who had helped save the greatest wonder of the world. Finch stood with his torch on full beam, scouring the walls for clues and evidently enjoying the moment. Femi just wanted to know the result. He pushed Finch in the back impatiently toward the box. Finch leant on a bent knee and placed his hands either side of the plain silver box. He bit at his lower lip in anticipation. His heart skipped a beat at the thought of what could be inside the chest and yet he didn't know how he would cope with the disappointment of finding it empty.

'Come, Mr. Finch! It is time – open the box,' whispered Femi, awaking Finch from his daydream. Without a pause, he started to open it up. It was stuck at first but with a little gentle persuasion, it opened without a sound. Finch took the torch and had a look inside. As he suspected, there were a few coins dating to the Ptolemaic age. That was a good sign. There was also a wonderful scarab knife, quite short and curved to a right angle at the bottom, the kind found in the Middle East. *Another good sign*, he thought to himself. There was a small piece of cloth which

21

had been wrapped around some tools of this man's trade. Working tools, a small hammer and compass. Surely this was Satyros. He searched more but that was it! Finch's heart sank. There was no clue as to where the Great Library may be hiding and nothing of any particular evidence that this was the great Greek architect. Finch sat back on his heels and put a hand to his face.

'Trinkets!' he said. 'Just trinkets.' There was silence and when Finch eventually caught Femi's eye, he could see that they were dancing in the half-light of the tomb.

'Mr. Finch – for a man who aims to seek out what is not yet ready to be found, you seem to capitulate all too easily,' said Femi. 'May I?' With that, he picked up the torch and shone it into the lid of the box.

When Finch realised the box was empty, he had let it fall flat on the ground and hadn't looked at the underneath of the lid. For there was wedged a papyrus scroll bound by a faded red tape. Finch gasped and found it difficult to swallow. He reached in and with the utmost delicacy, picked up the scroll. Its condition was incredible. He carefully undid the tie and unravelled the parchment. It was magnificent. As he unrolled it, he could see a huge amount of writing and a diagram. Finch had found what he had come for. He laced it back together and placed it in the box, picked the whole lot up and together they made their way back to the tent. Femi, appreciating the importance of the find, took a wad of notes from his pocket, paid the Egyptian foreman and waved the workers away. He scurried up the hill to the tent so as not to miss a thing. By the time he had got to the tent, Finch had already got the scroll out and had pinned it on the table, securing each corner down with whatever he could find. He scrabbled for his old notebook and pen and started to translate the words, making a note of everything. It was in remarkable condition and was written in the most perfect Greek. It read loosely:

'My father's life's work containing the Great Hall of Alexandria is now in its final resting place and I fear that my life is in grave danger. The Library lies in a country to the south-east of Greece, where the men are painted by the sun but have a great air amongst them. On an arid and vast plain to the east, it lies beneath the earth. A sunken hole and lagoon in a parched land overseen by a tower. Do not feign a dead end for seek and you shall find.'

Finch grinned and clapped his hands with delight. 'I have found it!' he cried.

Femi stared at him in bewilderment. 'My friend – I do not wish to be the man who shatters your dreams, but there is many a land to the east of Egypt that contains... painted men and I dare say a few oases at that. Do you know where this place is that the ghost of millennia past speaks of?'

Finch was unsure how much he should reveal to Femi, but his over enthusiasm got the better of him and he stood quickly and retrieved a map from a bag.

'Look here!' said Finch, pointing to the map. 'If you look south-east from Egypt, you are in this kind of area.' Finch was now pointing to the Middle East. 'Here, there is many a 'painted' chap! Now I had suspected for some time that it was somewhere there from research and various documents, but it was all hearsay. I think that it is in Oman. You see, Oman was known as Mazun and was the land of the Parthians who were a great dynasty. Now the Parthians and the Sassanids, who later took over from the Parthians, liked law and order and were great traders and more importantly they loved history and craved knowledge. Their leader, Arsaces I, admired the Greek civilisation and often modelled his own state on Greek ideologies. Ptolemy knew this and asked him for his blessing and protection to move the Library to Oman. The Parthians were strong and no one would waste too much time conquering a desert. It would be a secret that would be passed down from sultan to sultan and they would forever be the keepers of the Library, always knowing that under their lands stood the knowledge of the world. And so it was. This lagoon that they speak of, is, I think, the Bimmah Sinkhole, is now on the coastal road between Muscat and Sur. It is a truly amazing natural phenomenon and overlooking the sinkhole are the ruins of Qalhat. A square, now dome-less mausoleum of Bibi Maryam. This is where I think the Library is.'

Femi stared in disbelief. Finch, getting to grips with himself and realising that in his exuberance may have said too much, looked into Femi's eyes. 'Now you know what I know. What will you do about it?'

Femi straightened his back and turned, collecting himself. He had felt annoyed by an accusing Finch but allowed himself to calm before he answered. He turned and spoke calmly and collectedly.

'Mr. Finch, Jake, we live in a world full of deceit and hatred. Everyone trying to outdo everyone else for the sake of money, status or power and I too have been guilty of taking advantage of situations to line my own pockets, it is a weakness. There are some people though, occasionally, who still seek to respect the world for what it has to offer and to try and answer the secrets it hides so well. I may be an Egyptian of today but my heart is beating in antiquity. What you have possibly found is the greatest treasure, save for the Holy Relics that the earth has. If you could find this, it would be too wonderful to comprehend and yet I hope with all my heart that you fail in your quest, for this can only bring with it greed, sadness and fighting. For men will do anything for it and ultimately it will be the destiny of the Library to be destroyed. But, if you do find what you seek, all I ask in this corrupt world is that you keep it to yourself, save one man,

24

and tell him all that you discover, for that man will die a happy man.' Femi clasped Finch's hand in a double handed handshake and kissed the back of it, smiling as he did so. 'Our secret is safe.' He released Finch's hand and looked one last time at the parchment. 'What is this?' asked Femi, pointing to the bottom of the scroll. 'The writing is strange and different from the Greek.'

Finch stared down and saw that indeed there was more. How he had failed to see this first-time round was a mystery, but there under the Greek inscriptions was a language unlike anything Finch had seen before. And yet, just as someone who stares at an anagram can decipher it straight away, without a thought, the letters and symbols seemed to make sense to him.

ENOCHIAN:-

Ⲥⳑⳑⲟⳑⳍⳑⲟ ⳑⲩⳑⳤⳍⳑⲂⳍⲤ ⳑⳑⲒⲂ ⳤⲞⳑⳤⳑⳑ ⳤⳤⳑⳑ ⳤⳝⳑⳑⳌⳤ Ⲓⳑⳤⳑ
ⳑⲉⳤⲩ ⳤⲙⲩⲙⲟⳑⳤ ⳤⲤⳑⳤ Ⲓⳑ ⳑⳍⳑⳑⳤⲂ ⳤⳑⳑⳤⳤⳑⲟ ⳤⲂⲟⳑⲟ ⳤⳑⳑⳤⳤⲉⳤ
.ⳍⳑⳑⲒⳑ ⳑⲉⲉⳤⳑ ⳤⳤⳤⲤ ⳑⲤⳍⳤⳑⳤ ⲒⳑⳤⲉⲤ ⳤⲉⳑⲢⲤⳤⲂⳑⲉⳍ ⳤⲂⲟⳑⲟ

The Great Library, the greatest prizes. The chalice of Christ and the Casket of the Prophet Moses.

Finch played dumb; he liked Femi and semi trusted him, but he did not want to share this dream with him anymore. 'They look like a secret code, it's rather odd. Do you have any ideas?' he asked.

Femi just shook his head and wiped his beaded forehead. 'It is a language unlike anything I have seen. Still, if anyone can work it out then you, Jake, are the man to do it. What will you do now?' asked Femi.

'I will, with your permission, leave Egypt as soon as possible and head back to London to tie a few things up before I head to Oman,' Finch replied. 'May I take the scroll?'

'Of course and Inshallah, may you find what you seek in good health. Just let me know; yes?' Femi embraced Finch and made his way to the dig site, shouting at any remaining workers, causing them to scurry around like rats fleeing after a door to a darkened room had been opened. Finch wasted no time in packing up his belongings, taking particular care of the scroll. He got into his jeep and headed back to his hotel room and readied himself to leave Egypt and get back home.

CHAPTER 4

Things were going to start to get pretty frenetic from now on and Jake needed time to recharge his batteries and think about his next move. He was uncontrollably excited about his discovery but knew he had to do things properly and that meant planning. He had always lived by the seven 'P's, 'Prior Planning and Preparation Prevents a Piss Poor Performance!' But in his ears was another saying from a mate of his who served in the forces, which was, 'No plan survives first contact!' In other words, always have a back-up. Apart from his own eagerness, there was no real need for him to be in too much of a hurry. After all, the Library had laid dormant for a couple of millennia so a few more weeks wouldn't make too much of a difference. His only real threat was Femi. If he wanted to, he could spill the beans about what he had learnt to whomever, in order to gain world renown, fame, money and generally stuff Finch up in doing so. The way he saw it was that if Femi was to scupper his plans, he'd be screwed whether he was there or not. Besides, there was something in Femi's eyes which reassured him. He had started to trust him more, which was crazy as he was an Egyptian and his past dealings with them generally had meant that he learnt to be naturally wary. Jake wanted to get back to his base in West Wales and plan for his future mission.

He adored his cottage. It lay on a cliff overlooking a sandy beach on the Cardigan Bay coastline. From here, he could hear and smell the sea; the salty air gave him a cerebral enema and cleansed him. He loved to just sit and watch the world go by and then get into the bracing sea with his old bodyboard and reinvigorate his soul. There was something strangely magical about the place. Although most of his work was in London, where he owned a small flat, and around the world, he had always wished for a way to be able to permanently base himself in Wales. But although born a Welshman, he had never really called the Principality home until he bought his cottage a few years back and now he tried to get back whenever he could.

It was a long journey. Finch dumped his bags in the hall and hung his keys on the hook by the front door. It was good to be back. He turned up the boiler and flicked the gas fire on to breathe some warmth into the slightly musty walls of the cottage. His head was buzzing, his mind a whirl of possibilities, but all blurring into one undefined muddle as a result of his exhaustion. He made a cup of coffee and sat in front of the fire, staring into the flames. He held the parchment in his hand and unfurled it gently then stared at it intently. With this he knew that if the Library existed, as he was positive it did, that he could find it; but it was the phrase at the bottom of the page which puzzled him the most. Was it what the inscription said or was it that he could read the incomprehensible language in the first place?! What the hell was it? It wasn't Babylonian or Samarian. It didn't show any of the patterns that other ancient languages had presented, so what was it? But it said that it knew the resting places of what was obviously the Ark of the Covenant and what he suspected was the Holy Grail. Men had been after these for as long as he could remember – what archaeologist hadn't? It had never even crossed Finch's mind to actually search for them and he had always suspected that they were myths, or if not, had undoubtedly been destroyed years earlier. The Ark, it had been whispered, lay in Ethiopia, in a temple, but the priests would never allow anyone to verify it, and to force entry would be to start a massive holy war. As for the Grail, well the closest anyone had got to finding that were the Crusaders and Dan Brown!

Finch was too tired to take this in and before too long, he was out for the count, his coffee cup nestled into his lap and the parchment resting on the ground, fallen from the grasp of his limp hand.

CHAPTER 5

Finch was aware of a cacophony of shouting and a riotous melee. He could not see any faces but he was aware that much of the hatred and anger was being directed at him. It was dark and the air was thick with acrid smoke. There was a controlled confusion and worst of all… there was fire. He could feel the intense heat building not far from his face and was trying to move but he was held tight, bound, restrained. The crowd called to him in French, yet Finch could understand perfectly, although his grasp of the language ordinarily was average. Yet at this moment, it was as clear as English. '*Guillaume de Beaujeu! Vous êtes un salaud hérétique! Vous m'entendez Guillaume!*' They were calling him a heretic bastard and the bombastic assault continued. Finch was Guillaume. He knew it. He answered in French that he was a servant and loyal but it obviously made no difference at all. He could hear screaming from all around him and the noise levels grew. Then he could feel the heat intensify and the smoke filling his senses.

Finch suddenly woke with a shout and jumped. He was sweating and breathing heavily and more annoyingly had spilled his coffee over his trousers. He came to his senses fast and checked the parchment for damage and tidied himself up. He put the cup in the sink and took a handful of cold water from the tap and refreshed his face with it, ridding himself of any salty perspiration. It was so real! The dreams. And the fire! Why fire? Who the hell is Guillame de Beaujeu? This was starting to get to Finch. He knew he had to have a clear mind when tackling this next phase of the dig and to do this, he needed to find out what was haunting him so much. Everyone has nightmares, but these weren't just nightmares. These were real and it was starting to affect his life. Finch needed help.

He entered the sitting room and sparked up his laptop. He Googled 'Psychiatrists and Hypnosis' and found a name which jumped out of the page – 'Martin Wiltshire – Help with phobias, flying, smoking, nightmares, eating disorders.' *That sounds like a broad enough brush*, thought Finch. He felt acutely embarrassed to even consider this type of mumbo jumbo help – but he needed answers and this guy dealt with nightmares and phobias. Maybe he could cure him of his flame aversion? 'Bollocks! What the hell!' shouted Finch and took a note of the number.

The psychiatrist was based in Bristol. Finch had to get the train to London anyway and a pit stop in Bristol would be easy enough to fit in. If he could just sort this out and focus his mind, it would be worth its weight in gold. He took the number of the clinic and headed to bed.

Outside was a lone figure, watching Finch's house from the edge of a hedge line. He had been there all night and had watched Finch's every move since his return from Egypt. He wore a long First World War style trench coat and pulled an already rolled liquorice paper flavoured cigarette out from the coat's deep pockets. The silver ring on his right thumb glinted in the natural light of the moon as he lit the cigarette, cupping the flame and embers in the palm of his hand so as to not attract attention. He took a long drag and exhaled as he saw the lights extinguish from the top floor of the house. He pulled the collar up around his neck, put his cigarette in his mouth and buried his hands into his coat pockets. This was to be a long night. The stranger made his way in through the hedge and to the edge of a small copse where he could still keep eyes on Finch's property and made himself as comfortable as he could. He needed to know what Finch's next move was.

31

CHAPTER 6

Finch was up early and made his way to the station where he had already booked a train ticket to London Paddington. On the way, he rang the shrink's clinic and managed, luckily, to get a cancelled appointment for two o'clock that afternoon. This was perfect. A quick hour on the couch, cured by three and in London for seven! He still didn't really believe in all that claptrap, but he felt he had to at least try and get to the root of his troubles. Nothing else had worked and he needed all his wits about him for what was coming up. He had nothing to lose… apart from £50 an hour, but even that would be worth it if he could be put right.

The station was about a thirty-minute walk and it was a great chance for Finch to get a bit of fresh sea air before entering the oppressive atmosphere of the capital. He grabbed his satchel and small old-fashioned suitcase and headed off. As he got to the bottom of his path and closed the gate behind him, a figure from the edge of the copse was watching his every move. The stranger had had an unsettled night and was scratchy. He watched Finch with a furrowed brow, rolled a cigarette in his hand and lit up. He allowed Finch to get far enough ahead so as not to arouse suspicion and then followed him to the station.

As Finch got on to the train, he found two empty seats and settled in by the window, placing his bag on the seat next to him to prevent anyone else from sitting beside him. The train was fairly empty and so the chance of anyone doing so was slim. He pulled out his little black notebook from his satchel and looked at the strange markings that had been on the parchment. 'What language was this?' he kept asking over and over again.

He flicked over to the back of the book where he had written: <u>SHRINK: Flames, Dreams,</u> Guillame de Beaujeu, French, Symbols, Nightmares / real – smells and sounds, etc.

He took a moment to inspect his surroundings where he noticed a scruffy man in a thick khaki trench coat enter the carriage and sat a few seats down from him in a tabled four-berth seating arrangement. He sat in the outside seat and gave Finch a knowing look. It made him feel a little ill at ease. He returned a smile, the sort of smile you give when one has toothache, then left the man's stare and looked out of the window pulling his bags closer to him while he did so. He glanced again out of the corner of his eye at the dishevelled chap who had acknowledged him. Ordinarily, it would not have crossed his mind but there was something about him. He seemed to know Finch and there was a huge nagging sensation in Finch's subconscious that indicated that he somehow knew him. The chap also didn't really suit his clothes. He looked like your stereotypical anti-disestablishment anarchist, but there was an underlying distinguished look about the man which didn't fit his attire. Finch could see that the man was still trying to engage his eye, and he assumed that he was just some nut who had taken a dislike or indeed a particular penchant for him. Finch was perfectly well equipped to look after himself, but he really didn't want the hassle of a confrontation, so he fixed his eyes out on to the platform and awaited the train's departure.

The train pulled out of the station and he opened up the notebook once more and looked at the symbols. They just didn't make sense. He had brought a reference book of ancient languages of antiquity to try and shed some light on the subject. How he knew what it all meant was another matter entirely. Finch laid the notebook on the adjacent pull-down table and leafed through the book muttering to himself. He had been aware that the man in the long coat had passed by him, maybe to use the facilities, but paid no heed. Now, though, he had an overwhelming sensation that he was behind him. He shot round and saw the chap standing in the aisle, straining to look at the markings in the notebook. Finch wanted to tell the man to 'sod off' but instead, he snatched his notebook and closed it, placing it in his satchel.

The man remained and as cool as you like, just said in a stilted Welsh accent, 'Sorry, mate, no offence meant – I was just surprised to see that old language again; brought back a few memories of my own. Like I said, no harm meant.' And with that, he returned to his seat and watched for Finch's reaction, knowing full well that the juicy worm he had just dangled in front of him was too good to let get away.

Finch collected himself for a moment. He was angry but hadn't expected anything like that. He thought the bloke was going to either threaten him or ask for some money. But the articulate nature and content of what the chap had just said threw him completely. 'How the hell does he know about the language... does he know what this is?' Finch muttered to himself quietly. In a flash, he got up and walked over to the chap who had just engaged with him, though as he came closer, he averted his gaze and stared out of the window. 'Excuse me,' Finch said awkwardly to the stranger. 'Do you mind?' He gestured to be able to sit in the seat opposite him. The stranger looked right up at him and smiled, gesturing back for him to sit. Finch noticed straight away the man's eyes. They were strikingly blue, the only other person who had eyes like that was... him. There was a beat of silence then Finch broke it. He was trying to be cool but wanted answers.

'You said that you hadn't seen that language for a long time. Did you mean these symbols?' Finch had his notebook out and was showing them to the man. 'Do you know what language it is?' The man appeared completely uninterested. He looked out of the window and leant back, interlacing his fingers together.

'You don't recognise them?' The man sounded surprised. 'You of all people.'

Finch was taken aback. 'What the hell do you mean by that – do I know you? Have we met? You speak as if we are acquainted?'

'I know you, Guillaume, or as you are now… Jake? But we'll get on to that later. You want to know about the language, yes?' he continued. Finch nodded, completely thrown by the man's words and demeanour. 'You thought it Samarian or Babylonian. Could it have been Aramaic perhaps – the language of Our Lord Jesus Christ Himself – did you think of that?'

'It's not Aramaic!' retorted Finch sharply.

'Of course not! No offence meant. The language you see is the language of Enochian. The language of Angels. By the way, the name's Kris – with a K. Sometimes known as Thomas Bérard.' He held out his hand to shake Finch's.

Finch instinctively shook his hand, bewildered at what the man had just said. The only thing Finch could think about saying in answer to that was, 'Kris with a K!' There was a beat, then Finch erupted, 'What the hell are you talking about? Angel language? Look, I have been in this game long enough to know there is no such thing as an Angel language and why did you call yourself Thomas, what was it again?' Finch was all a muddle.

Kris was calm. 'So many questions, Jake. I called myself Thomas Bérard. I have two names because I was born Thomas Bérard but Kris is my name now and Enochian is very real – if you are so sure it isn't, why do you understand it? Which you do! You have indeed been in this game for a long time, hundreds of years in fact– but you were a warrior. You now dig for clues from the past to answer questions about the future. You have a good soul and are fired up about finding what you thought was the greatest find in history but now know that it is just a doorway to

35

the truly greatest prize that the world has ever beheld. It is a prize that must be found, for in the wrong hands, it would be catastrophic and only the custodians of the pure and righteous have the right and honour to take on such a task.'

Finch looked at the man. 'How do you know that? And what was all that other crap about?'

Kris laughed. 'I'm sorry, Guillaume — I mean, Jake'

Finch was getting frustrated. 'Wait, wait. Look, I need to know a few answers, if I may? How do you know me and these things and why are people writing angelic symbols on parchments thousands of years ago? How do I know what they mean? No waffle riddles or ambiguity, just tell me straight. What the hell's going on?'

Kris leaned forward and stared straight at Finch, trying to get an intangible connection. 'Answers, Jake? Will you accept them? Well, I'll do my best to enlighten you, if that is what you want, but you'll just think it all a load of old bollocks and think me a madman. Nevertheless, I will tell you what I know. Are you ready? The language on the parchment that you found whilst trying to find the Great Library of Alexandria was indeed a great find and will, I feel, take you to that most wonderful discovery, but as the parchment rightly says, the Library holds the key to a greater prize: that of the whereabouts of the Ark of the Covenant and the Holy Grail. It was written in Enochian, the ancient language of the angels; by whom, I cannot answer but it was written for you or men like you to find and get to the final prize and protect it before it lands in the hands of people who would wish to take advantage of it and use it for their own ill will. This leads on to how you understand the writing. You understand it because you are a custodian of the prize and it is part of your make-up. How do I know all of this and how do I know you? Because we are brothers of a time long ago, sworn protectors and members of a small but elite group, wandering through life

36

finding the answers to questions that were never told. We have a gift to look back through time and seek the truth so that we can succeed and protect the future.' He finished and kept Finch's stare. There was a pause and Finch leant back and looked around the train. He wiped his face with his palms and swept them through his hair and leant forward again.

'Now, I don't know what you are on, pal, and I don't know how you know some of this stuff, but you're right about one thing, that was the biggest load of bollocks I have ever heard. Stay the hell away from me.' Finch made to get up, when Kris grabbed his wrist.

Kris looked at Finch and said in a loud whisper, 'You know I speak the truth. I have been trying to find you for some time and have been recceing your house and had to wait for you to get back from your bloody dig in Egypt. But I found you. We were never meant to be apart. We are inexorably intertwined and need each other, as we need the others, and we have to be fearful of the ones that intend to take what is not theirs to take. You think you have stumbled into this. This was your... this IS your destiny. Don't be so ignorant! This is why you are here!'

Finch pulled his arm free and turned to return to his seat. He hadn't got two paces when Kris continued. 'You have dreams, don't you? Vivid, real dreams. Your senses reel with the tangibility of them. You know names, places, and situations. In all of these, there are similar people but at various stages of history. They are real. Yes! You have dreams. These are not just dreams, they are your past lives revisited, the brain cannot place all the facts and so you revisit times and places to answer questions. You can't change anything but you can help alter how you are in the future by learning from your past. Some can control this regression; others have no idea what they are doing – you being the latter. You have no idea what a big part of this puzzle you are and now you need to understand and take your position in the game, Guillame.' Finch stood stunned; he lowered his head and made his way to his seat. As he sat, Kris followed and stood over him. 'You have it? The birthmark? Top of your right forearm on the inside under the crook of your elbow joint? Yes? Does it look anything like this?'

With that, Kris lifted up his sleeve to reveal a circular red mark with a cross connected to the edge of the ring. Finch stared in disbelief at what he was looking at. He kept his gaze on the mark and after a bit, pulled his own sleeve up to reveal the exact same symbol. 'We are meant to be here – you need to understand this. Whether you like it or not, you need me and I need you! I will see you soon, brother.' Kris pulled his sleeve down and walked out of the carriage, leaving Finch void of all feeling. He was dumbfounded by what had happened. He needed a drink. He shot round to see where Kris had gone, but he had disappeared. Finch sat for the rest of the journey, dazed. The tannoy sparked into life announcing the train's arrival at Bristol Temple Meads. Finch gathered his gear and headed for the door. As the train pulled in, Finch opened the door and headed straight for the nearest pub and ordered a pint of Guinness and a double whisky. Kris watched him from a safe distance. Finch sat at the bar, staring into nothingness and trying to piece together the last few hours and what it all meant.

CHAPTER 7

Finch looked at his watch and realised that he should get a jog on if he was going to get to the shrink on time. What had happened on the train had shaken him and to be honest, he didn't know what to make of it all, but in any event, he was going to the right place. He hailed a taxi and made his way to the practice just off White Ladies Road in the Clifton area of the city. Not far behind him was Kris, keeping a solid eye on his newly found brother in arms. He got to the practice with about ten minutes to spare and enough time to check the place out. It was a Victorian terrace building and looked the part. Inside was clean but not clinical in that disinfectant type of way. The receptionist looked up at Finch as he closed the front door behind him.

'Hello. You must be Mr. Finch. If I could ask you to fill in this questionnaire and take a seat, you will be called up shortly.' Finch nodded. The woman behind the desk was in her late forties and still very attractive; Finch didn't want to talk as he felt very conscious that he was in need of professional mental help. Ridiculous really, as he knew that people who went to these sorts of places weren't crazy, just needed a little re-tuning here and there. He filled out the form, the usual stuff about name and address and contra indications. Then he sat looking at every part of the room in detail, wondering what excuse he would give the doctor as to why he needed this consultation. At one point he almost walked out, but as he was considering that option, the receptionist smiled and told him that he could go up to the see Dr Wiltshire and that was that. He was going.

The doctor was exactly what Finch imagined him to be; fairly short and portly with wild curly hair in small tight curls receding from the brow. His Timmy Mallet-esque large round glasses did nothing for his look. He was instantly likeable though. He shot up to greet Finch as he entered the room. He wore a brown hole ridden cardigan with brown elbow pads, blue pastel shirt, undone to the chest and Farah trousers. He beamed a great smile at Finch. 'Hello, sir! Please come in, be not afraid! Ha! Just kidding. Please come in! Have a seat.'

Finch sat on the large brown leather sofa and instantly felt more relaxed and returned the doctor's smile. 'Hello – I'm Jake,' he said.

'Ah yes – Jake Finch. Wonderful.' This last phrase was said overlooking his large glasses. 'You are an archaeologist – how wonderful! So there must be a strange but exceptional reason why you are here no doubt!' Finch laughed and nodded to himself. There was a beat of silence. 'Can I call you Jake?' asked the doctor.

'Of course.'

'Right you are, Jake it is then. I am Martin, I've been in the game for over twenty years and still loving it and I can promise you that nothing you say will leave this place or surprise me in the slightest; so, the stage is yours.' And with that he nodded at Finch and sat back in his armchair and swivelled slowly from side to side, awaiting Finch's lament.

Finch shifted uncomfortably in his seat and looked out of the window, searching for the words to explain his fears. They sounded so ridiculous now, but the earlier saga had thrown him out of kilter and his usual verbal eloquence had now eluded him.

'Ever since I can remember, I have had a fear of fire, whether it is a flame or raging inferno – it terrifies me and even the thought of the slightest flicker makes me feel really uncomfortable. The problem is that when I close my eyes, my dreams always lead me back to some fiery encounter and I wake,

40

shaking and sweating and unable to get back to sleep. Quite frankly, I feel exhausted. I've a few intense weeks ahead of me and it's important I have my game head on, so to speak, but it is starting to overwhelm me a little. I can't really think of anything else.' Martin tried to interject at this natural pause but Finch, lost now in his soliloquy, continued; he needed to really explain his feelings.

'The thing is, when I sleep, I dream, and it's as if I am really there. I know people always say that, but if you knew you were having a nightmare and it was all just a dream, then that would ease the sense of terror. But I am really there. The smells, the people, occurrences – all real. And not only that, but I also know the people and the historical situations. It's not just a manifestation of today's drama unfolding in unexpected ways. These are historical moments in time with me at the centre, with people and things I remember from the past. It's unnerving. The other day, there were faces and noise everywhere. People spoke in French and I understood it perfectly and my French really isn't that good. They called me a name I hadn't heard before but it was me. I was bound and once again flames were present. It is driving me crazy!' Finch finished, pleased that he had got the monkey off his back but still felt a little stupid and desperate. After a while, he looked up at Martin who was still looking at him, contemplating how he would respond to this open-hearted response from Finch.

'Fear,' he started. 'Fear is a funny thing. It creates biological changes in the body, which leads to a chain reaction of events which makes us feel and do many things. It is very real, and it is very hard to control, but we can. We can do this by pharmaceutical intervention or by training the mind to overcome this fear. I almost said irrational fear but there is nothing irrational about it when it is your fear. But the brain can be trained into overcoming problems and it helps us to deal with them in a much better way. The other way to tackle this is to look

41

at why you have the fear in the first place. For example, a man who hates flying may not actually be afraid of flight but it is the feeling of claustrophobia or not being in control or even the fear of death, which is the root of the problem – you see?' He stared at Finch for a reaction which he got in the form of a nod. 'Now, he may be like this because he was in an accident when he was young that he could not avoid as he was not the one in control or he was locked in a room or a lift for some time, unable to control the ability to escape. Now to your fear of fire – have you to your knowledge had any adverse encounters with fire?'

Finch immediately answered, 'No! Nothing! Never burnt or come close to having any ill effects from a fire. That's why I can't explain it.'

Martin sat back in his chair and considered Finch's response. It was obvious that Finch was an intelligent man, and a science-based individual and therefore more logical than many of Wiltshire's patients. As Martin contemplated Finch's situation and made some notes, Finch continued. 'I mean,' he said, 'The other day whilst on a dig I unearthed a parchment with some writing on it that I had never seen before. I have seen many languages and ancient texts and always managed to source or understand them but this flummoxed me. I mean, I had no idea and yet… I knew what it meant! I didn't know what it was but I knew what it said. Someone later told me that the language was something called Enochian, or something like that.'

'The language of…'

Martin interrupted, 'Angels.'

Finch shot a look at him and shouted, 'Yes! That's it! But how would I know that? Plus my grasp of French in the dream. It's crazy!'

Martin swivelled back around and pondered. 'Enochian is, I believe, a language which was recorded in some journals in the

42

late 16th century by a couple of gentlemen, their names escape me for the moment, but they believed that the language was given to them by angels for the use of magic. Now, it is highly possible that if the language was real, that it could have been around since the dawn of time – if you believe in all of that. As I remember one of the chaps… Oh come on, Martin,' he said to himself quietly. 'What was his name… Ah yes, John Dee! That's it! Yes, Dee wrote that this was supposed to be the language God used to create the world and speak to Adam but when Adam bit into the apple and was banished from Eden, he lost the language. The language was hidden from mankind but a book was recorded for humanity called… umm! Anyway, it was lost in the flood, conveniently, and that was that! How you are able to understand it is not logical, but not impossible. Maybe you should see a medium?' The last part was said with a large chortle and grin to lift the increasing tension in the room evident on Finch's face. 'Just kidding,' said Martin.

He was about to carry on when Finch asked him, 'If you evidently don't believe in all of this, why do you know so much about it?'

Martin smiled. 'Ah! I've been bubbled! In order to understand the psyche, one must look at all possible answers. I don't believe in ghosts but if someone comes here and tells me he is having something occur in his house, who am I to say it isn't true. There very well might be something happening. There are stranger things in heaven and earth than a fat nerd like me could ever try and explain. But what I must do is understand the different options and then work out what the best answer would be. To offer those answers, one must be prepared to know and understand all other avenues, however bizarre. Anyway, it does me no harm to understand it more. Not that I have to believe in it. You tell me that there was a language created by God which doesn't exist now. Well, that opens a whole argument about religion and personal thoughts, but I will never say it is

43

impossible, as who am I to say otherwise? Hmm?' Finch nodded, happy in the fact this chap sitting in front of him didn't think he was completely barking mad.

Martin stood and went over to his wall of books. An impressive collection of old and new spines laid out on the shelf in what can only be described as an organised chaos. He looked for a while and pulled out a red book and returned to his seat cradling the book in his arms. 'Jake. Have you ever heard of regression?'

Finch smiled a smile that indicated that he did actually think the shrink now thought he was mad. 'Regression. Yep. That's where you get hypnotised and then travel back to some past life where you find out you were either Gandhi or a milkmaid from Romania in the 15th century and that is why you hate milk! It's the sort of thing Paul McKenna does. It's parlour games stuff!' said Finch dismissively.

'Funnily enough, I think it has real merit. You surprise me, Jake, for a man who deals with so many ghostly echoes from the past, to be so disparaging about visiting it, is strange,' said Martin.

Finch rebuffed this quickly. 'You surprise me, Dr Wiltshire. A man who seems to be relatively cast in black and white, to now believe in souls and religion appears to be just as odd.'

Wiltshire smiled. 'Ah the parody or irony – whatever. It is odd. I myself am unsure about religion, and as I said before, who am I to say things don't exist. Religion to me is just a great way to start a fight! But, yes, when you talk about there being a soul and a life force and in this case a life force that lives on after the body's shell has gone, then you have to talk about religion in the same breath because something must have made the soul. Where does it go etcetera, etcetera? What I think personally is unimportant. In my position as a scientist, I have seen too many cases where the patients have been regressed and come out with

44

the most incredible stories. For example, men have been regressed into many lives and known the names of people who had existed and moreover knew their idiosyncrasies.

'It is quite extraordinary and it happens a great deal. I feel that in your case you may have had a traumatic occurrence in a previous life which has led you to be afraid of fire – maybe you had been the baker in the Great Fire of London? What do you say – has to be worth a try?'

Finch stared at Dr Wiltshire's earnest face. He did trust and like this man, but regression? The thought that he had been here before and that was why he had this hang-up now, just seemed to be far too much for him to handle – particularly today. Finch slapped his thighs, 'Martin. Look, just being here talking about my problems and not being made to feel stupid has helped a great deal. So, thank you. But I'm afraid regression and chanting or whatever you do to find out I was that milk-maid, is just one step too far!' Finch stood and put his hand out to shake Martin's hand. Martin stood and shook his hand and smiled and gave him his card.

'Listen, if you decide that you might want to give this "rubbish" a go, give me a shout. Who knows, it might just work! Very nice to have met you, Jake, and good luck with whatever it is that you are about to embark on. Though I have to say that if I could understand an unknown, potentially mythical language which was obviously key to the next part of my adventure, I'd probably want more answers,' Martin said with a grin.

Finch just replied, 'And an extra hundred pounds for the pleasure of it no doubt!'

'Oh touché – cynical, but touché, old boy!'

And with that, Finch left and, in his heart, he did feel better having spoken to someone out loud about his fears. Now, he had to get to London and start to figure out where his next move should be and put this distraction behind him.

Finch made his way to the railway station. The brevity of the last encounter with Martin Wiltshire had caused him to almost forget about that morning's revelations and he had not given Kris another thought but not too far behind him was the man he met on the train.

Kris thought it would be more prudent for him to talk once again to Finch on the train, rather than a coffee house out in the open. At least on the train he could grab his attention and speak to him knowing that he wouldn't run away or make a scene, so he stayed a good pace behind him and followed him to London.

CHAPTER 8

Finch settled down in his seat and thought a couple of hours' kip on the train would be just what he needed. He had no sooner shut his eyes when he felt the presence of someone sitting beside him in the cramped seats of the train. Without stirring, he knew from the smell of stale tobacco and musty clothes it was Kris. Still with his eyes closed, Finch spoke, 'What do you want? Not satisfied with buggering my day up once, you thought you'd come back for round two, yeah?' Finch now opened his eyes and faced Kris.

Kris, emotionless, stared straight back at Finch. 'You saw the shrink, you all sorted then? No? Didn't think so. Are you going to let him regress you?' he asked.

'How did you know we talked about regression?' Finch replied, suspecting Kris had somehow eavesdropped on the whole conversation.

'Because it's the only sensible plan of action and hopefully then you will understand who you are and the ability you have.'

'Oh, not all that again!' sighed Finch.

'Listen, Finchy,' Kris said, being provocatively informal. 'When are you going to realise all I have said is true. I give you all the evidence you need and still you stammer around like some stuttering goon. You need to understand and get onboard with this quickly or there is a good chance that someone will want you dead because of who you are or were. Incidentally, you are not Mr. Jake Finch but Guillaume de Beaujeu of Rocamador, France. You were the Grand Master of The Order of The Knights Templar 1273 to 1291 but on Friday 13th 1307, King Philip IV ordered the Templars to be arrested: *"Dieu n'est pas content, nous*

47

avons des ennemis de la foi dans le Royaume" – ("God is not pleased. We have enemies of the faith in the kingdom"). We were charged with numerous offences – everything from apostasy, idolatry, heresy, obscene rituals and homosexuality, financial corruption, fraud, and secrecy. Many of the Knights accused, confessed to these charges under torture. All these interrogations were recorded on a thirty-metre-long parchment, now kept at the Archives Nationales in Paris. You will see your name on that parchment, signed by your own hand. Many were made to confess that they had spat on the Cross: "*Je reconnais que craché trois fois sur la Croix, mais de bouche et pas de Coeur*" – "I admit that I have spat three times on the Cross, but only from my mouth and not from my heart." The Templars were accused of idolatry and heresy and burnt at the stake. You, me and countless others – that is why you fear the flames, Guillaume, because as a righteous and pious warrior, all your flesh was burnt from your body while you still lived because you were protecting the most powerful relics God had to offer this world. That is why you understand French in your dreams and understand the language of the angels, for we all spoke it to use as a code in the fight against the darkness. That is why we are brothers and there are many like us about. We are souls who find answers and leave clues through our many existences and until our quest is complete, will return to this mortal plane. We are The Renatus, Guillaume. We have no special powers, we can die as easily as any other man, but our gift is to be able to regress ourselves to any one of our past lives and look for the clues which will better our soul and help us put the pieces together of the greatest puzzle ever created: the whereabouts of the Holy Grail. It exists, Guillaume, and you're close to finding it and in the meantime, you will discover other mysteries about man's time on earth, but this will make you a target for men without such pure hearts. Men will seek to harm you so that they can earn the prize for themselves. And the Grail, Guillaume, it does exist and with it a power that only God can handle. It was never meant to be wielded by mortal hands. Just the thought of it gives men power over others. But the Grail, it is said, can give a man the ability to live forever, to be made immortal, to never die. In the wrong hands, this would have a devastating effect on humanity which was never Our Lord's plan. Therefore, we have to protect it – for eternity. Do you understand, Guillaume – do you now believe what I am saying?' Kris finished.

Finch looked at him as if he were mad, although he had a feeling that everything he said was right – he had always known deep down, a nagging feeling; he had just not fully known the facts and decided to bury his head in the sand. But now it did all make some sort of sense. The information that Kris had divulged, the dreams, the fire, his own character, his thirst for knowledge, the past. The scar! Finch sighed and nodded and it was as if he had been placed in a trance. Where it came from, he didn't know but he looked at Thomas Bérard and said, *'Oui Thomas, je comprend. Je commence à retenir. Les cicatrices sont profondes. Les Templiers Oui?* (Yes, Thomas, I understand. I am starting to remember. The scars run deep. The Knights Templar, yes?)'

Kris merely replied, *'Oui pour Les Templiers.'*

There was silence for some time. Finch's head was a blur. He had been so adamant that the 'hippy' who was sitting beside him had been talking such nonsense that he just couldn't comprehend what had gone on. But it did all make sense and no matter how blinkered he wanted to still be, the rays of truth kept bombarding him and he knew without a doubt that all that had just been said was indeed the truth and in many ways, it was a relief of mammoth proportions. 'Then I must now find what I am looking for with even more haste,' said Finch.

'*We,*' said Kris. 'For your quest is mine too. I don't care about the Library, it is a necessity to source our final goal; but, brother, you will need me as you will need others.' Finch initially shook at the thought of someone getting in the way of him finding the Great Library which he had spent so long looking for.

'You make it sound as if we are going to war,' Finch said through a half smile. Kris looked at him.

'In all your dreams, was there a man who showed a pattern, a similarity, a man who seeped evil and hated you with all his heart? Think carefully.'

Finch looked into himself and thought hard. There was someone, someone who always seemed to be his nemesis, but the face or name eluded him. He couldn't be sure. It could be that he was getting carried away with this whole story and making up a nemesis would be all too easy to do.

'I'm not sure – maybe I... why?'

Kris continued, 'There is a man who started his life at the same time as ours but instead of being one of us, he despised us and has always tried his hardest to destroy us through flesh or reputation. He is a Regressor but his heart is black. Many have fallen to him through the ages, including you and me. It buys him time and more clues as to where the Grail is. If he were to find this, he would hold uncontrollable power. He cannot be allowed to succeed. But he will do absolutely anything to stop us and take the Grail for himself. You must go back to your doctor and regress. You must! Get as many clues as you can about your past lives and learn how to control it yourself, as I can. It is possible to regress and visit any one of the lives lived before. One cannot change or interfere with anything in the past but going back can piece together clues you may have missed. Enough to give you a head start in this life. You must go back to the doctor. You need to know who is chasing you, who are friends, and any clues that will help us find the Grail. Yes?'

Finch looked at him and agreed. 'I need to go to London. I need a battle plan for the next move. Then I'll get back to Bristol.

I have to plan alone but will give you updates – you have a phone?'

'No – I will be there when you need to speak – this is all I am here for now. Good luck, Guillaume, it's good to be at your side again. It has been too long, *adieu*.' He placed a hand on Finch's shoulder and made his way to the carriage door and as the train pulled into Reading, he got off and didn't look back.

CHAPTER 9

In a smoky corner of a seedy watering hole in Egypt, a man sat at a table and opposite him, an Egyptian digger. A vaguely white dishdash covered with the day's excavations on it, the table also had a large bottle of whisky and an ashtray full of cigarette butts. Beside it, a carefully placed packet of Gitanes filterless cigarettes and an expensive silver lighter placed on top of the packet. The Arab was plastered. Full to the brim on free whisky which the stranger had been plying him with for some time.

The stranger looked wholly out of place. He was wearing a dark thin pin striped three-piece suit. His shoes were black leather brogues and immaculately polished. It was as if the sand particles were forbidden to touch the mirror-like footwear. His white shirt was starched to within an inch of its life and his tie was non-ostentatious and business-like. His dark thick hair was swept back and kept neat by a handful of hair oil. This man was calm and collected. He knew what he wanted and this little scene was a means to an end. He sat opposite the sozzled Arab, legs crossed and cigarette in hand, watching his every move, filling up the glass of whisky whenever it went below the halfway mark.

'Who was in charge of the dig? Was it Femi El Masri – that fat government man? Hmm? Who was the white man – what did he find?' The man spoke well but his accent had just the hint of French. Every part of this man reeked of authority. But his eyes were dead. Joyless. Nevertheless, he had a strikingly handsome look which disguised a vicious streak which could simmer for a while before exploding.

The Arab stared at the man and only reacted when he heard Femi's name. 'El Masri! El Masri! المصري – He the boss!' That

52

was enough for the stranger. This man was merely the indicator to ensure that he was on the right track. He stood up, his tall stature casting a menacing shadow over the drunk Arab. He looked up at him, fearful, but the stranger smirked and threw some money on the table as he left, heading out into the diminishing evening sun to find Femi El Masri. The stranger was Victor Mantz and he had business with Mr El Masri.

Finch was in his London flat sitting at the table, papers strewn everywhere. He liked to be organised. He also liked to be ready for any given situation that may arise. He was looking at the parchment and had re read it a hundred times. The question now was how to actually find the Library and do it with the blessing of the locals, particularly the Sultan of Oman. They wouldn't take too kindly having the greatest ever discovery unearthed from under their noses without being informed about it. This could be the sort of country that would cut your head off and ask questions later, and Finch wasn't interested in losing anything. Then again, if word got out about what was potentially hidden in the Omani desert, all hell could be let loose. No. Finch was going to have to box clever on this. He got out his old brown leather contact book which contained years' worth of names he had met and helped and worked with. Maybe there could be someone he had forgotten about who could guide him on this. He thumbed through the pages, mumbling to himself. Then he saw a blast from the past: 'Yousef Khalifa!' he shouted. 'That old bugger – maybe! Just maybe!'

About ten years ago, Finch had been addressing the Iraqi government about the possibility of trying to find one of the Seven Wonders of the World – The Hanging Gardens of Babylon. Their idea was to try and unearth great archaeological gems, improve tourism and also prove to the world that the Iraqi people had always been blessed and the knowledge of the

53

whereabouts of the Gardens within Iraqi borders would help appreciate that. Particularly important after the bitter taste the Gulf and Iranian Wars had left. As it happens, there was some inconclusive proof, but looking after Finch was a UN monitor from Oman. He was an ex-colonel in the Omani Army and a British wannabe. He had become close to Finch, making it a very personal job to ensure his safety. Khalifa though was fascinated with all things ancient and was convinced that Oman was the source of all Biblical legend. Blind love for his land with the optimism of an old English adventurer would have moulded his thoughts. His enthusiasm was contagious. After spending a month with him, he had declared that Finch was now his brother, though the two hadn't spoken since. But hey, isn't that what families do? Could he be trusted though, what pull did he have? Was he even alive?

Finch decided that he needed to at least touch base with Khalifa and find out where he was. Without giving anything away, Finch had to know that he had an ally with him out there – because the one thing he had learned was that when it came to religious archaeological finds, things always got funky. Throw this regression stuff into the mix and one could be opening up a whole can of worms! Finch found his last number and set about finding Yousef Khalifa.

CHAPTER 10

A dark shadow had followed Femi to the Cairo Museum. He needed to go into the office he used there to make a note of the various applications for digs within Egypt. He far preferred to work from the museum as it was detached from the various governmental bureaucrats and red tape, plus he loved to be surrounded by the artefacts of thousands of years from his beloved country. At times he would just sit in the main hall staring at the various finds and get completely lost in his own world. It would sometimes mean him not leaving the place until well into the early hours of the morning, but he was a man who could survive on little sleep, but it was worth it to be surrounded by all the echoes of the past. The figure watched as he opened the door and shut it very deliberately behind him. It was Victor.

He crossed the street and threw his smoked Gitane to the floor and made his way round to an alley that ran beside the museum. It was poorly lit and a tradesman's door was the best way to gain access. Victor surveyed it closely. The lock was surprisingly ordinary for a door to such a wonderful place. The room that lay on the other side of the door belonged to the cleaners. They would normally prop the door open and smoke, sleep and while away the day. The door that separated the room from the museum was a more substantial one entirely, but Victor had to get in. Normally he would have been more methodical, more professional, but time was running out and he needed to know what Femi knew. He had no idea of what, if any, other security measures there were, and whether smashing open this door would trap him and have the local police alerted from an alarm connected directly from the museum to the police station. A more direct approach was needed. He sidled his way toward the museum's front door and banged on it loudly and deliberately. Nothing. He did it again and still not a flicker from within. He tried again and this time, a middle-aged, over-weight guard opened the door tentatively. 'What do you want?' the guard asked curtly.

Victor looked at the man with his deep black eyes. 'I wish to speak to the man who just entered the museum – Mr El Masri. It's most urgent that I meet with him now.'

The guard looked at Victor suspiciously. 'It's late. Come back and see Mr El Masri in the morning.' The guard attempted to shut the door but Victor pushed his shoulder and body weight against it, preventing the guard from moving it an inch. Victor was assessing the situation. 'Is there someone… your boss, I can speak to about this please?'

The guard was visibly annoyed by this and again curtly replied, 'I am the boss here. There is no one else, and Mr El Masri does not wish to be disturbed no—' As soon as Victor heard that the fat guard was alone, he made his move. He pushed his shoulder inside the heavy door with enough force to knock the guard back on his heels. He was obviously out of shape and no match for Victor who was tall, fit and strong. As soon as Victor was inside, he sidestepped behind the guard and got his forearm around the guard's neck and applied pressure, then lifted the man off the ground so that all of his weight was being supported by his neck. The guard did his best to struggle but Victor was firm and strong. This was only going to end one way and soon the guard's body went limp. Victor dropped him to the floor and dragged him behind the reception desk out of direct sight of the doorway. He straightened himself up and started to make his way to the main hall, when he stopped and turned back to see the lifeless body of the guard. He walked over and took the Glock pistol, which was strapped to the waist of the dead man and put it in the waistband of his trousers. Then, with a sickening crack, he smashed his heel down on the dead guard's throat. 'No point

56

in being unsure,' Victor said to himself with a smile, clearly enjoying that final death blow.

Femi was in his office writing a letter to a prospective archaeologist who was seeking permission to start a dig to the south of the city. Femi liked to handwrite his letters. He was 'old school' and thought that a personal touch when dealing with these situations was far more apt. He only ever used a Montblanc Meisterstuck fountain pen and always used black ink. He had beautiful handwriting and took pride in the work of art he produced on his quality writing paper. He was in a world of his own, blissfully unaware of the drama that had unfolded in the reception area of the museum. He was brought back to earth with a prolonged knocking on his office door. 'Knock, knock, knock,' came a voice in a slightly stilted French accent. The door swung open, revealing Victor leaning against the side of the door.

Femi was calm. He sat up and put down his pen. 'Who are you; what are you doing here?' Victor looked down at him then smiled and put his finger to his lips to shush the man in the seat. He walked over slowly and sat in the chair opposite Femi. Meanwhile, Femi was feverishly looking over the stranger's shoulder, trying to see whether the night guard was about to arrive and eject this dark stranger.

Realising what he was doing, Victor said, 'You needn't concern yourself about being disturbed; I have, shall we say, given the guard the night off.' He smiled to himself and got out his cigarettes, putting one to his lips. 'Do you mind?' Victor asked as he lit the cigarette.

Femi looked bemused. 'Again, I will ask you. Who are you and what is it that you want? Can this not wait until morning?'

Victor ignored him and looked around the room. It was adorned with archaeological photos and framed insects and bugs, Femi's other great hobby. On the huge mahogany table, was a beautiful knife, recovered from a tomb Femi helped to unearth on his first dig and which, as a gesture of thanks, the government had presented it to him. It was gold, eight inches long with a simple slim blade and a handle that mimicked the hand that held it. Still as sharp as the day it was made, with small pieces of jade, onyx and opal inlaid around the top and bottom of the handle, that glinted in the dim light of the office.

Finally, Victor exhaled his cigarette smoke right at Femi and spoke. 'You are Mr Femi El Masri. You are Egypt's answer to the 'big red pen' — ticks and crosses and all that, when it comes to matters of digging in this squalid country – yes?'

Femi looked shocked at this man's tone. He wasn't used to being spoken to like that, particularly not in his own office. But there was something unnerving about him that made Femi nervous. Femi took a moment.

'Yes, I am! Now to whom am I speaking?'

Victor took a deep drag on his cigarette and leant back, brushing off some ash which had fallen on to his trousers with a couple of deliberate strokes of his hand.

'I am Victor Mantz. I am a man who is looking for something. Something that is of the utmost importance. And you, Mr El Masri, I am assured have the answers to some of my questions, and you will tell me what I need to know. I am not known for my humour, nor am a patient man. I therefore will not tolerate any lying or hesitation on your behalf. So you will tell me what I need to know. Do you understand me?' Femi stared back trying to assess the man sitting in front of him. Victor continued. 'I have been around for hundreds of years and will continue to visit this earth in various forms but now I want to stay as I am. I like me – this me – and I am bored with starting over again and again. I need to be on the first flight out of your squalid country tomorrow morning with the information I require and if you try and deny or resist me in the slightest, I will make your death a slow and horribly painful one. Do you still understand me?'

Femi nodded, understanding the gravity of the situation. He took out his linen handkerchief and mopped his brow and mouth. 'What is it you want to know?'

'The man you accompanied to a dig recently. A white man. Who was he?'

Femi recalled his name instantly. 'Finch. His name is Jake Finch.'

Victor stubbed his cigarette out on the floor beside him. 'Finch. Yes! Tell me what he was looking for. As I understand it, the tomb he uncovered was poor and the diggers you had working on the site were most disappointed with the results – seems a great deal of work for such little reward, but by all accounts, he was quite satisfied with what he found.'

Femi looked at Victor; he really did not want to say but the stranger's presence made him feel most uncomfortable. He said, 'May I?' Leaning forward, he opened the bottom drawer of his desk to reveal a half-drunk bottle of scotch and glasses. 'Would you like to join me?' Femi asked. Victor shook his head but indicated that Femi may continue. He poured himself an ample helping of alcohol and drained it, wincing a little at the taste. 'The tomb was that of a man around the Ptolemaic era, a builder or something. He had nothing much in his tomb and Finch isn't the talkative kind. All I know is that whatever he found in the man's humble possessions made him happy and he departed for England the next day. It's the truth – I swear to it!' Femi shouted, mopping his wet brow again.

'Oh, I believe you are telling the truth. Most definitely. I just get the feeling that you have just not filled in the blanks comprehensively enough. Yes, the tomb was of a worker – not of anyone of any wealth or power and certainly not a tomb that a drunk Egyptian worker would remember. Yes, he found something and yes, he was happy. I am just struggling with the bit about not explaining anything. After all, you are the man with the red pen. Wouldn't you have been ever so slightly interested as to why a man would be digging for such an uninspiring tomb and then be delighted when he found it bare, save for a few trinkets? Wouldn't the head of the Egyptian Archaeological Department have been just a little more inquisitive? After all, you are an expert in this field and would have had a natural interest – together with your naturally suspicious mind. Are you really telling me that you were satisfied with his explanation? Are you really happy with your answer, Mr El-Mas-ri?'

Victor was now standing and had come round to sit on the corner of the desk facing Femi and looked straight into his eyes. Femi shuddered and felt a surge of fear running up his spine. Femi leant away from the man and reached for his whisky bottle but before he could get to it Victor pushed it aside. 'It was the tomb of the head architect of Ptolemy. He had been tasked with building a copy of the Great Library of Alexandria somewhere in the East as Ptolemy knew it wouldn't be safe from thieves or natural disasters, so he had everything copied and moved. Only a few had knowledge of this.' Femi paused.

'Go on,' pushed Victor.

'Finch was looking for any clues that could lead him to the Library. He had been working on theories for years and this find was the culmination of a lot of work. He found a parchment which proved this was the man he was looking for and the existence of the Library – where it is, I do not know; I swear this to you on the word of Allah!' Femi paused again and looked as guilty as a child who dipped his finger into his mother's cake mix and been caught. Victor picked up on this straight away.

'And – what else?'

'Finch found what he was looking for and then on a parchment in a box found something else. It basically said that the Library was just the start and that it would indicate where the true treasure was – the whereabouts of... the Holy Grail. I know this because I was curious too and wondered why he was so content. The writing was in Eno... Enochr... some kind of language.'

Victor interjected, 'Enochian.'

'Yes! Yes, that was it! He told me everything and thanked me and asked me to keep this quiet. I agreed, as it would be a wonderful find. And that is all, I swear to you, now please... please go,' Femi pleaded with the man.

Victor stood and lit another cigarette, clearly pleased with what he just heard. 'Thank you, Femi – you have been most accommodating and enlightening. I must be leaving for London now as Mr Finch and I have business. We are old friends, going back a very long time. But you see, I think there is still more.'

Victor knew full well that Femi had told him the whole story but now Victor wanted to have some fun. He took the knife which was perched on the desk and studied it. 'It's beautiful and heavy – what man is capable of is astounding.' With that, he turned with furious speed and speared the blade through Femi's hand resting on the table. It seared through the flesh with ease and embedded itself firmly into the wood of the table. Femi screamed, as much in disbelief at what had just happened as in pain. This was the bit Victor enjoyed the most. He didn't have to do it as often now as he had in the past. He just liked to.

Femi was staring down at his hand speared to the table. He was sweating profusely and was in shock. 'Please! I told you all that went on between Finch and myself. You must believe me!' pleaded Femi. Victor removed his jacket and placed it on the back of the chair he had been sitting on.

61

'Oh I believe you. It's just that I have always enjoyed the art of inflicting pain. Sick? Yes, but everyone has their vices. At least I can admit to mine.' He tapped the whisky bottle in disapproval. 'Besides,' he continued, 'I had to kill the guard outside to get to you and you know that I did it and you also know where I am going, so ergo, you are a potential thorn in my side. Therefore, unfortunately, you must be silenced as well.' The realisation of what he had just said shook through Femi's body like an earthquake. He made to scream but Victor had snatched Femi's handkerchief and shoved it deep in his mouth.

He turned, smiling to himself and sauntered over to the door. From the outside through the gap could be seen the terrified face of Femi pinned to the table with his own handkerchief gagging his sounds. As Victor held the door, looking down the dark passage, he paused, 'It is one of life's most amusing quirks that only now just before a man's imminent death that one feels most alive. Enjoy it, it is rare thing.' He now turned to Femi. 'Now let us see if we can display you like one of your beetles, shall we?' The heavy door closed slowly and the muffled cries from the middle-aged Egyptian filled the room.

After a while, Victor opened the door and left the office with a swagger in his step. He was off to London. He knew he was on the right track at last and Finch was going to do all the hard work for him.

CHAPTER 11

Finch had taken some time to get his head together and had also arranged for another consultation with Martin Wiltshire following the last conversation he had had with Kris. He hadn't given too much thought to that whole can of worms, instead, he now had to work on his strategy for tackling Oman. The parchment was definitely pointing to that country and now he was furiously researching the Bimmah Sinkhole and the lagoon that lay beneath it. He had also managed to contact Khalifa. He was now, fortunately for Finch, living in Muscat and was working as a liaison officer between the Omani Armed Forces and the UK Security Services. His job was to try and get the Oman armed forces more involved with British army training and doctrine, sending forces and individuals over to the UK to train and learn the language. Khalifa was perfect for this role as he spoke superb English and was immensely charming. He had been thrilled to hear from Finch, and when told that he was coming to Oman, had not allowed Finch to even think about staying anywhere but his home. Finch was very coy at explaining why he was visiting and Khalifa could most definitely smell a rat. But with Khalifa potentially on side, it would at least make having a sneak peek at the sinkhole a whole lot easier. He would have to tell Khalifa more eventually but for the time being, he merely told him that it was a bit of business and pleasure and that he intended to do some diving at the dive centre in Muscat. Finch was an accomplished diver, having made many descents on various hidden sites in the ocean, but cave diving always scared him and he preferred someone with him, someone as accomplished as he was. He marked out the route to the sinkhole which lay on the coastal road between Muscat and Sur. Did the ruins at Qalhat have any clues hidden within it? And what the hell did all that

Enochian text mean? Was this really a Grail path? What power did it possess? All these questions whirled around his head but he was making headway. He scribbled relentlessly in his black notebook. He didn't want to be stuck in any way when he was abroad, so his planning was usually meticulous. Sometimes though, it was best to just get feet on the ground in the country and see it all with one's own eyes. What's more, Khalifa was going to help him with his visa, which was a great help as Middle Eastern red tape was always a nightmare.

It was seven o'clock and Finch felt he had earned a beer and so made his way to the Poulett Arms and prepared himself for a cold Guinness. As Finch entered the pub, in the background, out of sight, a dark shadow watched his every move with a calm calculated posture, a white filter-less tar-stained Gitanes marking the spot where he had just stood. The game was truly afoot.

CHAPTER 12

Finch got off the train at Bristol and was immediately met by a familiar figure. It was Kris. He was wearing exactly the same clothes as when they had first met and looked as unkempt now as he did then. 'Do you ever change?' Finch asked with a wry smile. Kris just shrugged and walked with him to the taxi rank.

'I'm glad you decided to go along with this, Jake. It's important. Listen to what your feelings tell you. Let the emotions overwhelm you and listen to the guidance Martin and I will give to you. When you can control your regression and use it for your own benefit without the confusion and the haze it is leaving now, it will open up a whole new world for you,' Kris said, looking straight at him, emotionless.

'Let's give it a go,' Finch answered with a slight sense of doubt in his voice.

When they got to the practice, Martin had rearranged his morning's clinic and both men were ushered straight upstairs without waiting. There, eager to get started, was Martin. 'Good morning, chaps! This is exciting. Regression!! Are you ready, old boy?' he continued without letting Finch speak. 'Sit. Sit. Sit. Or better still, lie back on the couch. Take your shoes off... or leave them on if you wish. Hands on your stomach. That's it, now... ahhh.' Martin was more excited about this than he had been in a long time. He now had to collect himself. After a while, he turned to Kris and said, 'What I intend to do is let him go back to a time of his choice, experience it and then see where we are. There may be names, faces, etcetera, we can work with and then if you could step in while he is still there and tell him how you... manipulate things, yes?' Kris nodded in agreement. 'Right, Jake. Relax and listen to my voice.' He turned to his table and started a metronome with a slow, methodical beat. 'Listen to the beat and let your body go limp. Concentrate on your breathing; think about it. Breathe in deeply for the count of three, hold it for three and then release for three seconds. Control your breathing and feel your body loosen. The air you are methodically breathing is flowing calmly around your body, relaxing you, slowing your heart rate and unplugging your mind from the tensions of the day. Listen to the beat and with every breath you take, control and exhale, you are going deeper and deeper asleep. Let yourself drift into a deep sense of relaxation where you are controlling your deep breaths.' Martin's voice was slow, rhythmical and calming. Even Kris, at one stage, felt like taking a quick nap himself. After a short while, Finch was out. 'Now, go back to a time, Jake. Go back to a time through the mists of the past where you have been before; any time, good or bad, a time that is vivid; go back and when you are there nod gently and look around you and be in that moment and when you feel happy just tell us what you see and where you are,' Martin instructed. After a short while, Finch gave a slow deliberate nod. Martin and Kris waited.

Finch drifted ever deeper asleep. He twitched in his thoughts and then he could see it. This was no dream; he was there. He could smell and feel everything. He was regressing.

He was on the edge of a field, the open ground stretched out in front of him. There was an old oak tree, large and shading him from the midday sun. He looked down and he could see his clothes. He was a soldier, that was clear. He had knee-high boots, trousers and a long thick coat. His musket was resting against the tree that was doing such a good job of keeping the sun off his face. In front of him was his hat and it reminded him of a Cavalier. He looked around and saw behind him an encampment. Tents and a fire with a pot hung over it. There were about a hundred men. Some sitting, some eating, some sleeping and some tending the horses. He recounted all this to the others in the room.

66

A voice came from behind him. 'You look like you are miles away. Am I disturbing you?' Finch looked round and saw a face he recognised. It was the same face he saw in his Bannockburn dream and so many dreams like this one. He had long hair and a ridiculous moustache with a pointed little beard. Finch stared at him before replying, 'Sorry, I was daydreaming. A day like today should be spent sitting, fishing and drinking wine.' The fellow laughed.

The man put his foot up on a small mound and rested his arms on his knee. 'You are not wrong, Jacob. Instead, I feel like a line sinking to the murky depths of some old pond because of the number of these buggers weighing me down.' With that, he pulled out a handful of musket shot and jiggled them in his hand. He then laughed and mischievously pushed them into the mud at the base of the oak tree. 'There. That should lighten the load a bit.' Then there was a shout from behind. A man on a horse. A sergeant perhaps.

'Hey – you corporals – Stand Too! Riders are approaching from the south.' Finch immediately took his musket and searched the horizon. The man standing next to him was Daniel. Finch instinctively knew his name. He could feel that not only were they serving together but were friends.

Martin interjected, 'What year is this, Jake?'

'It is 1649.'

'Ah, he must be part of the King's army in the English Civil War – how splendid! What do you see?' he asked eagerly.

Finch spoke quietly, 'In the distance, there are horses, coming this way. We are all stood too.'

Martin smiled. 'And are you a Cavalier or Roundhead – a soldier?'

Finch recanted, 'I am a corporal in His Majesty's 1st Dragoon Guards – protectors of the Crown against the pretender – Cromwell and his bunch of self-righteous bastards!' Finch could see some horses in the distance about three quarters of a mile away. He laughed and turned to Daniel. 'I will split that Roundhead into quarters with one shot – even from this distance!' Daniel laughed. 'You're good but not that good. Save it until you are sure, then let the bastard have it.' The horses stopped and gathered themselves at the bottom of a hedge-lined field. They obviously had the knowledge that the Cavaliers were in the tree line and were rightly hesitant. The sergeant who had spoken previously dismounted his horse and crouched between the two men. 'A recce party perhaps?' Finch peered again and could see that the men were dressed well and were no ordinary forward scouts.

'They appear to be more important than that. All mounted and dressed well and no one on foot? Is it a smoke screen to hit our rear or a show of intent?' Finch thought aloud. 'Well, whoever they are – they looked pissed off.' The sergeant indicated by nodding his head toward the riders who looked agitated. After a short beat, the sergeant whispered, 'These pig herders have had enough time now. Corporals. Take ten men – use the hedge line and stay out of sight and see them away.' Finch grinned.

'Yes, Sergeant!'

Finch recounted his story to the others in Martin's room, both fixed and listening intently. Finch and Daniel took ten men, ridded themselves of anything heavy and liable to make a noise and skirted around the field, shadowing the hedge line to flank the horsemen who numbered some seven in total. All were armed with pistols and swords, but more importantly, all seated on large horses. They got within fifty metres of the Parliamentarians and loaded their muskets. A quick volley and then a swift follow up would put an end to this skirmish. The muskets though were notoriously inaccurate and so the closer the better, but in a fight between a mounted soldier and a sword-wielding man on the ground, there really is only ever one outcome. They had to get this right. With muskets loaded, they could hear the enemies' voices and smell their horses. On Finch's word, they moved out from the shadows of the hedge and steadied themselves for their shot. This had to count. They rushed forward and out into the field and picked their men.

'Fire!' shouted Finch and with that the horsemen turned in shock at seeing twelve men on bended knee holding them in their sights. Their instant reaction was to counter the offensive move with a charge. They kicked their spurs into the horses' flanks and hurtled toward the musketeers. Finch fired and the others followed. He had singled out the man who was clearly their leader and the heavy shot hit true and hard into the man's face through the gap in his visor. The power of the shot drove him off his steed and he hit the ground hard – his face showing a small hole under his left eye, but leaving a massive exit wound at the back of his head, the helmet acting like a bowl, caught the man's brains and bone.

The others discharged their weapons and through the smoke and gunpowder, they could assess how successful they had been with their opening volley. Of the seven riders, three had been killed but four survived, one badly wounded through his shoulder but remaining seated. The Cavaliers knew the drill. When a mounted horseman made for you, one couldn't outrun him or have time to reload. It was fleet-footed swordsmanship that would save him. Finch grabbed the first three men beside him and told them to get to the hedge line and reload and carry on shooting. The others drew their swords and waited. One horseman veered off and followed the musketeers and managed to dispatch two of them without too much trouble. The last made it to the safety of the hedge and scrambled away, trying to find his spare shot. The horseman turned and joined the others. In front of Finch, he saw the thundering hooves of a bay coming straight for him, its rider screaming and pointing his sword at his throat. Finch feinted one way as they came closer and then lurched to his right out of the horse's path. As he did so he evaded the lunge of the rider but managed to swing his sword round and catch the rear Achilles tendon of the bay. The horse whinnied and stumbled throwing its rider off with force. Finch, who was lightly dressed and free from anything that would slow him down, jumped up to his feet and saw the fallen Roundhead. He was confused from his fall and before he could regain his composure, Finch pounced and drove his sword deep into the man's neck. He gargled and foamy blood spewed from his mouth before he went limp and dropped to the ground. Finch withdrew his sword and went looking for more work.

The injured rider had managed to guide his horse into one of the foot soldiers, knocking him down and finishing the job off by having the horse land on him with its iron shoes. Daniel was faring better. He had launched his sword in a javelin-like manner into the neck of the horse, throwing it into a mad panicked fury and up-ending the rider. He was no match for the soldiers that surrounded him and he was dealt with swiftly. The two riders that remained stayed calm; they knew they still had the edge even though there were still nine men against two. Finch barked orders to the others and decided to get his musket so that he could take the horsemen out from a safe distance. Thinking that the Roundheads would be concerning themselves with the others, he put his head down and ran for all his worth to the hedge where he had dropped his weapon. He got down on one knee and started to reload. At that point, he looked up to see Daniel running toward him, yelling – everything seemed to slow down. Daniel was being pursued by a rider and Finch frantically tried to speed up the loading of his weapon to help his friend; but, as the horseman came closer and readied his sword, a loud crack came from Finch's right and the horseman dropped out of his saddle and hit the ground, leaving the horse to gallop aimlessly into the field toward the cavalry line. The musketeer in the hedge line had picked his spot well and had shot immaculately. The other soldiers killed him quickly, but Daniel still ran toward Finch screaming. It was then that Finch realised why his friend was shouting. As he made to turn and look over his shoulder, Finch could hear the dull thud of horse's hooves kicking up the wet soil and a searing pain streamed through his chest as the point of a sword ripped deep into his back, tearing flesh, sinew and bone. It was as if the sword was super-heated and the pain was indescribable. The shock of the attack dumbfounded Finch. He could see Daniel running, shouting, tears in his eyes and spittle flowing from his mouth, but he could not do or say anything. Then a hard but blunted thud hit Finch on the back of his neck and everything went very quiet and peaceful and the world started to go dark. His head lurched forward and he was vaguely aware that it grasped on to his neck by the thinnest of organic matter, as the last electronic messages flooded his brain. He felt no pain and then there was nothing.

Finch had been giving a vivid narrative all this while, holding his audience in a trance. Suddenly, he went silent and then gasped for breath, his eyes red with tears and his brow thick with sweat. Martin collected himself quickly and roused Finch from his regressive state. The room was still and silent. It was Kris that broke the silence. He knelt before Finch.

'Are you OK?' he asked more purposefully than with any care.

'Yes!' Finch panted. 'I, I died – just then.'

Martin sat forward and stared at Finch. 'Bloody Hell! That was incredible – you bloody died! I need a drink.' Martin stood and removed an old book on the shelf which was hiding a half-drunk bottle of whisky and took an exaggerated swig. Finch, though, was surprisingly calm.

'It's true – we are real. That was real. I mean, I don't know how, but this is real!' Kris smiled and walked over to Martin and took a sip of whisky. 'Daniel – you recognised him, right?'

'Yes – I see him all the time – we seem to be mates,' Finch said.

'He is your soulmate. We need him – he is one of us. We need to find him,' Kris said, taking another ample glug of Martin's Famous Grouse.

'You know him, don't you? Who is he?' Finch enquired tentatively.

'All in good time, my friend – we need to go. You did well today, but it is only the start. Was the other one there?' Kris asked. Finch just shrugged. 'We need to find… Daniel. Thank you, Martin. We will need you again soon. Thanks for the drink.' With that, Kris turned and headed out the door with Finch, dazed, following him.

'We need to talk. And I must go to Salisbury Plain and find those hidden lead shot to just…' Finch fumbled his words.

'Just to be sure,' Kris finished his sentence. 'Of course.'

A few hours later, Kris and Finch were on the edge of Salisbury Plain at the place Finch had described so well earlier that day in his regression. Finch tried to orientate himself to where exactly the shot would have been buried all those centuries earlier. He felt a great feeling of déjà vu and it wasn't long before he remembered where the tree was. He walked up to it slowly and laid his hand gently on the bark. He knelt down and with a stick, pried the compacted soil apart. Kris lit a cigarette and stared across the field. All this was a bit of a charade. A vital step

72

on the path for Finch's recognition of the fact all this was indeed true. It didn't interest him. He just wanted to get to London so they could make efforts to find the person Finch described as Daniel, although Kris had an inkling of his whereabouts already. As well as finding Finch, he had researched the locations of other ex-Templars as well.

Finch kept digging until he hit something hard. He scrabbled away in the dirt and pulled out a couple of dirty round musket balls. He was gobsmacked. He felt quite overwhelmed with emotion and it was all he could do to hold back the tears.

'They're here. It's all true. It's incredible,' Finch said, looking at Kris who in turn stepped on the small, barely lit cigarette end.

Placing a hand on Finch's shoulder, he said, '*Nous sommes ce que nous sommes et nous sommes toujours le templier et nous devons finir ce qu'on a commencé. Toujours*' (We are what we are and we are still the Templar and we must finish what we started. Always).' Finch nodded and understood. He collected the shot and placed them in his pocket and the two men headed for London.

CHAPTER 13

Victor sat in the café drinking an espresso and taking no notice at all of the 'No Smoking' sign. He stared out of the window as if looking into the past. 'Excuse me, sir. Would you mind not smoking? This is a non-smoking café. If you would like to smoke, I can get you a table outside.' The waiter was courteous yet confident in his manner. Victor looked up at the man with his dark sinister eyes and smiled a sickly smile. He took a final deep inhalation of the cigarette and handed it to the waiter, staring at him. The waiter, a little bemused, reached for the half-smoked cigarette. Victor grabbed the wrist of the young waiter and pulled him in. Victor had great strength and the waiter was a waif of a man. He exhaled his smoke into the young man's face and released his grip and turned to continue staring out of the window. The waiter retreated to behind the counter, unsure of what to make of his encounter with the tall stranger. Victor sipped his coffee. Life was not worth living if it didn't consist of extremes and so the strongest coffee and cigarettes were just the tip of the iceberg.

A man walked into the café and spotted Victor straight away. He looked around suspiciously and sat alongside him. 'You have news?' Victor whispered in a low voice. The man who was thick set but had a weasel-like face obviously revered Victor but showed no fear.

'Yes, sir. Finch and Kris are in London. They are looking for Finch's friend.'

Victor knew what the man was talking about and interrupted him. 'They are looking for Renaud?'

The man nodded '*Oui*. Renaud de Vichiers. They need him. Would you like this to be prevented?'

Victor, who was still looking into the middle distance and not speaking directly to the burly individual, said, 'no. They must meet. It is important. Finch must find the Library. Stay in the shadows and tell me everything. Particularly when he leaves the country. But be discreet as I need Finch, and I need him to succeed. Go.' With that, he slid an envelope he produced from his breast jacket pocket across the table to the man. A hefty payment for his troubles. He picked it up and disappeared as quickly as he came. Victor finished his espresso, savoured the taste and dribbled a large glob of spit from his mouth into the small cup. He had his eyes fixed on the waiter as he did so and smirked. He placed the cup down and walked over to the waiter. He stood in front of him, menacingly and whispered, 'Do not ever speak to me again, you are a worm.' This was followed by an enormous, backhanded slap right across the young waiter's face. The hand, adorned by Victor's weighty gold ring which together with the force of the slap, sent the waiter flying behind the bar, knocking him senseless. Not content, Victor lifted the man up and placed his head under the steamer attached to the coffee machine. 'I smoke where and when I like, little worm!' And with a dash of his hand, twisted the handle round, sending a jet of scalding hot steam onto the waiter's head and face. Victor let go, leaving him to slump to the floor. He removed a Gitanes and lit it, throwing the match at the waiter. As he did, he sneered, '*Ver*! (Worm)' and left the café happy with today's business.

CHAPTER 14

Finch sat at his computer in his London flat and leant back on two legs of the chair. 'How the hell do I go about finding a bloke I don't know anything about apart from the fact he was called bloody Daniel in the 1600s? Do I get someone to sketch what I remembered him to look like and post a picture on the net in the hope that someone will recognise a drawing of a scraggly haired moustachioed Cavalier in dodgy clothing? I mean... How?'

Kris, who was standing on the balcony overlooking the Thames, looked at Finch. 'You know, I never remembered you being such a whiney bugger. I found you, Jake, and I haven't spent my time with my thumb up my arse dreaming of just Jake Finch. I can find people and I know exactly where the person you know Daniel as... is.'

Finch stared at him. 'Great. And when were you about to share this information with me?' Finch sneered.

'About two minutes ago! If I may.' Kris ushered Finch out of the way of the computer and set about finding Daniel. Finch got up, exacerbated.

'Is everything a bloody mystery with you?' Finch sighed.

This merely warranted a sharp response of, 'You're the archaeologist – you work it out. There you go.' Kris sat back as Finch came round and stared at the computer screen. 'Daniel!'

Finch immediately turned and headed to look at the screen. but just before he could see the elusive face of Daniel, Kris shut the lid.

'What now!' Finch sighed.

'Right! Before you see the photo, you need to know something,' Kris said, stuttering his words, knowing that this conversation was not going to be an easy one.

'Right….and?'

'Well, the soul regeneration thing isn't a precise art. The truth is, I just don't know how it really works, but sometimes you recognise the old person and sometimes it is not so easy, though there are definite traits' Kris continued.

'So - Daniel, or what was Daniel may look a bit different?' Finch said, not really looking surprised.

'Yes! You got it. So just keep an open mind,' Kris said, slowly opening up the screen.

'Oh come on Kris, just show me, it's not as if he's the Queen!' Finch grabbed the laptop and looked at the screen. 'You seem to have gone off the page?' He handed the laptop back to Kris.

Instead of taking the computer, Kris pushed it back to Finch, 'Nope, that's the right page old boy. Meet…Daniel."

'What! But it's a woman and as I remember it, Daniel was definitely a bloke. Not a Danielle but Daniel, you know winky and doesn't need to sit down to wee!!' Finch said, still reeling from seeing the photo.

Kris paused and stood, 'Well there really is no getting away from the fact you have a brilliant mind. Yes, she's woman. And if I may say, a very beautiful woman. Plus, if I am not mistaken, there is definitely a kind of Rihanna look about her?'

Finch stared at Kris with incredulity.

'Oh, don't be such a misogynist Jake! So, he's a woman. I don't know how but he is. I mean, I've never regenerated as a chick but it obviously happens. But it is definitely him.'

'How do you know? You were looking for Daniel and found Karin — there just may have been an error in your bloodhound skills Sherlock!' Finch's voice was now raising in tone.

'Look moron! It isn't the first time I have done this and I knew from the start that he was a woman, I just chose not to tell you before, as I suspected that you may act like this.

'Like what?'

'Like a bigoted buffoon. The great Jake Finch. Conqueror of the sand, jungle and decoder of the past — Uber man! How could he possibly need the help of a woman? Well, tough shit pal. This is Daniel - was Daniel and we are going to find him, I mean her and she, he, she is going to help us and you are going to be nothing but encouraging and charming, because without his -ah! Her help, this won't work! Got it! Shit! Anyone would think we're born in the Middle Ages.' Kris was more exhausted than angry by Finch's manner.

'Well apparently, according to you, I am!' retorted Finch, crashing back on the sofa and looking like a spoilt child.

Kris moved over and sat on the edge of the couch. 'Look at her eyes. Isn't it a little unusual for a black woman to have such incredible blue eyes? And if you read her bio, she's like some all-action adventure lover. Sounds like anyone? I appreciate this is not what you expected or wanted but it is what it is and whether you like it or not, that is Renaud de Vichiers, and we need to speak with her...him.'

With yet another fumble on what to address Karin as, the two men laughed and broke the tension.

'Let's just go with Karin.' Finch smiled. 'I didn't see this coming. I think I need a pint.'

The two men got up and Finch grabbed his coat. As he closed the door, he recalled the previous conversation and stopped. 'And for your information, I am not a misogynist or a bigot. Just happy with my own company!'

Kris laughed and turned to him, 'That my old friend is the same thing. Come on, it's your round!'

After a pint and sandwich, courtesy of Finch the two men made their way to Wandsworth. As they got off the tube, Kris briefed Finch.

'So, Renaud de Vichiers, AKA Karin Edwards, lives at thirty-five Dolphin House, Wandsworth. Just around the corner.' Finch stared at the 'LinkedIn' image of the woman on his phone. There was no mistaking that she was a striking and athletic looking woman, but she bore absolutely no resemblance to Daniel whatsoever. It would be one thing to try and convince a guy that he was the regressed soul of a Knights Templar and get them to drop everything to come on some quest, but a successful woman, well that was going to be nigh on impossible.

'So, what is the score with her? Is she married? Kids?' Finch enquired.

Kris lit the cigarette he had been rolling and like some sci-fi space computer, started to reel off the life of Karin Edwards.

'Karin Edwards was born in 1986, which makes her 35 years of age. She was raised in Edinburgh until she left school and studied at Oxford for a degree in English. Her father left the family when she was three and is now deceased and her mother, with whom she was close to, died eight years ago. She has no relatives, an ex-husband that she can't stand and no boyfriend. She currently works for a Country Magazine as a writer but is trying to write a novel and make it as an author. She was an amazing Pentathlete in her time but she gave it up when she broke her ankle skiing. She owns a small cottage in Provence and strangely enough, speaks fluent French. As far as I am aware, she isn't a vegetarian and doesn't drink out of pint glasses!' Kris said smugly. 'Oh and has a strange scar on her left arm very similar to the one that you and I have.'

'Bloody hell, Kris. You forgot to tell me whether she had a crap this morning!' Finch was amazed by the information rolling off Kris' lips. After a pause, Finch asked, 'Do you think she knows? Does she know about you, me, the Templars and the regressions – can she do it? Is this going to be 'Mission Impossible'? Ultimately, are the police going to be called for two middle aged men trying to coerce an attractive woman into getting into a car with them? I guess it would have been easier to bring a puppy or bag of sweets!'

Kris laughed and spluttered on his smoke emanating from his mouth, 'Charlie said meow, meow, meow!' he said, doing his best impression of the cat from the 'Stranger Danger' ads of the 1970s.

It was good to see Kris laugh; it was the first time Finch had seen him lighten up and it made him seem more human.

'I am sure she knows, deep down. As we all do. I have no doubt that she has been waiting her whole life for us and I am positive that she won't be half as much of a pain in the arse as you were to convince.' Kris laughed out loud again. He was obviously enjoying this part of the adventure.

Karin stared out over the River Thames from her eighth-floor apartment. As Finch had alluded to before, she was a beautiful woman and in great physical shape, all apart from a slight tendency to shift the weight off her injured ankle. Not so much of a limp but a delicacy on each stride. She looked out of the flat sipping her coffee, lost in the ripples of the flowing water of the River Thames. She had a fire, a yearning somewhere, but even the need to find that fire, yet alone re-ignite it, had faded some time ago. The coffee wasn't hitting the mark and it was nearly 'gin o'clock'. Opening the fridge Karin saw that the basics of tonic and lime were nowhere to be seen and on closer inspection the need for gin was rather essential as well. She grabbed her purse and made her way to the local store.

Finch and Kris stared up at the apartment block from outside the 'Buy Wise' store opposite. 'That's it then, is it?' asked Finch. Kris just nodded as he rolled some tobacco into a Rizla. 'Right, number thirty-five! Let's go,' Finch said, talking more to himself than engaging with Kris. They hadn't got more than two steps when Karin emerged from the building, heading straight towards them. 'That's her. That's her. And she's heading this way,' panicked Finch. Kris looked at him in sheer bewilderment.

'What's up with you? You've been in many a scrape throughout your life and you're running about like a little girl, panicking because a woman who doesn't know what you look like and doesn't know who you are or even that we are looking for her is going to the shop behind you? You've changed, Guillaume! Keep calm and follow my lead.' Karin came closer and walked past the two men without the merest flicker. Kris was his usual aloof self. Finch, on the other hand, stood looking at the wall from a yard away. As Karin entered the shop, Finch couldn't help himself. He needed to look at this woman, his apparent long lost soul mate. He followed her into the shop and idled behind her. As Karin eyed up the tonic water, Finch stared intensely.

Knowing that this strange man was blatantly staring at her made Karin feel more than a little uncomfortable and she looked up and gave a forced grin toward Finch. Almost instantly, Karin gave a double take. She thought she recognised him but could not figure out how.

Finch saw that she had flinched at seeing his face and made for the door. Karin watched the man head outside, wracking her brain about how she knew him. When Finch got outside, Kris was waiting. 'Columbo you ain't!' Kris sneered.

'She saw me and she flinched – I think she knew who I was.' He ignored Kris' quip.

'Look, let's just let her get back to the flat and we'll follow her there. It won't do anyone any good talking out here. Agreed?' Finch nodded and waited for Karin to emerge.

A few minutes later, she walked purposefully past the two men and headed back to her apartment. Finch and Kris followed.

A short walk later, Finch and Kris were outside Karin's flat. Finch looked at Kris for confidence but he just wanted to get on with it. While Finch faffed, Kris took the initiative and rang the doorbell impatiently. A few moments later, the door opened with Karin looking suspiciously at the two men who looked more than a bit strange loitering outside her door. Karin had clocked Finch's face from downstairs in the shop and took a step back. 'Yes, can I help you fellows?' Karin asked slowly, keeping her foot wedged behind the door and the chain attached, while at the same time trying to find her hockey stick which she kept behind the door.

Finch cleared his throat and was just about to speak when Kris interrupted sharply. 'Hello, Miss Edwards. My name is Kris and this stuttering buffoon is Jake. Do you think we may come in and have a word with you about a very delicate matter?'

Karin looked puzzled, trying to make sense of what this dishevelled man had just said. 'No. No, I'm sorry it probably isn't the wisest thing to let two blokes I have never met before into my flat for a chat. No – say what you need to say,' Karin replied in a more imposing manner than her initial riposte.

This time it was Kris' turn to be cut short by Finch 'Look, Karin. We know who you are and I know you are wondering who the hell we are but we really need to speak to you. I know it's not a good call to let two random weirdos into your flat but I swear we are not mad, not interested in robbing you or anything like that. We have been looking for you for the longest time imaginable, well a few days in reality but anyway, we really need to speak to you.'

Finch spoke most earnestly and Karin felt a sort of connection with him. She couldn't help thinking that she knew this guy from somewhere. Not from their shop encounter but there was something else niggling her as to the identity of the bloke. She stood there eyeing up the two men. Before she could start to make sense of it all, Kris whipped his sleeve up and showed her the scar of the Templar cross on his arm. 'Plus, we have something in common, brother…. urm sister?' Karin stared in disbelief at the mark Kris presented to her. There was a long pause and Finch was about the speak when Karin unhooked the chain and opened the door.

Karin watched the two men walk into her flat and she left the door slightly ajar. She was ordinarily a sensible woman, but in that instance, it just seemed the right thing to do. She just hoped she wasn't going to regret it. Kris and Finch went into the L-shaped lounge with a kitchen at one end and a balcony at the other; the lounge was barely big enough to house a sofa against the wall. Karin caught up with the two men as they scanned the room and tried to get her words out.

'That, that thing on your arm, you showed me just then. How did you get it?' Kris brushed the question aside and nonchalantly told her he was born with it and carried on looking at the flat.

'It's the same as yours, Karin. You have it. I have it. And dopey balls here, has it. And if you would just relax and get us a

83

drink and let us sit down, I can explain why we are here and what this scar has to do with anything. Oh, and Karin… breathe!'

Karin didn't know whether she was coming or going. Her head was a whirl with questions. 'She steadied herself, realising at last that these men didn't at least seem to pose an imminent danger to her wellbeing. 'Coffee? Tea? Something stronger?' asked Karin. By this time, Kris and Finch were seated on the sofa.

'Whisky,' Kris ordered followed by Finch asking the same. Karin disappeared into the kitchen and then emerged with three large whiskies. They sat and drank a good dollop of booze and after a short while in a much more relaxed atmosphere, Karin broke the ice.

'Right, guys. I'm sorry to ask again, but who the fuck are you people? Do I need to start screaming? And just in case, I have a knife on me and I am a black belt at Ju Jitsu, ok!'

'No you're not Karin, but I believe you about the knife; you were always good with a blade,' Kris grinned.

Finch looked at Kris in wonder at his brashness but he was keen to try and appease his old friend.

'Look, Karin, we are not here in any way shape or form to threaten or harm you or make you feel uncomfortable. We would have spoken to you outside but this isn't the conversation for eavesdroppers and you would have just walked away. What we have to say to you is either going to blow your mind or you'll just think we're crazy and call the police. So, all I ask is that you hear us out and then the floor is all yours. OK?'

Karin took another slug and settled back into her chair staring at Finch and Kris. She had the same piercing blue eyes. A detail that hadn't been wasted on Finch.

'Ok astound me. What is this all about?' Karin replied, wishing she had kept her hockey stick with her to go with the knife.

Kris started to explain to Karin who she was, whilst Finch just sat staring at her, transfixed. Half because she was an attractive woman but half because he felt a fondness for this stranger that he couldn't explain. A soul lost in time that he had known for centuries.

Kris had gone through pretty much the same spiel that he had given Finch the first time they met. When he had finished, Kris leant back in his chair as if waiting for an appraisal of his performance. They both looked at Karin in eagerness waiting to see whether she either bolted for the door in terror or whether she was interested enough to find out more.

Karin sat as still as a bronzed statue and looked at the two men, her eyes flitting from one to the other. After a short while, she took a large glug of her whisky and leant forward resting her elbows on her knees. 'You know, I suppose most people would think that the explanation you have so eloquently given me was the biggest load of rubbish ever concocted and that they would have to be a complete idiot to believe, even for one second, that any of your story was true or even had an inkling of truth. And in theory, my next move should be to fend you off long enough for the police to get here. Normally, I am most people. But, but…' Karin hesitated. 'There is something so familiar about you both, particularly you. Jake?' Finch just nodded. Karin continued as she rose from her seat and wandered behind it, looking puzzled but slowly piecing everything together. 'You have a look, a smell, a… something. I feel like I know you and the weirdest thing, which is going to sound bizarre is that I have dreamt about you. In strange times. You may look slightly different, but it's you all the same.' Kris and Finch looked triumphantly at each other as if they had cracked some unbreakable code. Karin

85

continued, 'That on its own is strange, but the scar, our eyes and a strange yearning that I haven't completed something I was meant to do. It's uncanny!' There was a long pause while everyone in the room took stock of the situation. Karin poured herself another drink and offered some to her now guests. 'So I am a Knights Templar? I thought they were supposed to be a bit odd. Not all good – I mean, I've read about them. Plus, weren't they all men and if you hadn't noticed, I'm no man!'

Kris took the lead again. 'The Templars have been vilified for centuries. Used as a convenient scapegoat for any of the world's problems. The truth is that we were pure and sacrificed our living selves to do God's will and to protect all the Church's true relics that, if taken by the wrong hands, would wreak misery on mankind. But do not think for one moment that we were total saints. We were merciless warriors, crushing anyone who stood in our way. And we were good at it. Particularly Guillaume here. You, Renaud, were not too bad either.' Kris sat back and started to feel more relaxed.

'Renard. That was me?' Karin asked.

'Yes, Renaud de Vichiers. And yes, you are no man, and I am not going to pretend how all this works now but for some reason, you have regenerated into the body of a woman, but you are no ordinary woman. You have the heart and tenacity of a lion. You can never lose who you really are and you are and will always be a Templar. A warrior,' Kris said but with genuine emotion.

Karin smiled and liked the thought of what Kris had said. Maybe this was the purpose she had been searching for, for so long. The missing parts of the puzzle.

There was a pause while Karin took stock and Finch and Kris waited for her reaction.

'Awesome! A warrior monk – Knights blooming Templar! I'm sorry but that's bloody brilliant, although a little trippy!' Karin exclaimed and the three of them laughed and raised a toast. 'Look, I don't know whether this is for real. It seems a little too absurd, but at the end of the day, there are too many coincidences and at the moment my life sucks so, what the hell!' There was silence then Karin spoke. 'So what does this all mean? There has to be a reason why you told me this, right? Am I like an immortal or have powers?'

Finch looked at Kris once again and said, 'You'd better take this one.' Kris stood in a dramatic manner and untethered his coat in a most theatrical manner. 'Not quite. In a nutshell, we are immortal, or rather our soul is. Everyone has a soul, but it hops from one different person to the next, reincarnating and the déjà vu feelings people experience are old long-lost memories. Our souls dictate our physicality, usually, but it shapes our being and personality. Throughout the ages, we have looked similar and acted the same. You may have the body of a woman but you are still Renaud. Your eyes and manner. This will continue to be so until one's soul dies.' Finch leant forward at this point as he hadn't heard about a soul dying before.

'Your soul can die? I mean OUR souls can die?' Finch pointed out.

Kris continued, 'Yes. There is a way to kill a soul. You see, there has always been good and evil. Souls are born good and bad. There are those like us who have wandered the earth for years and our souls are pure, for we try to be pretty decent at all times, fearless in thought, word and deed. The flip side is that there are those who are naturally evil and they will do all they can to get as much power for themselves, to impose their will over others. And then you have the middle ground. The people who could be either or. This comes down to nurture. A good upbringing keeps people on the right track but a bad start and

87

they go the other way. It is not an exact science, and it is always about keeping the balance. There are some souls who are as old as us but darker than the night and these are the souls it is our job to rid the world of before they get the chance to seize the ultimate object of power. Our gift is to be able to regress ourselves to any time we have lived before and learn from our mistakes or sequence of events so that we can be better prepared and ready ourselves for the ultimate battle. We cannot change the past, but we can change our future by preparing for it in the best way possible. We have come together because of this quest, because the time is close at hand. And this is where you come in, Karin, and Jake will fill you in with all the details later, but we are on a journey, and we need you. Jake has found what he thinks is the resting place of the Great Library of Alexandria – the books that the Greeks and the rest of the ancient world revered. But this is just the beginning, for this will lead us to the greatest discovery of the world, the final resting place of the Holy Grail. Christ's chalice. And it is a chalice! We have all held it at one time and died many times over for it. It is what has made us what we are over hundreds of years and what we have fought for, and it holds immeasurable power. Should it fall into the wrong hands, well the results would be unthinkable, and whether one were a believer or not, the outcome would still be the same. Darkness for eternity. The holder would live forever and dictate the fate of mankind until the end of days and we would have failed.'

Kris stopped and stared out across the Thames. Finch stood and addressed Kris.

'Kris, is there something you are not telling me. Are we in danger?' The mood turned and the jovial atmosphere was now deadly serious.

Kris spoke out into the London air. 'There is one that I know of who would and has done everything to get his hands on this prize. At the moment, he calls himself Victor Mantz. He is

88

as old as we are but he is rich, powerful, cunning and his blood runs black with hatred and disdain for all things. He is a Regressor and is well skilled at the art. If he were to succeed, we would all die once and for all and the world would stare into an abyss of bleakness forever.'

'And this man is also a Templar?' enquired Karin. There was a pause and Kris turned to his friends.

'This man has a pitiless soul and wherever you have been over the centuries, he has never been too far away. We are like magnets and are drawn inexplicably to one another. He has nearly always beaten us. He is the reason why we cannot fail. Think back! Think of all those times you have been repressed, hurt, humiliated and even killed. Who do you think delivered you the blow to send you on your way on Salisbury Plain? It was him. And he is no Templar, yet still bears a sign of his past: a cross. But his is black. He was there at the beginning, but he didn't wear the white jupon and red cross of God. No, his war uniform was more terrifying.' Kris stopped.

Finch, sensing that Kris was deliberately pausing to prevent telling who this man was, interrupted frantically. 'Kris, who is he? Tell us!'

'He was a man of God who had all the power in the world. He was Pope Clement V. Clement ruled with a violent and repressive fist. Anyone he thought was a heretic, he would burn but sometimes it was just a convenient excuse. His annihilation of the Templars was all about money and power of which he wanted more, even though he had it in abundance. When he died, even God showed His displeasure at his wretched life. While his body lay in state, a thunderstorm developed and a lightning bolt struck the church and set it alight. How ironic! The fire was so intense that when it was extinguished, his entire body was almost destroyed. It was Clement who was the one who burnt you both at the stake in 1307.' The room fell silent. Finch slumped into the chair and Karin was speechless.

'I was burnt as a Templar for my faith,' Karin said to herself in a whisper.

'We all were,' Kris responded, 'hence our unnatural fear of open flames. It was 1307, October. Friday the 13th. The Pope had declared all Templars heretics and demanded our souls be purged. We had been on the run for years and every man wanted the bounty placed on our heads and an assured place in heaven given to them by the Pope. But he knew that with us out of the way his power would be unbridled. We killed many and tried for the longest time to defy this man, but eventually we were caught, tried, tortured and burnt. But you, Jake, for you Victor took a personal pleasure in igniting the pyre himself and laughed as your skin blackened and blistered in the flames. However, he failed, for with our deaths, we took our secrets and our faith, and not once in all the time under duress did anyone deny God, betray his friends or cry out in pain. We were perfect to the last. A fact that has always riled Victor and throughout the ages we have pieced together our past lives in order to be where we are today. The "signed" confessions were not ours but were forged. None of us would have signed something which denounced our faith, knowing full well we would all be slain anyway. So, you see, this is our destiny. We have no choice and we now have each other and we must see it through and, be under no illusions, we must succeed.' Kris finished; he had spoken with fire in his belly and now tears welled in his eyes. The three looked round and Karin broke the ice.

'Well, I may be new to all of this, but I'm in. This is extraordinary and I am totally with you!'

Finch stood and blurted, 'Of course. Completely!'

Kris just repeated, 'Completely.'

The three souls embraced. Kris, realising his cool demeanour had been breached, released from the hug. 'Well, that was easier than I thought. I had visions of having to leg it while you called the rozzers!'

Karin laughed. 'Well to be fair that would have been a more sensible thing to do than to let two shabby blokes into my flat and believe that I, a thirty something, young black woman was the reincarnated soul of a Knights Templar! Come to think of it – what the hell was I thinking!'

For a moment, it felt that the realisation that this was a little farfetched was about to get the better of Karin, until Finch piped up. 'Well, it's too late now, you said you'd help and you would just be a big fat liar if you didn't, so there!!'

The three laughed at Finch's childlike reposts and readied themselves for an adventure of a lifetime. This lifetime.

CHAPTER 15

OMAN – THE GREAT LIBRARY

The plane touched down at Seed International Airport, Oman and there was Khalifa waiting patiently to meet Finch. Khalifa had used his considerable contacts to get visas for Kris, Karin and himself and accommodation at the fabulous dive centre in Muscat, as his own house couldn't accommodate all three guests. Finch had been quite airy with the true reason he had come out to Oman, but Khalifa was nobody's fool and could smell a lie a mile away. Nonetheless, when Khalifa saw Finch, he cheered and embraced him like a brother. 'Ah, Mr. Jake – I did not ever expect to see you again but, Inshallah, you are here and I am very happy. Everything is taken care of and you are my guests in my country. It is good to see you, my friend. So good. And my English is even better – I could even pass for a country gent, no?' Khalifa beamed at Finch and slapped him heartily on the back and let out a roar of laughter. He was a big man and his character larger still. Finch was more pleased to see him than he had thought.

'Colonel,' as Finch liked to call him out of respect more than anything else and Khalifa liked it. 'Let me introduce my two comrades, Kris and Karin; they are professional colleagues of mine.'

Khalifa looked at them for a second and shook their hands eagerly. 'Friends of Jake's are also my friends. Come! Let us get out of this awful place and drink and eat and enjoy Muscat's finest hospitality,' beamed Khalifa. With that, the three were ushered into a long, blacked-out chauffeur-driven Mercedes Benz and taken to the dive centre.

The dive centre was about fifteen kilometres from the airport and when they arrived, Finch, Kris and Karin were taken aback by its incredible beauty. Wooden buildings on the beach, decked out in luxurious style, offering an incredible view on to the beach and the sheltered blue cove. With the sun dancing off the still waters, it was a vista of pure paradise. At its hub was the centre itself which offered a bar and food.

Karin was like a little girl having just unwrapped her dream toy at Christmas. 'This place is amazing. Why haven't I been here before?' asked Karin.

Kris replied dryly, 'Because it's sodding bankrupting to stay here!'

Karin just scoffed. 'Kris, smile and take that ridiculous coat off. Just chill and have some F-U-N.' Kris wanted to join in with the humour and allowed himself a wry smile with Karin but then returned to his more usual sombre and morose self.

'Remember, Karin. We're here for Finch. This is work, yeah?'

Karin nodded in agreement but added, 'Yeah but it would be great to have a swim though.' And with that, she ran down the beach fully clothed and hurled herself into the crystal blue waters, shouting as she went. This tickled Kris, who was half tempted to join her. While Karin and Kris checked out the beach, Khalifa pulled on Finch's arm and took him into the bar alone.

'A beer and an orange juice please,' he said to the waiter. Then he turned his gaze to Finch. 'We have been friends for some time now, Jake, and you make me very happy to allow me to help you and to see you once again, but please, As the English say, "I wasn't born just yesterday," no? So tell me, Jake, why are you really in Oman with two strangers? And please, Inshallah, the truth.' The drinks were delivered on cue and Finch took a long sip of the cold refreshing beer.

'I'm sorry, Colonel, I haven't been straight with you. It is just the fewer the people that know, the better.' Finch was still being very cautious over his words. Khalifa nodded but he wanted more. Finch still wrestled with whether telling Khalifa the whole story was a good move but he figured that he would need this man's help at some point, and he couldn't or even wouldn't assist if he didn't know the whole picture. Finch rubbed his face with the palm of his hands and began.

'I have found a clue that could lead me to possibly the greatest archaeological find this world has ever seen and it is hidden right here in Oman,' Finch whispered, taking another sip of his beer, his eyes flitting all over the place, searching for flapping ears trying to hear what was being said. Khalifa was silent and again indicated with his eyes that more information was required. Finch continued, 'It is quite possible that the Great Lost Library of Alexandria, that was spoken about in classical Greece, is not far from here – hidden from human view for a few millennia. Until now.' Khalifa put his drink down.

'Are you saying that the library is real and still exists and it is here in Oman?' Khalifa sounded incredulous. 'But how could that be? It was in Alexandria and was, as I recall, destroyed by the Romans when they invaded Egypt,' Khalifa argued.

Finch's eyes lit up at the thought once again of finding the Library. 'Yes, I know. It's hard to believe, but I have proof that Ptolemy had the Library moved in advance, in order to protect it in its entirety,' continued Finch. 'And I will need you, old friend, to help me confirm it. Just think what it will do for Oman.'

94

Khalifa swung him a look to say in no uncertain terms not to patronise him, which Finch got very quickly. Nevertheless, he was intrigued. 'Gosh! The Library? Here? Unbelievable! You know we will have to keep the Sultan informed about this. It will be impossible to keep anything from him and if I am seen as being disloyal then I would be ashamed, so this has to be done,' Khalifa confirmed.

These were not the words Finch wanted to hear, as he had hoped to keep all of this strictly below the radar. But he appreciated that this was the sensible course of action and there was no one better to try and persuade the Sultan and the powers that be to help this quest, rather than hinder it.

'I will do it, my friend, but I can tell you, and don't ask me why, but he will not like it and will want to see you in person, OK?'

Finch agreed to let Khalifa handle things, but all Finch wanted to do at the moment was finish his beer and get his head down.

The rest of the day was a blur of food and beer, but after a good sleep, Finch and the others were refreshed and rested. He rose early as he was keen to go and recce the sinkhole and see what lay before him. It was five o'clock and the sun was just starting to gently poke its head up over the horizon. Both he and the other two were all eager to get going. The journey from the dive centre to the sinkhole was about forty-five minutes by car. Khalifa had hired him a white Toyota 4x4 and it was just the job for Oman's unpredictable roads. Not a word was spoken on the way, all three wondering, in their own way, what lay beyond the opening.

Suddenly, Kris piped up, 'There! Up on the hill,' he shouted, pointing to a stone ruin being glazed in orange by the morning sun. Finch looked over and saw it. It was indeed the ruins of

95

Qalhat, the dome-less mausoleum of Bibi Maryam. It looked splendid and even better in real life. That alone would have been a spectacle enough to see but it was just a marker leading the way down to the Bimmah Sinkhole. Finch took the 4x4 up a rough track to the foot of the Qalhat ruins. He was in work mode and he removed from the boot of the vehicle his cap and satchel, which contained his trusty notebook, torch, knife and various articles he had collected that always came in useful when on a dig. With the car locked, they made their way west along a narrow path that took them over a rise and away from the road. As the group edged over the hill, their hearts thumped hard in their chests with the anticipation of seeing the sinkhole, but it was just a false crest. Sensing the disappointment, Finch took the lead.

'Come on. It's around here somewhere. Sinkholes don't just disappear.'

The others followed in silence. They walked for a further five minutes when, as they crested another small hillock, they saw it for the first time: a rocky sinkhole in the middle of the desert. It was innocuously magnificent. Finch couldn't contain himself and broke into a jog to get down to the opening. He peered over the edge of the rocks and looked down to see a greenish turquoise bowl of clear water. It was a place mentioned in all tourist books and more recently a set of concrete steps had been constructed leading down the shale to one side, to allow greater access for the reams of tourists that traipsed through the desert to have a dip in this glorious oasis. All those tourists had no idea at what may be lying underneath. They all just stood staring at the beauty of it.

'Let's get down there,' Karin shouted eagerly and now it was her turn to trot on towards the steps and down to the water's edge. Finch and Kris followed, although Kris broke into a quick saunter, as he didn't do running. They eventually got down the steps to face the hole. Finch scoured the walls of the sinkhole for any clues to the whereabouts of an opening, but it was just a sheer rock face and any shadowy crevasses were just slight folds in the rock making illusions in the morning sun. Finch lifted his cap and scratched his head. He was just about to say something when the surface of the lake erupted like a bubbling cauldron. The lagoon foamed into a frenzy until a black head appeared, breaking through the water's shimmering skin and then, he saw the glint of the sun reflected in a diver's mask. They all squinted to get a good look at the aquatic burglar.

The diver removed his air regulator from his mouth and called, 'I thought you said you were an early riser, my friend. It's almost noon.'

'Khalifa. It's Khalifa! What the hell are you doing?' Finch's shouts echoed around the chamber, reverberating in their ears. Khalifa had now swum over to the men on the shore, and sat in the shallows, removing his mask.

'Since you had met me all those years ago, I became something of a diving enthusiast and rather enjoy the solitude and silence of being underwater and exploring the great expanses of the ocean or small watery tunnels under the earth. So, after we spoke, I decided to see if I could be of some assistance in your quest. I kitted up this morning and have been hunting around down there for an opening.'

Before he had finished his sentence Finch was champing at the bit. 'Well? Well? What did you find? Is there an opening? A chamber? A tunnel? Is...' Finch was struggling to get his words out.

Khalifa looked at Finch with sombre eyes. 'I am sorry, my friend; I saw nothing.' Finch's look said it all. He was certain that this housed the Library or was this some thousand-year-old practical joke? He was just about to respond when Khalifa broke into a roar of laughter.

'Your face! Oh, I am sorry, my friend, but it is not often a poor Omani can get the better of a British gentleman. I am sorry. Finch, there is a hole in the wall. Hand carved about twelve metres down. It turns into a passage and continues on. It is the only opening in the wall and so must be something significant. I didn't go any further as it is always unwise to venture into such a place alone or without string. The water level must have risen over the centuries, hiding the opening from the public.'

Finch was still struggling to know whether to laugh or cry. Instead, he kicked Khalifa and kissed his head. 'You are a turd, Colonel! But I love you! Yes!' exclaimed Finch loud enough that it rang around the bowl. Karin and Kris were grinning like Cheshire cats and embraced Finch warmly.

'What now?' asked Kris.

'I'll get my gear from the car and follow Khalifa down to the tunnel. You guys stay topside and keep your eyes open. Let's get this party started.'

Within moments, Finch had run to the vehicle and brought his diving gear down to the opening of the sinkhole, where he started to change. It was still early, and the tourists hadn't appeared yet. As Finch hurried to get changed, Kris wandered over to Khalifa.

'Colonel. Are those two men with you? They have been there for the last few minutes and seem to be very interested in our movements.' Kris was pointing to two Omani men dressed in 'dish-dashes' smoking and observing the scene.

'No. They are not my people. They look like nomads being nosy. Pay no mind to them. It is nothing.' Khalifa waved it away as if swatting a fly. Kris, though, didn't like the look of them. They were showing more interest than just mere passers-by who happened to be watching the activities of some men in the lagoon. He decided to go and confront them.

98

'Hey, Karin. Over here. I need you!' he called. Karin looked up from where she was sitting with her feet in the water. She dried them off and without a word, caught up with Kris. As they got to the top of the concrete steps, the two Omanis headed back to their beaten-up truck and drove off to the east. That was just the reaction Kris didn't want to see, because it meant only one thing. Other parties were interested in what was going on and that spelt trouble. Kris and Karin made their way back down to the lagoon having seen off the voyeurs.

'Who were they? Locals?' asked Finch as he prepared to dive.

Kris lit a cigarette. 'No. This wasn't just some innocent passers-by coming to have a look. These guys were sent to watch us.'

'Government or local authorities maybe. You know how protective people are. Maybe they are just looking for a quick handout?' Karin enquired.

Kris shook his head adamantly. 'No. These guys have been sent to report back to someone about our movements and didn't want any trouble. If they were the authorities, they would have made a song and dance and we would probably have had to call upon Khalifa to sort things out.'

'Besides,' Khalifa interrupted, 'if it was the authorities, they wouldn't be dressed like Marsh Arabs and I would know all about it.'

Finch looked round at Kris. 'Who would want to know our movements, Kris? You seem pretty sure.'

'Victor,' replied Kris. 'He will want what we are looking for and will be on our tail. He wouldn't want to make any scene or intervene yet. Why do the work yourself if you can get a professional to do it for you? No, we are OK for now, but as this ball starts to roll, we will need to be more careful about what we

99

do and will have to watch each other's backs. We all know what he is capable of and with such a big prize at stake – well, it doesn't take much imagination to see what he would do to anyone who stands in his way.'

Finch tested his regulator and torch and grabbed a roll of string. 'Well, if we are OK for now, we need to make sure we get what we came here to find. Ready?' He turned to Khalifa who now had his mask back on and gave an "OK" sign with his hand. The two neoprene-clad men submerged to find out what lay past the watery tunnel.

CHAPTER 16

The water was crystal clear and the opening in the rock face was easily visible from under the surface. The doorway opened up and appeared to come to an abrupt end about ten feet into it. A design characteristic which no doubt had deterred many a prospective swimmer before, as it looked without any doubt, that the passageway ended there. But it didn't. It snaked back on itself and then returned round on its original course, an optical illusion that would have outwitted many. The tunnel was now pitch black as the ambient sunlight had disappeared and both Khalifa and Finch turned on their powerful torches. Meanwhile, Finch also secured a piece of string to a rock on the tunnel's side. This was usual practice for cave diving and would serve as their lifeline back, should they get disorientated. The passageway was bare. Just two walls about four feet apart and six foot high with absolutely no clues that this was leading anywhere in particular. In most instances, in Finch's experience, there was always a glyph or something pointing you in the right direction. Even if it was a sign, warning you to turn back. This, though, was more of the same. Finch had four hundred metres of line with him and he started to wonder whether it would be enough as the tube appeared to be never-ending. They stopped and looked around and checked each other. Khalifa's eyes sparkled in his mask and gave the "OK" sign once more and the two men carried on and all the while Finch became more and more concerned that this was going to have a disappointing ending.

The reel of string was getting dangerously close to the end, which meant they would have to turn back. Finch noticed that the air bubbles expelled from his regulator were starting to break on the water's surface which meant they were not so deep anymore. Then, through the darkness, the torches' beams

101

highlighted what appeared to be a step leading up. As they got closer, it became apparent that there was a set of stone steps leading out of the water. Finch kicked on and broke the surface of the water and took his first look at the underground cavern. He wasn't sure what to expect but what he did see left him cold and empty and disappointed beyond words. There, in front of him leading up from the submerged steps, was a large cavern. The rock walls were rough on all sides, bar the one directly in front. This was smooth going up to the roof of the space which, when it met with the flat wall, was about eight feet high. It was solid rock. Finch removed his fins and scuba gear and made his way up the steps. The air was stale and heavy. This room had probably never seen the light of day and he was more than likely the first man to stand here for a thousand or more years. Khalifa hurried to join him and the two scoured the area for any clues as to what this place was and if there were any other chambers. They trod carefully on the flat stone floor.

Finch shone his bright torch beam all around the cave. At its highest point, it stood about fifteen feet and was only about sixty by ninety feet with the steps leading down into the water from where they had just come from. It was Khalifa that broke the silence. 'What is your assumption, my friend? Was this the resting place of the Great Library?'

Finch bit his top lip in bewilderment. 'No. It can't be. It's far too small to house the scrolls, books and documents from the Library. If what we read is to be believed, you would need a room a hundred times as big. And just to plonk it here with such relatively easy access. No. This can't be it.'

Khalifa shone his torch around again looking for any other niches in the rock. 'But where then? We are in the right place, yes?'

Finch nodded. 'Yes, yes, we are here all right. Or at least I am pretty sure we are.' Finch headed toward the flat rock in front of the steps and patted it with his hand and tapped it with his knuckle. 'This has to be an opening of some kind. It's too out of sorts. Rough rock everywhere and a flat wall. But there doesn't appear to be any trace that it can be opened. No cracks, no seams, no nothing and this wall is solid. Maybe there is a trigger or key. Khalifa, let's look around for something unusual that would house a... something to open up the door. A hole in the floor or a button to push... anything.' The two men scoured the cavern, inspecting every inch of it. After a while, Finch slumped on the floor, resting his back on the flat wall. 'I know the Greeks were clever but this is ridiculous!' Finch exclaimed.

Khalifa was staring at the floor and noticed that it was well worn. 'The Greeks went to all the trouble of moving the Library here to keep it safe, and a great man was in charge of building the new resting place, it was probably his finest moment and would not want anyone to find it. Therefore, anyone capable of building this place must have a brilliant mind and would not want to disappoint his Pharaoh, so this key must be well hidden so that it would not even lend a clue that there is something else here. So we must think like a Greek, yes?'

Finch looked at Khalifa and smiled. 'You're absolutely right. Where would a brilliant Greek hide a key?'

The two men took one more look around and then resigned themselves to the fact that they would have to go back, not only empty handed but empty minded. They pulled their scuba gear on, re-attached their fins, checked their regulators and returned to the lagoon following the string which was guiding their way. The swim back seemed to take half as long as getting there, as Finch's mind was awhirl with questions. He was still trying to figure out where the hell an opening to a further chamber could be, as there just had to be one, when he and Khalifa emerged into the bright Omani sunshine.

As the two men broke the water's surface and adjusted their eyes to the striking daylight, they saw Kris and Karin standing and looking uncomfortable, an INSAS assault rifle aimed right at their heads. There were about ten men, dressed in army fatigues, all armed and looking unimpressed. Finch and Khalifa swam to the side of the lagoon, a trail of weapon barrels tracking their every move. As Finch got to the edge and removed his regulator a major in his early forties greeted him in perfect English.

'Mr Finch. I hope you enjoyed your dive in our sinkhole, it is quite beautiful. My name is Major Rami Amela of the Royal Oman Army. I am the Sultan's ADC. Would you please dress yourself and accompany me?' Finch looked confused and started to undo his kit.

Khalifa swam to the water's edge, spitting out his regulator. 'Major Amela, I am Colonel Yousef Khalifa and I am escorting these gentlemen as my guests; there is no harm done here. Remove your weapons from my friends immediately!'

The major stepped back and saluted the colonel. 'Colonel, with the greatest respect, I must ask that you join us. My authority comes directly from the Sultan himself. Please.'

Khalifa was stumped. He couldn't talk his way round an order from the Sultan. Both men hurried to get changed. When they had done so, Major Amela indicated to a soldier to collect the scuba gear and headed off towards Finch's car.

'One of my men will return your equipment to your car and follow us. Your keys, if you would be so kind, Mr Finch.' Finch tossed the car keys to the soldier and the other armed men hurried up and out of the sinkhole. Once they had emerged, they were confronted with four blacked-out Humvees.

Karin looked at Finch. 'Well, did you see it?' she whispered, overly excited and seemingly completely oblivious to their predicament.

Finch shook his head. 'Nope. Not a sausage.' Karin was just about to follow it up with another question when she was interrupted by the Omani officer.

'Would you please accompany my sergeant. Colonel, please go in the second car and, Mr Finch, you will ride with me in the lead vehicle.' All went to their respective cars and the convoy began.

'Are we being arrested?' Finch asked.

'No. The Sultan wishes to ask you a few questions personally and what the Sultan wants, it is our pleasurable duty to accommodate his every whim.' It was obvious the major did not want to engage Finch in small talk, so he sat in silence for the journey to the Al Alam Palace in Muscat. He was sitting in the back of a blacked out military vehicle at gunpoint and yet all that Finch could think about was where that entrance could be.

The vehicle arrived at the heavily guarded gate, which swung open when the guard commander recognised the major. It continued its way to the front of the palace where it stopped abruptly. The major got out and opened the door, ushering Finch inside. The palace was stunning and they all marvelled at the sheer decadence of the place. The sort of wealth on display was bordering on the vulgar but nevertheless impressive. There had been so much to take in, both at the site and here, that it hadn't even crossed Finch's mind as to the nature of the Sultan's request to seek an audience with him, until now. This was new territory for Finch and he felt incredibly uncomfortable. Then it dawned on him. Was this man going to stop him in his tracks and deny him the chance of the archaeological discovery of the millennium? Did he know already? Should he lie? All these questions but he had not had time to prepare himself. He cursed his absent-mindedness and did his best to weigh up the situation.

'Wait here,' the major ordered. Finch, Karin and Kris did as they were told and looked not unlike three naughty school kids awaiting the wrath of the headmaster. Colonel Khalifa was nowhere to be seen. In front of them stood an enormous set of doors, ornately decorated and heavy. All around were statuesque soldiers, immaculately dressed and stood to attention, ready at any point to do whatever the Sultan dictated. They waited for what seemed an eternity, but eventually the doors swung open and the major appeared. 'Gentlemen and lady. You will be introduced and stand before the presence of royalty. Protocol dictates you bow your head when you are introduced; you speak only when spoken to. Do not touch any member of the household unless invited to do so. Do not offend him in any way. Speak the truth. This is most important. Failure to adhere to anything I have said will have dire consequences. Understood?' The three nodded and followed the major into the room.

The room was positively spartan in comparison to what they had seen. Business-like and cold. There was a thick carpet, a couple of sofas and chairs, a table with water and glasses and a large picture of the Sultan with an unfurled flag of Oman. Again, they waited for someone to come. Finch felt agitated as it was precious time being wasted, when all he wanted was to get back to the sinkhole and look for clues to the whereabouts of the Library. Eventually, a connecting door opened and in walked the Sultan of Oman, Qaboos bin Said al Said. He was without doubt a regal looking man. Distinguished and powerful. He was followed closely by the major, five guards and a couple of aides. The Sultan greeted each of his guests in turn. '*Salam aleikum.* Hello. A pleasure to meet with you and thank you for coming.' Each bowed and their hands were shaken and each awkwardly answered without much conviction. 'Sit, please,' the Sultan said indicating for the three to sit on the sofa. There was an uncomfortable silence and the Sultan looked at Finch and his friends intently but with a pleasant smile on his face. 'You must be Mr Finch. Am I correct?' The Sultan spoke quietly, directing his question straight at Finch.

'Yes, your… umm,' Finch mumbled unsure at the correct response.

The major interjected sharply. 'You will address His Royal Highness as Your Majesty!'

Finch quickly replied again with the correct ending. 'Yes, your majesty. I am.' With that, the Sultan whipped round to the major and spoke to him in Arabic. The major nodded and stood.

'His Majesty would like to speak with Mr Finch in private. Will you please come with me?'

Karin and Kris looked at each other and Finch for re-assurance. Finch just nodded and smiled and the two were escorted out from where they had come from. The Sultan stared at Finch, who met his gaze unflinchingly.

'Why are you here in my country, Mr Finch?' the Sultan asked without moving his eyes from Finch's.

Finch paused before answering. He thought about coming out with some spurious story and act the ignoramus, but the Sultan was no fool. He probably knew everything already and just wanted to test him. Finch cleared his throat. 'I'm here, your majesty, in search of one of the Ancient Wonders of the World, as I believe it rests in the sacred earth of Oman.'

'And what is this wonder please?' the Sultan enquired. Finch paused.

'The Great Library of Alexandria. I believe that Ptolemy had it moved here in his reign so that it could never be destroyed by people who would not understand its importance to mankind.' Finch spoke with authority. The Sultan looked neither surprised nor elated with this news. He re-arranged his dish-dash.

107

'The Great Library? If my history of the classics are correct, I thought that the great Julius Caesar destroyed it in 48 BC. He razed it to the ground. Perhaps not intentionally, as he was a learned man, but nevertheless he wiped the Library from the face of the earth. Is this not so?'

Finch nodded. 'Yes, it is, your majesty, but I believe that Ptolemy, fearing the destruction of the Library and together with his reverence for all things devoted to Alexander the Great, had the Library copied and the originals moved to a subterranean library here in Oman, hence keeping it safe for eternity and only a sacred few ever knew about what he had done.'

The Sultan sat back. 'You have proof about this?'

'Yes,' Finch answered, not allowing himself to say more than was necessary.

'You appear to have done your homework, Mr Finch. Tell me, do you know why Oman specifically? Why not somewhere closer to home in Africa or even back in Macedonia in honour of Alexander himself? It seems a little odd,' said the Sultan. Finch was taken aback. It was an obvious enough question and yet one he neither knew the answer to, nor had thought to prepare an answer for.

'I suppose Ptolemy must have had connections, powerful trusted ones and that no one would dare to invade here or think that such an important asset would be hidden in these surroundings.' Finch thought that if anything, a bit of flattery would do the trick.

'A good try. But you do not know? Right?' the Sultan replied and before Finch could answer, he continued, 'Maybe, it was that. Or maybe Ptolemy's favourite wife was Omani. After all, we have some of the most beautiful women in the world, or maybe there was an alliance or friendship between Ptolemy's wife and her brother, who just happened to be the Sultan of

108

Mazun, the land of the Parthians. Maybe he was a great ruler of a powerful race in a large country with unforgiving and barren lands, so perfect for a great treasure to be hidden and so therefore maybe a secretive alliance was formed only to be known by the few. Descendants running through history. Maybe you are right. Maybe?' The Sultan smiled. Finch was visibly working out what the Sultan had just said. 'We are the same, you and I, Mr Finch. I know what you are. Lift up your sleeve,' ordered the Sultan. Finch did as instructed. 'The mark you hold is that of the Templars. That, together with those piercing blue eyes could only mean one thing. This mark on my own arm is the mark of the protectors of Amman – the great secrets.' The Sultan rolled his own sleeve up, revealing a mark. It looked like an Egyptian style 'eye' with crossed swords through it. 'We all have our own secrets, Mr Finch,' the Sultan said quietly.

Finch was dumbfounded, though he shouldn't have been, given all he had learned over the past few weeks. After a pause, the Sultan spoke once more.

'Do you control the power to regress in this life yet?' Finch was still staring at the Sultan's arm, lost in his own thoughts, but the Sultan repeated the question.

'Um. Yes, I have regressed, but it is all still quite new to me and I am not able to control where I go.'

The Sultan unrolled his sleeve, covering the scar and leant back. 'I will tell you my story if you will permit me to take a little more of your time. I know exactly why you are here and what your progress is. Many years ago, Ptolemy did have his library at Alexandria replicated and the originals moved here because of the alliance formed with his brother-in-law. It was an ingenious ploy, an act that should leave mankind forever in Ptolemy's debt. For until you walk in and see and become a part of the Library, you will never understand the power and intrigue it possesses. The Sultans were tasked with the honour of protecting the secret

109

of the Library as it would not do anyone any good to know about it. Of course, mankind would want to know it exists and what it held and no doubt scholars would give their eye teeth for it. I am also sure that mankind would learn a lot from the manuscripts. But with a find such as this, there is great responsibility and there would always be someone who would want it and would see the financial gains to be had, and with that comes jealousy, greed, anger, violence, destruction and death. Then all the good work that Ptolemy and my ancestors have accomplished for thousands of years would be for nothing. No, it would not do anyone any good.'

Finch leant forward, fearing the worst. 'So, if you have no intention of allowing the world to know about this, majesty, and my friends and I know about this place, what do you intend to do with us?' There was uncertainty in Finch's voice now. The Sultan stared at him.

'Oh, you know it is there hypothetically and I know it is there in reality. But you have been to the room yourself through the sinkhole. There is nothing there and there is no way on earth that anyone would ever find anything if they ventured in. There are no clues – nothing. So, who would believe you? It would just be another story for conspiracy theorists to talk about at conventions and you would go slowly mad knowing what you think you know and no one believing you because you would never be able to prove it. Mainly because the only way you could even start to prove the theory would be by entering MY country and asking permission – which I would never give you. But you must not fear for your life, Mr Finch – you are safe and the reason you are here is because there is more to this story than meets the eye.' Finch moved so far forward he was struggling to keep his buttocks on the chair. 'We had met through the ages Mr Finch, there are things and people that one is drawn to, our paths have crossed many times and each time you have always proved to be of a pure soul. This is important for me to know this. As custodians of the past, we are also naturally pulled towards the objects that wish us to find and protect them. That is why you are now here in my presence in Oman. This is your destiny. You still look bewildered by the events you are experiencing but you must surrender to them and understand that this was all supposed to happen. The Library is only one wonder to be unearthed. There are secrets hidden within its walls which need to be uncovered and by the right men. One of those men is you, Mr Finch. These secrets need to be answered for if the knowledge falls into the wrong hands, then all is lost and our existence have all been for naught. So, I will help you, Mr Finch, and you will help me and you must never tell anyone of your discoveries. Never tell anyone of the location and as quickly as you have found what you are looking for, you must forget it and never return or breathe a word of it again.'

'Or?' Finch asked.

'Or you will die,' the Sultan finished off.

There was silence. Then Finch took a hold of himself. 'That room is empty and you said yourself, there are no clues on how to get in. So where is the key?'

The Sultan leant forward and pulled from his neck a medallion made of clay about five inches in diameter. It contained forty-five different symbols occurring 241 times, all in hieroglyphics. 'This,' he said, 'is the Phaistos Disk. It has been passed down through the generations. No one knows what it says, but it is the only way you can gain access to the Library. I am too old to swim through watery chambers, Mr Finch, so I will entrust this with my major who you met earlier. He knows what he needs to know and will not ask questions, but I trust him with my life and he will go with you. Tell no one, Mr Finch, then trust no one. It is only your Templar code which will keep you safe and find what you have been sent on this earth to find, before it's too late.' Without any time to respond to the Sultan, he had got up and made for the door. Before he left, he turned to Finch one last time. 'Always so many questions and not enough time, at least not in this lifetime. Good luck and succeed, Inshallah.' And with that he left.

Finch met up with the other two outside. The sun was bright and high in the sky and Finch's head was spinning. His two comrades looked at Finch expectantly. He was just about to explain when Major Rami met with them.

'Lady and gentlemen, I will meet you at the sinkhole at 0800hrs tomorrow morning. The Sultan will give me the key and we will begin the quest in hand. Until then. And, sleep well, for I feel that a good night's sleep will be hard to come by after tomorrow. The car will take you back to the dive centre – your vehicle will be there waiting for you.' Rami bowed his head and left them.

Finch, Kris and Karin got into the vehicle and it wasn't until they had reached the relative privacy of their hotel room that Finch explained what had been communicated to him by the Sultan. Karin was still very new to this and found it all incredible. Kris looked at Finch and gave a slight smirk.

'It's all coming together,' he said quietly and smiled to himself.

A knock at the door shattered the silence, frightening them; they all felt vulnerable after the day's occurrences. Kris stood by the door and indicated Finch to stand behind it, ready to dispatch anyone who had intentions of violence.

'Yes?' Kris asked. The voice from behind the door was familiar and the sense of relief was tangible.

'It is me, Colonel Yousef. Please let me in.' Kris opened the door suspiciously but was relieved to see that it was indeed Yousef. He looked rattled and irritated.

'Are you all OK? I have not been told anything. Are you leaving? Did they hurt you?'

Finch walked over and shook Yousef's hand warmly. 'Colonel, we're fine. Today's events have been quite surreal.' Finch informed Yousef of the Sultan's conversation in a very edited version, missing out the bits about the key and his regressed past. He trusted Yousef, but it would not be wise to say too much, and besides, if he genuinely didn't know then he would be safer in the long run. The group went and enjoyed a well-earned drink and sat listening to the gentle caress of the sea on the sandy shore. The colonel took sip of his sweet tea and wiped his mouth with his hands. 'Jake, the two men today who were watching us, they were not Omani authorities and they were too precise in their movements just to be nomadic voyeurs, which can only indicate that there is another interested party about to join in the fun. Yes?' Finch looked at Kris in the hope that he might shed some light on the matter.

'Yes. You are right, Colonel. I think we are being monitored every step of our way. There is a chap called Victor, I am not sure if I told you, but he is most definitely here in Oman and will be watching our every movement. He basically wants what we want and is letting us do the work for him; it hasn't been in his interest to get involved yet but I don't think his first move is too far away. We need to be on our toes. He's bad news and apparently capable and willing to do anything. We watch each other's backs fervently from now on.' They all let their own thoughts take advantage of the silence of the evening and all looked at one another in a quiet assurance that they would not let each other down.

CHAPTER 17

Finch, Kris and Karin were awake and up before the sun had broken on the barren horizon. No one spoke in the car on the journey to the sinkhole. The atmosphere was tense. Today they would see with their own eyes the hidden wonder of the world which was the Great Library of Alexandria. There was also the thought that they may not be alone and that their lives may be at risk. Finch pulled up at the lagoon. Khalifa's car was already in situ. It was seven o'clock, an hour earlier than they had arranged with the major, but Finch needed to check out the lie of the land. They parked up and Kris got out of the car and after an over-exaggerated stretch grabbed Finch's shoulder in reassurance and took his post as sentry overlooking the sinkhole. Karin helped Khalifa with the scuba gear. Finch was still edgy, scanning the horizon for any prying eyes. The hour seemed to pass ludicrously slowly, but at five to eight, a dust cloud could be seen on the horizon heading their way. Two blacked-out Humvee all-terrain vehicles were making their way toward them. Pretty much bang on the dot of eight o'clock, the vehicles drew up and out stepped Major Rami. He removed his sunglasses with a theatrical flourish and looked at Finch.

'Good morning. Are you ready to do this?' he asked, enjoying his role in this piece of theatre.

'Yes,' Finch answered. 'Who's diving?' he asked.

'Just me and my corporal. He is coming just to "watch our arcs," so to speak,' Major Rami replied, pointing his sunglasses at a stocky and humourless corporal. He had turned up with eight soldiers, all physically fit and equipped for a war. 'I'll leave the rest up here as top cover. I believe we may be expecting company,' Rami continued.

114

'Fine,' Finch replied. 'Colonel Khalifa and I will be diving. Karin and Kris will remain up top with your guys.' Rami nodded in agreement. Then all four collected their equipment and headed to the water's edge.

As Finch passed Kris, he muttered, 'Stay alert, buddy, I am not sure if I trust this guy and then you might have Victor to deal with as well.' Kris nodded and Finch knew that Kris was not underestimating the gravity of what he had just said.

Finch, Khalifa, Rami and the Omani corporal suited up and entered the water on the way to the submerged tunnel leading to the chamber. On the side of the sinkhole, Kris kept watch on top of the ridge whilst Karin stared into the crystal blue waters of the lagoon. The Omani soldiers stayed with the vehicles and appeared to be totally uninterested in what was going on.

After a while, Finch and the dive team had arrived at the steps leading up into the cavern. Finch emerged first, followed by Khalifa and then the two Omanis. Finch whipped his flippers and scuba gear off and peered around the room again hoping to solve the mystery of how the doorway would open before the major revealed its secrets, but Finch was flummoxed. When Rami had discarded his scuba equipment, he looked at Finch and smiled.

'You still not worked it out yet, huh?' He unzipped his wetsuit and removed the red clay looking disc from his neck. 'Sometimes, things are supposed to remain hidden,' the major said, holding up the disc. He walked over to the face of the rock in front of the men and held the disc in such a way that the characters on it, which started from a labyrinthine entrance were facing the steps. He then placed the disc directly in line with the steps about five feet up the wall and waited. Finch held his breath. The wait seemed eternal and then from deep within the

115

wall there was an audible loud clunk. The wall came to life and moving parts from inside it began to groan in a rhythmical order. Then after a shudder, the first two steps leading up to the chamber fell away and dropped, encouraging whoever was there to follow them down into the stone wall. The room was a red herring. Rami replaced the disk around his head and made his way down the steps. The three other men followed him. They walked along a short corridor of stone for about twenty metres and then Rami stopped. 'Welcome to the Great Library, gentlemen. The Library of Alexandria.'

Finch rushed to get past him and shone his light, trying to pick any shape out with his Maglite torch. It was powerful but in what seemed to be an enormous room, it had little effect. Rami turned and with his lighter, lit a torch which in turn lit a small channel of oil which ran in a well-constructed rut around the room at about waist height. The oil took and the yellowy firelight lit the room up in all its glory and only now could Finch really take in the size and importance of the find. Finch looked up and was dumbstruck.

There in front of him was a mass of honeycombed chambers leading on into one another, each side containing diamond shaped alcoves which housed thousands of scrolls. Where there were no scrolls, the walls were washed in white plaster which had naturally faded through the passage of time but bearing that in mind, were still remarkably fresh. What was even more beautiful were the many friezes which adorned the whitewashed walls. Pictures that depicted glorious individuals, battles and gods, telling a story from Greek legend and great victories by Alexander himself. Finch tentatively brushed his fingertips over the pictures and imagined the time that they were given birth. The Library was a labyrinth of scrolls and pictures. Finch had butterflies in his stomach and could hardly contain his excitement. So intense were his feelings he could feel a tear roll down his face and drip onto the cold stone floor. He ventured down an aisle, his hands spread outward from his body in an attempt to touch everything he passed. He stopped at one shelf and gently picked up a scroll as if it were made of the thinnest pond ice. He liberated the string holding the rolled parchment together and with the most delicate of caresses, unfurled the paper. It was in immaculate condition and it was hard to imagine that these were so incredibly old. He saw with his own eyes the Greek lettering in hand crafted writing and his heart missed a beat. He didn't even think to translate the text; he just couldn't comprehend what he was experiencing. He wandered around the space in awe. His reverence was shattered as Khalifa joined him.

'It is more magnificent than I could ever have expected.'

'It is remarkable! It is real!' Finch just couldn't express himself. He forgot about his other quest – the real quest. To search for the clue that he was supposed to find to lead him toward the Holy Grail. It didn't even cross his mind.

They had been in the chamber for an hour and it felt like minutes. And when Major Rami told him that he had to return to the surface, he could not believe it. 'But why? Why so soon?' asked Finch, perplexed and with a sense of pleading in his voice.

'It is not good to be in here so long. The air is stale and it does not do the Library much good to experience the change of atmosphere. Come. We must go now,' Rami replied. Before Finch could put up any verbal defence, the stocky corporal ushered all out of the chamber and before one knew it, the flames were doused and the darkness once more shrouded the Library. The men walked up to the depressed steps and, once all had emerged, Rami passed the disc over the wall once again and the steps closed with a definite clunk. Finch was devastated. He had uncovered the greatest find of archaeological history and one he had spent the vast majority of his life researching; he had been given a taste and then had had the plate stripped away from him.

'Will we be able to come back?' Finch asked. But Rami ignored him and climbed into his scuba gear. Finch repeated his question again, but again Rami continued readying himself for the return and then told everyone to get going. Finch was fraught. They needed to return.

On the return journey, Finch's mind was a flurry of questions which needed answering. He didn't want to believe that his brief encounter with the Library was all he was going to be allowed to have. Besides, the Sultan needed him to unearth some of the Library's secrets. He could see the sun penetrating the surface of the lagoon and its warmth felt wonderful on his black wetsuit. As his head broke the water's surface, he was flabbergasted at what he saw. There in front of him and surrounding the sinkhole from above were about thirty men, all armed with semi-automatic weapons and all looking like they meant business. Finch scanned the horizon eagerly to see where his two friends were. Then he saw them, their hands cuffed behind their backs and on their knees and being overlooked by a couple of locals with weapons. Sitting just to the side of them by the water's edge was a man dressed in black being shaded by another man holding an umbrella. Finch removed his mask and swam to the side, following the major and his corporal.

'What is the meaning of this. Do you know who I am? I demand you lower your weapons and stand down. Immediately!' the major shouted at the man in black as he furiously tried to escape the clutches of his cumbersome scuba equipment. The man in black was Victor.

When Rami had finished talking, Victor raised his finger to his lips and hushed him. He sat in his chair and crossed his legs, his hands clasped in a relaxed fashion on his lap.

'Yes. I know who you are, Major Rami, and I know you are the Sultan's representative here. Your men are safe and are being watched at the top by your vehicles. My business is not with you or your Sultan, Major, so please leave and allow me to speak with Mr Finch in private.'

The major, now free from his gear, walked up to Victor with his corporal guarding his back and stood menacingly over him. 'Finch is our guest. He comes with me. Tell your men to stand down!'

Victor looked up at Rami. He was becoming irritated. 'Major. You are in no position to dictate terms. Take your men and go, otherwise my patience will ebb. Do not test me. Finch stays as do his friends; now go. I will not repeat myself.' Victor gave a signal to the armed men and there was a definite re-aiming of guns on to the Omani officer. Rami composed himself for a while and looked at Finch.

'I will go, but I will return.'

Finch, who by now was standing in his wetsuit, acknowledged Rami and watched as he made his way up to his Humvee vehicles. 'You guys OK?' Finch asked Karin and Kris. Victor interrupted before they had a chance to answer.

'They are fine, Mr Finch, or is it Jake? Jake sounds far more informal. We need to speak, Jake, and this is the best way to get your attention.' Victor signalled one of the armed men to take Colonel Khalifa and handcuff his wrists and put him with the others. 'Colonel,' Victor said, lowering his head with a mock sense of respect.

'You have it,' Finch replied.

'Good!' Victor slapped his thigh and stood. 'But not here. Too open and quite frankly the sun is a little hot to be able to think clearly, yes? Take them to the vehicles. Finch travels with me,' Victor instructed his second-in-command who barked orders at the armed men in Arabic. All made their way to the waiting vehicles and left the scene in a cloud of dust.

119

CHAPTER 18

Rami had now returned to the palace and sought the Sultan. He explained what had happened and the ire was clear to see in the Sultan's face. 'Find out who he is and bring him to kneel before me. Make sure Finch survives and then bring him to me also.' The Sultan was in no mood for small talk and disappeared, visibly furious.

The vehicles pulled up outside an old tavern on the outskirts of Muscat. Disused and barren, it was a perfect place for the sort of conversation Victor had in mind without drawing attention to oneself. Everyone got out of the vehicles and Finch, Karin, Kris and Khalifa were bundled into a back room. All were bound to chairs and sat in a line. The room looked like some poor scene from a 'B' movie. Empty and dimly lit. Victor's henchmen lined the walls, their weapons slung. They were all reasonably relaxed as they had got their captives to this place and the chance of escape was slight, to say the very least. Victor sat at an old table to the side of the four captives and while sparking up a Gitanes indicated that he wanted Finch at the table with him. Two burly men came from leaning against the wall and lifted Finch and the chair to the table. Finch felt incredibly vulnerable as his hands were tied behind his back and he expected to be given a good shoeing at any minute. But surprisingly, he didn't feel afraid. The adrenaline must have been coursing through his veins or he must have been under-estimating Victor's intentions. Victor inhaled deeply on his cigarette and blew the smoke directly at Finch.

'Hello, Guillaume. Thank you for joining me. I'm sorry the ambience and décor isn't more distinguished but needs must.' Finch was feeling angry and bolshie.

120

'Who the hell do think you are! Kidnapping us. Do you have any idea how powerful that major is and who he represents…?' Victor held his hands up to quieten Finch down.

'Ssshh. Yes. Yes. I am very well aware of who Major Rami is. It is of no consequence. I don't like small talk, Guillaume, as Mr El Masri would confirm, if he could.' Victor allowed himself a little chuckle. 'Let's get down to business. The only reason you are all still alive now is that I want something that you do not yet possess but are in the process of acquiring.' Finch shot Victor a defiant look and was just about to argue when Victor continued, 'And please spare me the "I don't know what you're talking about" routine. I know EVERYTHING! And I intend to get what I desire, namely the Grail! Oh, I know you have found this library and I am sure it is marvellous, but it is not what I want. You know how to get it.' Victor sat back and studied Finch.

Finch looked round at his friends for inspiration, but they looked bemused. 'Well, Victor, isn't it? If you know everything, you will know that this morning was the first time I have seen the Library, which incidentally is what I have spent years trying to find. You will know that I only spent about an hour in the Library which is clearly not long enough and therefore have absolutely no idea about how to find the Grail, and in sending Major Rami off with your shoe up his arse has pretty much made it impossible for us to get back into the Library at all. So, a word of advice: it's not really advisable to come into someone's country and piss all over their favourite rug!' Finch stared defiantly at Victor, who stared back. He was in no mood for games. He had started out in a buoyant mood and everything seemed to be going well. But his demeanour had blackened and now he was getting angry.

'Well then, Guillaume. It appears that you have some work to do. I am not a man who appreciates disappointment and I like to hold all the cards. We have known each other for a very long time, Guillaume. You and your pitiful Templar values. At least now they might just benefit me for once. Who knows, if you do this, I may consider not burning you and your friends at the stake again. Oh, how I love a good barbecue!' Victor had leant forward and lit a match under Finch's nose. This made Finch instinctively retreat, which brought a wry smile to Victor's face.

'It will be impossible! The Sultan is the only man who can open the Library. Do you think he is going to help us in any way now? You must be out of your tiny mind. The moment any of us show our faces again, his ARMY will dismember us where we stand. You screwed this up for yourself – for everyone!' Finch's temperature was rising and he shouted the last salvo through gritted teeth directly at Victor. Victor shot up, catapulting his chair backwards.

'How dare you speak to me like that!' Victor released a vicious backhand swipe across Finch's face, his ring catching his eyebrow, nicking it and causing a trickle of blood to flow down his face. 'I allow you to live. I do! You have one week, Guillaume, to find out how to get back into that library and find the Grail, or else your friends will suffer. I appreciate it is a difficult venture and so you may keep the help of your more unkempt comrade.' Victor pointed at Kris. 'But I will be accommodating Ms Edwards until you have some news. If there is nothing, then I will make her last few hours on this earth fairly unpleasant.' Finch swung around and looked at Karin. Karin in turn looked defiant. Finch understood. 'Go to hell Victor, or should I say Clement. You need me to find this thing - I am the only chance you have. And besides, you know everything right? Then you know that we are just time travellers. Our souls jumping from life to life. The regression gives us pointers. We are all ready to die for our beliefs. We always have been. We will just fight another day. So again I say – GO TO HELL. We will always hold the upper hand.' Finch looked pretty smug. He was convinced that he had called Victor's bluff. And in truth he was ready to die. He was feeling more and more confident in the knowledge that he could retrace his steps from this life and come back again as someone else in the next life. Pain was momentary. Victor studied Finch. He walked in a circle around him and took the Glock pistol from one of his guards. 'Oh what a brave little soul. You Templars are really full of surprises. I am not messing about. This bravado will be short lived. A car will take you back to your hotel and I will be watching you with Ms Edwards – I wonder if she agrees with your gung-ho attitude. She is very new to this and perhaps she would prefer to spend a little more time in this life than get ready to face the next; mind you, she may come back as a man and not such a beautiful woman. I might even give you longer so Ms Edwards and I could get to know each other a little better? Hmm??' Victor was standing behind Karin and stroked her disturbingly. He signalled a guard to turn Finch's chair toward them. 'You have one week.' Victor turned to Khalifa on the end. 'We don't need him.' And with that, Victor shot Khalifa in the back of the head, his face exploding in a red pulp. 'Ah what a shame, he does not regress. We wish his soul Godspeed. One week, Guillaume.' With that, Victor was away with most of his guards. Karin was gagged and taken with him, while the other two were unbound from the chairs.

Finch stared at Khalifa, shocked and shaking. 'Goodbye, old friend. I am so sorry,' Finch whispered. Kris attempted to comfort Finch but the guards had pistol whipped them and bundled them into the back of the waiting cars where they made for the dive centre.

CHAPTER 19

Finch and Kris sat in the bar of the dive centre nursing a cold lager, still dazed by the events earlier. They knew to have expected Victor, but they hadn't thought for one moment that he would kill Khalifa. Finch felt wracked with guilt and blamed himself completely for the fact that he was now dead. Kris could see what was going through Finch's head.

'It's not your fault, Jake. Khalifa was a soldier. He may not have thought there was any immediate danger, but even if he did, do you think for one moment that would have stopped him? You need to focus. Look, Victor hasn't changed; he is still the malicious spawn he was six centuries ago and we have to be up for this. There's too much at stake. And they have Karin. And be under no illusion, he will gut her in an instant if he thinks we are playing him. So we have to man up here, bro, and get back into the game.' Finch cradled his drink and nodded.

'Victor is going to pay. I swear I will see to it he does!'

'Good,' Kris replied, realising that Finch was back with him. 'Now we need to get to the palace and see Rami and the Sultan. We have to get back to the Library. The Sultan would have heard all about what has happened and will be shitting feathers at the fact that he has been chinned off by some white foreigner in his own country. When we tell him about Khalifa, he will be in our pockets, right?'

Finch looked at Kris long and hard and finished his beer. 'Come on, let's go.' The two men got into their vehicle and headed off to the palace.

As they drew up to the palace gates, the guards were on full alert. The two men were pulled out of their 4x4 and searched and held at gunpoint in the guardroom. 'Look, we need to see Major Rami Amela. He is expecting us. Call him! You'll see,' Finch implored the guard commander who stared at him impassively. 'Do it now!' Finch screamed.

The commander picked up the phone and dialled a number and spoke to someone in Arabic. Finch and Kris waited with bated breath. The phone was replaced and he stood staring at them both. Then in Arabic, he muttered something to the men in the room, which merited a quick response. The weapons were lowered and the atmosphere mellowed immediately, though when Finch went to shake the guard's hand, the weapons were brought tight immediately. Kris and Finch stood anxiously. The door of the guardhouse opened and the sergeant, on seeing the officer, sprang to attention. It was Rami. There were no immediate pleasantries, just a look and a motion with his hand to follow him. The relief felt by both men was tangible. Rami held the door of a black Humvee open for Finch and Kris to get into and they sped to the palace. Finally, Rami spoke.

'I am glad you are alive. And I am sorry not to have been of more help at the lagoon. The Sultan wished to see you both.'

Finch leant forward. 'They shot Colonel Khalifa. And they have our friend as a hostage.'

Rami's eyes flared. 'I am sorry for your loss,' he said plainly and carried on driving stony-faced, though inside he was raging uncontrollably at the fact a fellow countryman had died and he had not been able to help.

Rami, Finch and Kris made their way to the same reception room they had met the Sultan in on the last occasion. Rami disappeared through the far door and returned with the Sultan a few minutes later. Finch bowed as he approached and the Sultan acknowledged the respect. 'I heard about what happened today and I am sorry for your loss and may he live in eternity, happy and safe, Inshallah.' The Sultan fidgeted and settled himself in the chair. It was a pleasant greeting but he wanted to get to the bones of the matter. 'Today I have been greatly insulted by this man and he shall pay for his disrespect, but in the meantime, we have to box clever and I will help you any way I can.' These were exactly the words Finch wanted to hear. The Sultan continued. 'You may go back to the Library with Major Rami and some of my men as protection, but as I understand it, that may not be wholly necessary. But you will have them anyway. Search the Library for any clues and then return to me, for only then will I tell you what I think you will need to know. Be sure, Mr Finch, to know you have an ally in this house. This is the start of a great and perilous adventure for not only you but for all our sakes. Go back to the Library and use your skills to find what you seek; the rest of the pieces of the jigsaw will be waiting for you on your return.'

The Sultan finished and had no interest in hearing from the two men. When he had concluded his business, he rose and escorted by Rami, left the room. Finch and Kris stood up as he did so and looked at each other. No sooner had Rami left the room, he had returned.

'Come on – we have lots to do. There are wetsuits and scuba gear in the vehicle. We will head to the sinkhole immediately. Any questions? Then we go.'

Rami led the way and Finch felt a sense of relief at being told what to do. Some responsibility had at last been taken off his shoulders. They got into the Humvee and Finch started to mull over where an antiquarian architect would hide something of great value in an already secret library, that Finch had failed even to gain entry to in the first place. This though wasn't totally

126

new ground. He had spent his whole life figuring out ancient puzzles. Now he faced the greatest puzzle of them all.

CHAPTER 20

Karin sat on the sofa in the hotel room that Victor had rented. She wasn't bound in any way and had the run of the room. As Victor had pointed out, if she escaped, Victor would just catch up with them all at a later date. He could kill them at any time. He always knew where to find Finch and this quest meant that Finch wouldn't stop until he had found what he was looking for and a quest always leaves a trail. Besides, there were eyes watching Karin everywhere. She would get as far as the pavement outside, before she would be set upon like a group of hyenas devouring their prey.

Victor entered the room and sat in the armchair opposite Karin. 'Renaud de Vichiers. It's been too long, Renaud. Too long since we have enjoyed an intimate chat. I know that you have only just realised your part in this game and the whole notion of regression and the past lives thing is all a little too much to bear, but safe to say – we have history. I think I shall continue to call you Renaud. It would just seem strange to call you by any other name. It may be odd given your current incarnation, and such a fine one at that, but to me whatever your external attributes - you will always just be plain old Renaud. You have guessed by now that I was Pope Clement V and I was the one who ended your life as a Templar, so I will understand if you hold more than a little grudge. The burning was the easy part; it was the torture prior to that which I personally enjoyed and you, Renaud, were so strong. Maybe it is the power you all possess in those blue eyes. Extraordinary! You are all freaks. Our paths have crossed throughout time and here we are again like some dysfunctional family. Renaud – do you know why I seek the Grail so much?' asked Victor.

Karin stared, pretending to be completely uninterested in Victor's conversation and shrugged her shoulders, 'Dunno. But I'm pretty sure you're gonna tell me though, huh!'

Victor continued. 'You see, Renaud, the Grail holds immense power. Some think it is made out of a metal unlike anything found here on earth and has properties that can make a man immortal, and that Jesus Christ was, as a man so pure of thought, that he was the only one worthy of its ownership. Others think it is the chalice used by Jesus at the Last Supper and possesses a God given power. Some mix them all together and come up with what they want to believe to suit themselves. I think that whatever the story is, that it holds an unspeakable power. The power of immortality. I was made to live forever, Renaud. I have been doing this for centuries but each time my soul takes a new guise. Well, I quite like this one; it is much more like the original! I want to be me forever and know the thoughts and intentions of men. I believe that if I possess the Grail I will at last be free from the Templars. For if I were to strike you down, then your soul would finally die, never to return. Your light would be extinguished for eternity. Those blue eyes would at last, lose their sparkle. Though, as we are speaking plainly, I just want it because it's there to be taken and I want the sheer unadulterated power and to have every worm on this planet bow to my every whim. Well, who wouldn't? That's why I want, nay, need that cup and it is the only reason you are still alive. I need Finch to find it.'

Karin chuckled to herself. 'Wow! You are such a tosser and so lame! All this wealth and power and you need a passed over archaeologist to do what you evidently can't do yourself. Your soul is diseased Victor, and it will catch up with you. You can't beat God and you certainly can't hide from Him. I may not know much, but I know that the universe survives through a delicate balance and whatever you give out, you get back tenfold and you will get what is coming to you one way or another.' Karin had got up now and was looking out of the cobwebbed window. Victor got up too and stood next to her and lit a Gitanes.

'Oh, I have a dark soul. Don't you worry about that. My existence has been a catalogue of atrocities. There are good souls and bad souls and ne'er the twain shall meet. I can live with that, and I can live happily in the knowledge that soon your soul will be forever withered and dead.' Victor had been almost standing over Karin. Foreboding and unnerving. There was a tension now that was turning more sinister. Victor ran his fingers up Karin's spine, causing her to pull away and shudder, repulsed by the feeling. Victor snatched violently at her hair and yanked her head back so she was looking straight into his face.

'Such a pretty thing you have become Renaud. Maybe you need a man to teach you a lesson in respect and perhaps you may enjoy it. Hmm?' Victor pushed his face millimetres from Karin's and sniffed deeply, smelling her scent. He tilted his head and looked at her body and smiled. 'Nice! Very pleasant indeed.' Karin had shown such defiance, but now she was scared and vulnerable and Victor knew it. 'But no matter what ridiculous facade you may keep, you will always be Renaud and you make me feel dirty just being in the same room as you. Though in future, maybe one of my guards could have you as a present, no?' He released his grip, smirked and walked away.

Karin wanted to talk and say something glib, but Victor had chilled her to the core. Instead, she whispered under her breath, '*Pura Regnabit Aeterna.*' Where it came from, she didn't know. Victor stopped and turned his head back, hearing this pathetic quote. 'The pure will reign eternal – perhaps, but then again, perhaps not.' Victor left with a smile, leaving Karin to contemplate what had just happened. This was as real as it could get and she was afraid of Victor.

CHAPTER 21

Rami, Finch and Kris with twenty or so Omani soldiers got to the sinkhole. Finch, Rami and the same corporal who dived with them before, plus another stocky soldier, wasted no time in getting their wetsuits on and preparing their scuba gear. Rami barked some orders at the soldiers and made their weapons ready, taking their posts around the lagoon.

Finch called to Kris, 'Are you sure you don't want to come?'

'No – if God wanted me to breathe underwater, he would have given me gills; besides, I would only be in the way. If Victor wanted us dead, it would have already happened. I'll just sit here and smoke if it's all the same with you.' Kris slapped Finch on the back and found a convenient stone to make himself comfortable against.

Rami, Finch and the soldiers checked their kit one more time before descending into the clear water and made their way back to the Library. Major Rami took out the disc and opened the door to the Library and in an instant the four men had illuminated the hall. Rami positioned the two guards at the doorway and turned to Finch. 'What are we looking for?'

Finch sighed and looked at Rami, 'I'm not sure. It hasn't been the best preparation for an archaeological dig. Satyros, Ptolemy's architect, was a very clever man and in his tomb was some indication of a greater prize. He must have concealed it well as he was a man of rare talent. He wouldn't, I don't believe, have hidden something that could have been destroyed by fire or an axe if the place was ever discovered or uncovered during a natural disaster. Look at the walls and floors; look for any unnatural joins; look for objects that stick out or holes that could be pushed to release a door, but don't touch anything without consulting me, for all we know, a place like this may hold as many scorpions as it does flowers.'

The two men made their own way around the Library, each armed with a powerful Maglite torch. Finch was almost literally fumbling in the dark. The place was vast and he was looking for a needle in a haystack. The building of the Library was so impressive. Everything was cut to perfection and trying to see any cracks or signs of imperfections in such artificial light was impossible. Never before had Finch felt such despair. He was normally upbeat on digs, as he knew that some clue could be dug up at any moment; it was just a matter of time, hard work and patience. The hours passed by quickly and they had got no further. Rami met up with Finch. 'Should we remove all the scrolls and check behind them?'

'No,' replied Finch. 'It won't be that obvious. Besides, if the scrolls were stolen or burnt then it would be obvious to find. No. It's more subtle than that. Let's just keep looking.' Finch was trying to sound convincing but it wasn't working. Rami continued searching. Finch was studying the walls. As well as the faded whitewashed plasterwork, were wonderful murals depicting Alexander, battles, gods and Ptolemy. The level of skill and craftsmanship was almost unbelievable. Ptolemy had Satyros killed, his only crime being that he knew too much. What he should have done was venerate him so that his name would have gone down in history with such geniuses as Pythagoras and Archimedes. This was a work of art and of sheer brilliance. Oh, what it would be to have the time to digest this place properly. To read the scrolls, understand the art and the design of the Library. He muttered away to himself, questioning himself at every turn. He stood in front of a mural of Ptolemy with Alexander. The expressions and body movement were extraordinary. It was a story from the pages of history; it was tangible. Then it hit Finch. The murals all had real people, apart from the gods, in them. Maybe a man of Satyros' standing would want his vanity to be pandered to, so that his face and name would be remembered. Perhaps there was a picture of him in here and if so, perhaps he was the key to unlock the clue as to the location of the Grail.

Finch scoured the walls with his torch. He had to read the pictures and what they depicted. Then at last he came to one that caught his eye. There in the top corner, was a small picture of Ptolemy ordering a man to go forth. In the foreground the same man stood with a measuring stick in hand, pointing to where his workforce should go. This picture was all about this particular individual, the builder of a monument or building. The builder of a Great Library. Finch looked closer and closer, squinting at the detail. Like many of the other pictures, the eyes were accentuated and looked overly large for the man's face, but they were striking and he appeared to be looking slightly down, like a naughty schoolboy. A strange look, given the heroic stance and story he appeared to be telling. Finch put his hand to the wall and rubbed his hand gently over the mural. Nothing. It was flat, with no flaws at all. The floor and the wall were immaculate. Finch continued to self-narrate his progress and thoughts and only stopped when Rami approached.

'Have you got something?'

Finch rubbed the wall again lightly with the palm of his hand. 'This is Satyros. I am sure of it. The man who created this masterpiece. It must be hiding something. His vanity wouldn't allow for anything less.' Rami patted the wall as well and merged his powerful torch with that of Finch's.

'It is perfect in every way,' Rami said in awe at the beauty of the mural. Finch clenched his fist and started to knock on the wall, straining his ears to hear any change in sound. He tapped all over but all sounds were that of bone on a solid rock wall. Finch was getting frustrated and his knocks became more vigorous until the last one was more of a punch than a dab. Finch suddenly stopped and stood back. The last punch on the wall felt different. He went back to the same spot. He tapped once more and again, it felt strange. He peered at the eyes on the wall and again knocked with his knuckle. The plaster here was not as solid as the rest of the wall, though it looked identical. Finch started to press the picture with his nail and as he did so, it depressed the drawing. There was something there. The rest of the picture was on plaster and rock. This was plaster and a void. He put a finger over the eyes and pressed hard and as he did so, the plaster started to give under the pressure. The other eye looked the same and behaved in the same manner. This had to be the key, Finch thought. He kept pushing when eventually there was a loud 'clunk'; Finch stepped back to get a better look. There was something moving in the wall, slowly but deliberately. Then another 'chunk' and a small drawer revealed itself at the floor under the mural. It was brilliantly concealed. The edges of the drawer had been covered over with a substance which masked any interruption in the rock face and floor. It was marvellous. Finch bent down, closely followed by Rami who was so overtaken with what he had just seen that he was in the way.

'Rami, I need to see this,' said Finch irritably.

Rami shrank back, still fascinated. Finch put his fingers in the drawer and pulled it open. Inside was a metal-ended rolled up scroll of faded brown parchment, and an ordinary, more tatty scroll, with a small amount of writing on it. Finch unfurled this first and read it.

The language appeared at first glance to be Greek. Finch took the parchment over to the flame and squinted at the jaded lettering.

'Θυμηθείτε – Ζωή αιώνιος για την καθαρή ψυχή του. Εμπιστοσύνη στο Λόρδο ο Θεός.' (REMEMBER – 'Life Eternal For The Pure Of Soul – Trust in The Lord God.')

Finch searched the paper for anything else but that was it.

'Brilliant!' Finch sighed to himself. Life eternal for the pure of soul! Finch was frustrated but was doing his very best to keep a lid on his temper.

'What is that?' Rami asked, pointing to the more elaborate scroll. Finch shrugged and gently pulled open the parchment. Rami waited for an answer, but Finch was silent, his eyes dilated and trying to catch his breath.

'Bloody hell – it can't be?' Finch once again was talking to himself.

'What have you found, Jake?' Rami again asked.

Finch peered at the paper close up. It was incredible. 'It looks like the missing piece of the Piri Reis map.'

Rami looked at Finch blankly. 'And this is good, yes? What is the Piri Re—?'

Finch interrupted. His initial disappointment had left him and he was glowing. 'The Piri Reis. It's a map. It was thought to be compiled in the early part of the sixteenth century by an Ottoman admiral and cartographer of great skill. Only some of the original map remains and was on display in the Library of the Topkapı Palace in Istanbul, but it disappeared in the 1930s and hasn't been tracked down since. This is the remaining part without a doubt. I mean, there was talk that he got the map from somewhere else, you know, just literally bastardised a few maps from India, Arabia, Christopher Columbus and more importantly from Claudius Ptolemy, the Greek geographer and cartographer who lived in Alexandria during the second century AD, because the map was so far ahead of his time. This confirms that the map must have come from around the time of Ptolemy. This is amazing.' Finch was lost in his own thoughts.

'So what is the point of it? Is it a treasure map or an early atlas?' Rami enquired.

'This map,' Finch continued, 'is a map of huge detail and shows that world travel happened a great deal, but the mystery of the map is that it shows Antarctica in great precision – an as then undiscovered continent. In fact, it is the talk of all Ufologists that the images on the map were taken from the sky by satellites or even spaceships, as the basic knowledge available at that time can't explain such a staggering correspondence with the reality on the ground. This map is incredible. It shows a correct application of longitude and latitude. These guys knew their astronomy, geometry and astrology at the same time. This is spectacular and could even literally be out of this world.'

Rami looked at Finch, unimpressed. 'The Sultan will want you to brief him on this. We have found what you have sought. We go.'

Finch's heart dropped at the thought of having to leave this gold mine of knowledge and mystery once more, perhaps never again to be allowed to re-enter it, as indeed he had found what they had set out to find. Whether it answered any questions was another story entirely. Finch knew that saving his friends and finishing this quest was more important than this library, however spectacular it was. Finch nodded, waterproofed the scrolls in a dry container and the men made their way back out of the Library and to the watery passageway. Rami wanted to be the last out, and Finch loitered at the doorway in an attempt to take one last look at the Great Library of Alexandria. Then they entered the water and left that wondrous place to be consumed by darkness once more.

When Finch and the others emerged from the lagoon there were no nasty surprises to greet them, everything was as it was when they had departed. Kris sauntered up to Finch and helped him with his tank.

136

'Did you find what you were looking for? Are we any closer to being able to leave this bloody country?' It wasn't like Kris to possess such brevity and Finch smiled, appreciating the thought.

'Yes, I think we did, sort of. It's just a case of filling in the spaces and I have a feeling that is going to be done for us imminently,' Finch responded, flicking his head over in the direction of Rami. Kris just nodded and pulled Finch to his feet. The men dried themselves, changed and all headed to the palace once again for a 'debrief session', as Rami called it, with the Sultan.

They met the Sultan in the same reception room as before. The Sultan didn't keep them waiting long. When he entered the room and made himself comfortable, he looked over at Major Rami. 'Major, would you mind leaving the room for a while. I wish to speak with Mr Finch and his friend alone.' This was not a request from the Sultan, however cordially it was delivered. It was an order. Rami rose and bowed toward the Sultan and left the room. The Sultan's gaze now switched to Finch and his intense blue-eyed stare. 'Tell me, Mr Finch, what did you find in the Library?' asked the Sultan.

Finch, who had been holding the same waterproof container he had in the chamber, opened it up and pulled out the inscribed parchment. 'I found this in a small drawer hidden beneath the plaster. It is an inscription which reads, 'REMEMBER – Life Eternal For The Pure Of Soul – Trust in The Lord God'. It is written in Greek. Does this mean anything to you?'

The Sultan took the paper and mouthed back the inscription Finch had just read out. 'I do not believe so. It means nothing to me,' the Sultan replied blankly. 'Is that it?'

Finch then retrieved the scroll containing the map. 'There was also this.' He unfurled the map and placed it very delicately on the table in front of the Sultan.

The Sultan recognised it immediately and baulked at the sight of it. 'The Piri Reis map,' the Sultan whispered, touching the edges very delicately with his fingertips.

'You have heard of it?' asked Finch.

The Sultan rose from his seat and made his way to the door. 'Wait here,' he ordered. Finch and Kris did as they were told and gave a wry look at one another. Within five minutes the Sultan had returned holding a similar scroll and offered it to Finch. 'Open it,' instructed the Sultan. Finch did so and took a sharp intake of breath. It was the missing parts of the map, reuniting them made a finished article.

'How did you get this and why?' Finch asked.

'How I got it is not important. Why? That is another matter entirely.' The Sultan sat over the map looking deeply into the remarkable drawings. 'Mr Finch, I am sure that a man of your calibre will know much about this map and so I will not teach an old dog new tricks. But what you might not know is the true relevance it holds. Many thought that this was the work of some Ottoman cartographer in the 1500s. But in truth, it was plagiarised by him from the original that lay deep within the Library and would take a man the longest time to find. What this man did do though, is also incorporate some other information gleaned from Columbus. I am a guardian of the Library and we have been entrusted for thousands of years to guard its secrets and this is one such secret which was used some time ago; it was my duty to reclaim it. What is more interesting about the map is not only the accuracy of it but the inclusion of Antarctica. But for you it also charts a place which will be of vital importance to you for your journey. What is more incredible is that it charts the

138

lines of the world grid.' Finch was engrossed in the Sultan's words.

'What is the world grid? I have never heard of it.'

The Sultan sat back in his chair and continued. 'The basic essence of a world grid is the division of the surface of the world into a mathematically predictable model. Plato once wrote that the earth, if viewed from above, would resemble a ball sewn from twelve pieces of skin. The Egyptians were so in advance of their time, in science, astrology, astronomy and maths, that Egypt became the centre of the known world. Egypt was 'Zero', the epicentre. Many other cities and major places of importance cited their foundations using Zero as a marker. The centre of the Piri Reis map is – (24° 06' N, 30° 00' E) – Egypt. There are a list of important places built on this grid such as Giza, the Great Pyramid, Xian Pyramids, the largest in the world, Southern Japan, "Dragon's Triangle", has enormous seismic activity, Algerian megalithic ruins, Megaliths at Axum, the Coptic Christian centre in Ethiopia, Bimini, the Bahamas, Bangkok and Angkor Wat, Lima, Peru, boundary of the Nazca Plate, Pisco the Candlestick of the Andes, Nazca Lines and Easter Island and its megaliths. This is not just coincidence and these are given to us by a higher form. The Egyptians were clever but this is far beyond the limits of their own abilities. There is a place that you will need to find which will help you understand more and realise that we have never been alone.'

Finch sat back and thought hard. He looked at the Sultan and collected his thoughts. 'Your Majesty. Sir! I wanted to find the Great Library of Alexandria more than anything else in the world. I hoped it existed. I knew it existed and now I have found it and for whatever reason I will never be allowed to speak of its existence or even enjoy the fruits of my labours by being able to digest the seeds of wisdom hidden in those catacombs. Prior to that I got found by this man,' Finch pointed at Kris who just

139

looked baffled, 'and am told that I was some great Templar Knight in the past along with a few others and tasked with protecting God's artefacts. Then I get told that there is a bigger prize to find and that this was somehow my destiny. The bigger prize being the greatest prize known to mankind – the Holy Grail, whatever that may be. I find out that I can regress and learn from the past. I find out that you have always known about this library and are from a long line of protectors and now I am finding out about maps, aliens and there is someone out there who wants to kill me and my friends for the power held in a relic, which may or may not exist. With the greatest respect, I am a little out of my depth here. Does the Grail exist? What is it? Is it real or alien, is my faith going be tested after 800 years?! I just don't know where to start.'

Finch's breathing had become erratic and he was looking pale. The Sultan smiled at Finch and rang a small bell beside him. Instantly, a servant entered the room and bowed. The Sultan spoke in Arabic and within minutes, a decanter and three ornate goblets appeared. The servant poured the wine from the silver jug and handed one each to Finch and Kris. The Sultan was poured water. He lifted his glass to Finch and Kris and drank. Finch and Kris returned the toast and took a rather more undignified swig from that of the Sultan. The servant left the room.

'I am told a drop of wine can soothe even the most furious mind,' the Sultan said calmly. 'You are here, Mr Finch, because fate has led you here. 800 years of living and dying and passions and knowledge have led you here to me with your friend, that is irrefutable and cannot be explained. Inshallah – as God wills. The Library was always just a stepping-stone on your journey to what you have been created to pursue. The protection of the Holy Grail. For this, men will do anything, as you are finding out. And you must see it through the intricate windings that destiny has in store for you, and it is up to you to call on your wisdom

140

and experiences of hundreds of years to guide you on your journey. You may fail and then the journey may begin again at some time when you are ready. The soul goes on and your soul is indeed pure but I feel that you are ready now. As for the Grail. It is real, and it is not some metaphoric sentence for what we should seek to achieve in life, but a tangible chalice, used by Jesus Christ at the Last Supper. It was given to him not through luck but destiny. He himself was sought, because he was the purest of souls and he was put on this planet by a higher being to save the souls of men. His was so pure that men would happily lay their lives down for him. But the bad seeds of man were forever corruptible and so the cup was hidden and men such as yourself were created to ensure relics of such power would never be placed in the hands of evil men. Warrior monks who would die to protect mankind and the legacy of Christ.

Now I can see you are fighting between faith and whatever else there might be, so let me help a little. Jesus was real. FACT. He was a beacon of hope and pure goodness. FACT. For anything good there is always bad. Yin and Yang and eventually the bad overwhelmed the good. FACT. The Grail possesses the ability to let a man live forever, if that is his wish. To look into one's soul and manipulate people's thoughts. He who has the Grail can kill a man's soul, and so it is an unearthly power that only the bearers of a true faith can comprehend – whatever that faith may be. If your nemesis gains control of the Grail, he would eradicate your souls forever and send a dark message into the hearts of men. This cannot be allowed. The Grail was forged from a metal unknown to man and so can have only come from somewhere not of this world. It really is no secret that alien beings have been visiting us for millions of years. The evidence is all around us, in the pyramids, in the hieroglyphics in all civilisations. They are just vastly more intelligent than us; they don't want to be seen. So you ask, is there a God or is it alien knowledge? My response is that the answer to that lies within us all, but for me of course there is a God – Allah. He is the one who makes a butterfly beat its wings and take flight with beauty and grace, on a wing so thin you could blow a hole through it. He is the one that forms our souls and moulds our thoughts. Jesus was His son. There is nothing to say that an advanced alien life form has just helped God with some of the more tangible difficulties of our existence. The two can live in harmony. So, Mr Finch, never question your faith, but you still have some doors to open before you can answer your own questions.'

The Sultan finished and was glowing and relieved to have imparted his knowledge. Finch's mind was awash with the unanswered questions of 'Why?' He sat in a daze.

The Sultan leaned forward and rang the bell three times and it was Major Rami that entered. All it took was a nod from the Sultan and Rami disappeared. 'There is a private jet waiting for you at the airport. Major Rami will take you there via the dive centre to retrieve your personal belongings and then you will fly to Bermuda and meet a man by the name of Varni. He is a monk and is part of a long line of monks who are of my order, dating back millennia. He will be wary of you. Give him this.' The Sultan gave Finch an envelope that Rami, who had re-entered, had given to him earlier. 'Inside is an exact copy of the Phaistos disc. You will appreciate that I cannot give you the original. But I have signed it as well so he will not doubt you. Give this to him and he will help you find the Grail.'

Finch could see that the Sultan was preparing to leave so he hurriedly asked, 'Why Bermuda? It seems a long way from Oman.'

The Sultan smiled. 'If you look at the map you will see that Bermuda lies at the very heart of a grid and in an important lay line in the balance of the world. The Omani Khanjar – our curved dagger that we carry and is present on our flag – comes from Bermuda. It was given to us many years ago to remind us

142

of the importance of the area and what it means to our people, potentially a gift from the same place the Grail came from. It is in the same shape of the island. Everything has a reason. Everything has its place in destiny.'

The Sultan stood and shook hands warmly with Finch and Kris. 'Gentlemen, the road ahead is exciting but very dangerous and Inshallah you will be victorious and you will have an ally here. We will keep our eyes open for your friend and with Allah's help she will be OK. May God be with you.' With that he left.

Rami drove the pair to get their gear and headed to the airport where a private jet was purring on the runway awaiting their arrival.

Rami's men loaded up the jet with Finch's and Kris' things.

'It has been a pleasure, Mr Finch, and the Sultan wanted me to give you my number to keep me informed and for you to call if you needed anything.' Rami for once had a tone of warmth in his voice and shook his hand with meaning.

'Thank you, Major. It has been an incredible trip. Thank you.' Kris smiled and nodded and gave him a slap on the back rather than a handshake. Finch and Kris got on the jet and strapped themselves in. No sooner had they sat down when an attractive stewardess offered them both a glass of champagne.

'With the compliments of the Sultan; your wish is our pleasure,' she said, smiling. For once it was Kris that perked up.

'You know things are picking up a bit, Jake. Not much, but just a bit.' The two toasted Karin and Khalifa as the jet roared into life down the runway and left Oman for the island of Bermuda.

CHAPTER 22

The man wandered cautiously over to where Victor was sitting. It was a typically hot and arid Omani day, yet Victor wore his blue suit, white shirt and tie, his dark sunglasses catching the eye of the approaching messenger. His black hair was slicked back and there was not the slightest bead of sweat upon his brow. His Gitanes cigarette disintegrated slowly under another long inhalation and his long drink of vodka and tonic stood fizzing slowly. A welcome bit of cool relief in contrast to the baking sun. The man stood nervously in front of Victor. He was just another stooge who had come to give him news of Finch's progress.

'Yes!' demanded Victor.

'I have news, sir, regarding the man.' The local's voice trembled as he spoke. Victor's demeanour and presence had that effect. Everyone who knew Victor got an understanding of how brutal and callous he could be. A smiling assassin if ever there was one.

'Well. Go on,' Victor hissed. 'The two men found something in the chamber and went back to Sultan Quaboos' palace and have taken a plane to Bermuda. They left this morning. Sir.'

Victor stopped smoking and sat up in his chair. 'Bermuda. Why Bermuda? Do you know what they found?'

'No, sir,' replied the Omani, fearing that this inadequate information would get him an audience with Victor's rage. Victor digested this information and straightened himself out. He turned to the messenger and smiled and tapped his face sarcastically. 'Good – you can finish that,' he said pointing at the vodka. He then walked out to a waiting car and sped away to where Karin was housed. The Omani's shoulders dropped as the tension ebbed away and he breathed a deep sigh of relief.

Victor opened the door to Karin's makeshift cell, for that is what effectively it was. 'Ms Edwards. It seems that our mutual friend Mr. Finch values your friendship. Either that or he has decided to take a well-earned break in more cordial surroundings. Why would he have gone to Bermuda, do you think?'

Karin got up from the sofa. She was looking tired but was still defiant. 'How the hell should I know? Maybe he has had enough of the desert,' Karin snapped.

'Come, come now, Karin. Let us not fall out. It doesn't become you to be so abrasive and rude, and besides if you keep this up, I may lose my otherwise patient attitude and decide that you are a waste of my resources, so why don't you stop with the attitude and be just a little more helpful – understand?' Victor's voice sent a chill up Karin's spine and her earlier bravado eked away.

'I have no idea why he's gone to Bermuda. I haven't been in this loop long enough to know what the hell is going on. I am completely in the dark. He must have found something in the Library which indicated a need to head there,' surmised Karin.

'And you don't have any idea at all what he could have possibly found?'

'No. Not a clue,' Karin answered glibly.

Victor believed her. He had interrogated and tortured enough people in his lifetimes to know when someone was telling the truth or not. Victor made his way to the door and beckoned in a small weasel-like individual, a strange looking chap of European descent who looked completely out of sync with the Arabs and muscular bodyguards that were surrounding Victor.

'Go to Bermuda. Follow him and keep me informed of his every move. Do not let him slip away and do not disappointment me.' The man bowed and scurried away like a rat that had just been released from its trap back into the wild. Just before Victor left, he turned to Karin. 'Do you trust him – Finch?'

Karin instinctively answered straight away and without any hesitation. 'Yes.'

'But you don't really know him. He might just go, find the Grail and meet you in the next life and leave you to me in this.'

Karin just replied, 'I feel like I have known Guillaume forever. He will be back!' Victor gave a derisive smirk, shrugged his broad shoulders and left the room. The door bolted securely behind him.

CHAPTER 23

BERMUDA

The plane prepared itself for landing. Kris was out for the count, his mouth wide open and his eyes rolled to the back of his head. Finch sat very much awake looking out on to the blue ocean. He had slept well during the flight but now his thoughts were heavily on the job in hand. What did the message on the parchment mean and why did they have to come all the way over to Bermuda to see a monk, only to have to probably head off halfway round the world again? It was disheartening. The thing that played on his mind more than anything else though, was what the Sultan had said concerning Jesus, God, the Holy Grail and the existence of extra-terrestrials. After all, what was he actually saying? That Jesus was just a good guy who had what sounds like a magical cup and the support of aliens? That was ridiculous. It went against everything Finch had ever known. He was a Christian and more importantly he was a member of the Knights Templar. He died many times in the name of Christ and God. He didn't want to believe that ET was the key to eternal salvation. It made him even more determined to find the answer, which was now burning inside of him. It bothered him. He felt empty. He felt like a shadow of sadness had enveloped him and nothing could make things right again. He needed to find his God again and proof that things were as they always should have been. Eventually he kicked Kris who woke abruptly with a snort.

'What's the matter? What's going on?' Kris stuttered trying to get his bearings after such a deep sleep.

'We're almost here,' Finch replied. 'Listen, have you given any thought at all to what the Sultan said about the Grail?'

Kris looked him in the eyes and they were intense. The question had stirred him like a bucket of cold water being poured over one's head. 'Yes. It's all I've been thinking about. But it comes down to faith. My faith has never been in question. Never. And some Royal Omani soothsayer isn't going to change that. Aliens! It might be true, but it doesn't change the fact that Jesus was real. Pure and good and was the Son of God. Whether he met ET along the way isn't here or there. God is God and Jesus lived and the goodness of man will always come from His divine will, and it is up to people like us to uphold that. As we always have, Jake.' Kris' gaze was still solid and unflinching. He meant every piece of what he just said.

Finch leant forward in his seat to meet his gaze more intensely. 'But what if we found something out we don't want to know, Kris? What then? I can't even begin to think about it.'

Kris relaxed back in his chair trying to defuse the tension from the conversation. 'If we do, then we do. But for me it changes nothing. You may be a scientist or an archaeologist or whatever it is you do in this life, Jake, but we have always been warrior monks. Templar. Greater than all these men on earth. You should not concern yourself with what may come from our findings because, as I said, it changes nothing.'

On cue, the fasten seat belt sign bleeped followed by the pleasant hostess who cleared away the glasses and prepared the cabin for landing. Finch hadn't been convinced by Kris' argument, but he liked his passion and unwavering belief. Finch though, was more practical and he needed answers to questions he might not want to know the answers to.

148

The Sultan had been a good ally and had sorted out their Bermuda liaison. As the private jet taxied to a halt they were met at the foot of the steps by a shady looking man, who resembled a poor pastiche of an FBI undercover agent in the seventies. Finch's eyes were adjusting to the bright sunlight of the Bermudan day and he shielded them against the glare of the sun as he made his way down the steps of the jet. 'Mr Finch? My name is Rodgers. I represent the Sultan of Oman. I have been briefed and appreciate that time is of the essence. I will instruct the jet captain to ready the aircraft for a departure and await your return. In the meantime, please get into the vehicle. We will get you through US Customs and then take you to your meeting.' Finch shook the man's hand and before he had the chance to ask him anything, he had skipped up the steps past Kris and made for the captain. Finch shot a look at Kris and smiled. They packed their respective bags in the back of the purring black Mercedes Benz and waited. Rodgers returned in a flash and headed for the customs gate.

'Mr Rodgers,' Finch started, but was immediately cut off.

'Just Rodgers, please.'

Finch continued. 'Rodgers. You are taking us to meet with Varni the monk, yes?'

'Yes. I have instructions to take you to St George's Unfinished Church, where you will meet with Varni. I shall wait and then return you to the jet where the captain has been instructed to take you to wherever you may wish to go. After that you are on you own.' No sooner had he finished speaking than he was out of the car and signalling them to follow with their luggage.

Kris leaned forward from the back seat and whispered into Finch's ear, 'Friendly little chap, isn't he? I wonder if he got his arse hole sewn up that tightly before he got the job or after?'

149

Finch chuckled and both men gathered their gear and followed him into the building. After a few rudimentary questions and a whisper from Rodgers in the ear of the Customs officer, the two were through the process in quick time and soon they were on their way to see Varni.

CHAPTER 24

It was a gorgeous day with a refreshing easterly breeze, which gave a pleasant respite from the heat, and for a while Finch's mind was still. He was just enjoying looking at the scenery and allowing the air from the open window to blow through his hair. It was wonderful. Kris on the other hand was fidgety.

'Who's this Varni then, mate, and how far away is St George's?' he asked, leaning forward. Rodger's expression didn't change and it was impossible to read anything in his face as his eyes were masked behind a ludicrously large pair of brown Ray-Bans.

'The journey will take us about an hour, due to the roads and speed limit. The whole island is only about 53km squared. I have heard of Varni but never met him. Some kind of strange monk. Never been into religion. That's why I live out here. Any other questions?' Rodgers sighed.

Both Finch and Kris had thought they had broken some ice with this officious chap but that last comment made them realise that he wasn't interested in conversation or small talk. Finch again shot Kris a look in his passenger visor mirror and just caught sight of him ticking to himself in the back. They both decided to sit back and enjoy the ride.

Finch was still looking out of the window, taking in all the beauty this small island had to offer, when Rodgers told them they were almost there. Finch looked up to see the church. It was a good-looking piece of architecture with just the sides of the walls remaining, no roof, and nature having its free rein of growth inside.

Rodgers pulled up outside the ruined church and turned off his engine and sat motionless. There was an uncomfortable silence. Kris leaned forward and tapped Rodgers on the shoulder. 'So sorry to trouble you, but do you wish us to get out, or what are we supposed to do?' Finch looked disapprovingly at Kris but before Finch could utter a word Kris followed up. 'Look Jake. If you haven't noticed, this place is a bomb site and this bloke is being as helpful as a chocolate teapot, while Karin is still in Oman somewhere, probably spread eagled on an old table, so excuse me if I'm getting a little edgy!' Kris was evidently being affected by the humidity and heat and his usual benign mood was starting to boil over. Rodgers flicked a cursory glance at Kris in the rear mirror as he sat back. Finch looked at Rodgers knowing what Kris had just said mirrored his own feelings.

'Mr Rodgers, I mean Rodgers, you are here with the blessing of the Sultan to help us, yes? So where do we go? It is rather urgent that we don't waste time.'

Rodgers still looked straight out of the front window and bleated, 'Go to the church and Varni will meet you. It is not difficult, Mr Finch.' Finch got out of the car and opened the back door for Kris, expecting him to release a left hook into Rodgers' nose.

'Come on. Let's find this monk and get out of here,' Finch whispered and they hurried up to what looked like a doorway of the old ruin. As they entered, the feeling that overwhelmed them was one of absolute serenity. Although they were in an empty shell of a church it was obvious to both men that this was a sacred place. Their base Templar emotions were fuelling both men's veins once more and each of them took a small moment to indulge in the peace and tranquillity the place had to offer. Finch looked back from staring up at the heavens and saw a small old man dressed in the traditional dark brown robes of a monk from the Benedictine order. He had a kind but sorrowful face and skin like old leather.

'God bless you, my sons. You are most welcome in this house of God, gentlemen.' Kris acknowledged the monk with a cursory bow but Finch introduced himself in a more amiable manner.

'Hello, sir. My name is Jake and this is Kris. We have been sent—' Finch was cut short by the monk who raised his hand to interrupt Finch mid stride.

'I know why you are here, Mr Finch, and all about your mission, as it is indeed a quest of the highest importance. I have been briefed most comprehensively by the Sultan. You have friends in high places, gentlemen. I appreciate time is of the utmost importance, but would you mind walking with me. It would not be proper to discuss such matters in this most sacred house of our Lord.' The monk turned and exited through a rear archway and headed into the thick wood which bordered the church on one side. Finch and Kris followed, slightly sad at having to leave the surroundings of the church so soon. The monk seemed to float gracefully over the ground. Just past the edge of the wood was a passage which led to a doorway heading into the slope of the hill. The monk pushed open the door. The two men followed and saw in front of them an underground chamber. A dimly lit room with an altar and a crucifix on it at one end and a table and chairs at the other. Another room led off to the side with a bed, kitchenette and lavatory branching off that.

'Does this come with the job?' Kris asked.

The monk smiled. 'I am the guardian of the church; I therefore must be nearby and this affords me the closeness and privacy required to be able to fulfil my role.'

153

As the men scanned the room Finch asked, 'Varni, that is you right?'

He nodded in acknowledgement.

'Why you? I mean, I am trying to piece together this story and I am just trying to work out why Bermuda, why you, why could we not have done this on the phone? Why are you the key to the door of our next journey?'

Varni smiled and offered the men a seat at the table. 'So many questions. And all of them most valid.' Varni grinned. 'The Lord's Road is never an easy one.' Varni sat at the head of the table and placed his arms in the cuffs of the opposite sleeve. 'This is not a conversation that can be had over a telephone. We are dealing with a quest between good and evil. You are warrior monks, Templar, and it is your responsibility to do God's work – besides, I like to look into a man's eyes and see his soul before I unveil my own secrets. You also needed to ask yourself some questions. This quest is going to open doors which you may wish had stayed shut and only you now can answer those questions which will emerge. So yes, you had to come out here.' Varni leant forward and poured three glasses of water and pushed them towards his guests. He took a sip and continued. 'Why do I possess this knowledge and therefore fit into your particular jigsaw? I too come from a long line of protectors of the secrets of Christ. I just prefer now to be a peaceful being. There are few of us still about and soon our kind will be even fewer. We were entrusted with some of the greatest mysteries of this earth, and to act if these were to be placed in the perilous hands of evil. It all sounds a little far-fetched, but you of all people should know that good and evil are all too real and I am sure your friend in Oman will be too aware of it also. That is all you need know about me. As for why Bermuda – well… the weather is quite conducive to a happy life.' Varni winked at Finch. 'Many centuries ago, in about 1510, a Bermudan monk went on a

154

pilgrimage throughout the South Americas in an attempt to spread the word of God. He too was a Regressor and had been a defender of purity in our land and like many, was as good a warrior as he was a priest. He stumbled upon a cave deep in the heart of the South American country of Ecuador, which housed a treasure which was unlike anything mankind had witnessed before. The Library of Tayos. He could not understand what these artefacts were and felt that no good could ever come from them if they fell into the wrong hands. The language was incomprehensible, but each item seemed to resonate a power and beat which was mesmeric. In his general ignorance of what he had found, he took one of the pieces of metal and destroyed the entrance to the cave in an attempt to hide it from the world. From the metal he… hmm, borrowed… he made a dagger. He had seen rudimentary maps of Bermuda and it indeed resembled a dagger. He encrusted it with precious stones and when he had finished, he realised that what he had created was a dagger that beat to the rhythm of his own being. It never dulled and never lost its edge. It was spectacular. A few years later Bermuda became unstable and the monks were forced out. The monk, who went by the name of Peter, had an overwhelming urge to head to the Middle East and spread the word of God. He boarded a ship and went on a huge pilgrimage. Ultimately, he ended up in what is now Oman. He felt very close to Christ there and as a mark of respect, Peter presented the knife to the Sultan. He was awestruck by the beauty and power of this ornament. He was dumbstruck, but he also revered it and was so delighted he made Peter part of his court and used to talk for hours with him on Christianity and Islam. Peter, though, died not long after he presented the blade and in respect the Sultan made the blade known today as a Khanjar, a national symbol representing purity, devotion, the warrior spirit and protection. That is why Bermuda.'

155

The men drank and Finch thought on what Varni had said. 'I'm sorry to rush you but, what now?'

Varni stood and walked over to the drawer and pulled out a red velvet piece of fabric which had been wrapped neatly around an object. 'Here, you must take this. Take your plane to Armenia and find the Etchmiadzin Cathedral. It is one of the earliest Christian places of worship in the world. There you will find Father Dimoculous. He is the Father in charge of the cathedral and Guardian of the Treasures. He will not welcome your visit and nor will he allow you to fulfil your request. That is when you must give him this.'

Varni opened up the red velvet cloth and inside was a piece of old wood. Both Finch and Kris looked at it blankly.

'I know it doesn't look like much, granted, but this will open your door in Armenia,' Varni concluded.

Kris picked it up quickly and with little regard. 'What is it?' Kris said with his usual abrasion. Varni looked at him awaiting his reaction.

'That is another actual piece of the Ark that Noah built during the Great Flood.'

Kris stopped his flippancy immediately and handled the object with a little more respect.

'The Ark?' Finch asked. Varni nodded.

'In the room of the Holy Relics in the Etchmiadzin Cathedral there are many wondrous relics from history. But there is one, which takes pride of place among them all. A piece of the Ark. Father Dimoculous is the Guardian of the Ark. It is the most revered piece in the Armenian Church and highly protected. It is encased in gold and silver and has the cross of our Lord Jesus Christ on it. According to the 4th and 5th century Armenian and Greek historians, it was said that a bishop of the

Church named James, led a group of pilgrims up the side of Mount Ararat. Whilst on their journey, the going was tough and they fell asleep. While he was asleep, an Angel of the Lord visited James and said, 'you will not make it up to the top of the mountain to see the Ark but as a reward for your efforts I give you a piece of the Ark.' When he awoke there was indeed a piece of wood under his head. And so, the relic has remained at the cathedral ever since. If you give him this, he will know instantly that it is a missing part of the Ark. This will allow you access to see the relic and you will need it, for on the back, written in an ink that can only be read under ultraviolet light, are the exact co-ordinates to the cave at Tayos. You will know what to do for yourself when and if you get there. After you get these co-ordinates, you must then proceed and obtain an object equivalent to the Rosetta Stone. In other words, as the stone was vital to our understanding of many a language, the object is the key to unravelling the questions in the cave. This will be found only in one place and one place alone. Ethiopia.'

Finch's eyes looked up and he understood what Varni had said. Kris saw Finch's reaction to this but was none the wiser.

'Now, I think it is time that you two were leaving. After all, you are against the clock. Yes?' Finch was still thinking when Varni got up. 'By the way, gentlemen; do not allow the Father to know why you seek the Ark. Embellish a story, for the Cave at Tayos is not for just anyone. It is a secret that should remain just that.' Finch nodded and all three headed for the door. 'I will leave you now, Templars. Go in peace with love and trust in the Lord.' Varni made the sign of the cross and shook both men's hands with meaning. Finch smiled and thanked Varni. Kris patted him on the shoulder in a way only Kris could. As the men left, Varni wished them luck and watched as they exited the wood. Once out they saw the po-faced Rodgers waiting in the car in the exact same position as he had been in when the two had got out an hour earlier. This time Kris, who evidently still had a beef with

Rodgers' attitude, got into the front seat, meaning Finch had the rear.

Niceties aside, Kris looked at Rodgers. 'Right! Back to the plane and make it quicker than you were getting us up here – got it?' Rodgers belligerently took his time doing up his seat belt and then conducted a very precise 'Mirror, Signal, Manoeuvre', although there wasn't another car within miles of where they were. Finch, on the other hand, sat in the back trying digest all that Varni had just said.

Rodgers pulled up to the airport and the Omani private jet. Finch got out of the car and thanked Rodgers. Kris on the other hand just sneered at him.

Rodgers sat looking forward completely unperturbed by Kris' expression. Finch, sensing a little tension grabbed Kris by the arm.

'Come on, Kris. Let's go. Leave happiness to his own thing.' The two men boarded the plane and Finch briefed the pilot, who then in turn briefed the Omani embassy to get a special visitors' entry visa in motion. Otherwise, it would be a very brief stay.

Once settled on the plane and airborne, it was the first time that Finch was able to get to grips with what Varni had told him. He had a chance now to plan his next moves and think about Karin and Victor. It also gave him the chance to wrestle with his own emotions and think about his own questions of faith and the potential reality of what they might unearth.

CHAPTER 25

Karin sat in the darkened stuffy room in Oman which was now her prison cell. Victor had treated her fairly, making sure she was fed and watered regularly and even supplied her with wine. Every now and again he would come in and survey the room and ask Karin questions about Finch and then leave. Victor entered the room, this time accompanied by two heavyset men. The mood was slightly different. Victor sat down and lit a cigarette, but his normal composure had appeared to have evaded him and he seemed irritable and jumpy. 'What do you think Finch is up to now?' Victor asked Karin in a rhetorical manner. 'My man in Bermuda tells me they went to see a monk in the north of the island and has now jetted away somewhere else. As we speak, the information I need is being... extracted... and we will know more. He is a clever one. No. He is a devious bastard! He would be a good ally if it weren't for that pathetic moral squint he has. That you all have!' Victor spat the last phrase from his lips.

Karin sat and shrugged her shoulders flippantly. 'I don't know, but Finch is good. He'll get you what you need. I'm sure of it.' Karin's flippancy visibly annoyed Victor who was trying his best to control his temper.

'Yes. He is good. But I wonder if he thinks as much of you. I mean, you two have only just met. You might be lost souls etcetera, but you're just a woman who has been brought along for the ride.' Karin was starting to feel very wary. Victor got up and went to the window. 'You know, gaining information from people in the good old days was fun and easy. You see, a man can only take so much pain before he tells you the very secrets of his heart. Women, they are stronger all together. You Templars, though. You were all different. You could twist a man's thumb 360 degrees and watch the tears run down his face and see his teeth clench together and he would not utter a sound and then, when it was too much to bear, his light would just extinguish. It used to make me explode with anger and I used to mutilate the corpse in spite. I once took a man's ears off and made him eat them before taking his eyes out with a hot poker to get some information about the whereabouts of other Templars. The man didn't make a sound. But his pain was written all over his contorted face. At least that was some consolation. You people cannot win this. I will win. As I always do and when I do, I will end the line of Knights Templar for eternity.'

There was a pause. Karin wanted to show some kind of belligerency, but she was afraid. Victor looked at the two burly men and nodded. On that signal, the two grabbed hold of Karin, dragging her over to the table. One man held Karin firmly from behind in a neck choke hold whilst the other held one arm tightly and the other palm down flat on the table. 'Your manner offends me, Karin. You may be a woman but you are no lady. So just in case you have any doubts as to who holds all the cards here or whether Finch thinks he can mess me around. I am going to teach you a lesson in being humble.' Karin's eyes were wide open and her heart was beating like a deranged clock. Victor went out of the room and returned shortly afterwards with a hammer and nails. Victor looked at Karin and grabbed her chin and inspected her face closely. He then rubbed his thumb over her sweating brow and tasted her sweat. 'Ah! The taste of fear,' Victor whispered. 'Now splay your fingers!' Victor ordered. Karin did what he said. 'I want you to know that I do this, not because I have to, but because… I want to.' With Karin's fingers spread on the table Victor placed a nail in the webbing of Karin's hand between the thumb and her finger. The anticipation was awful and Karin looked down not thinking that Victor would actually hurt her, after all she was just a bit of a guarantee in case Finch failed to deliver. But he was being true to his word – so why would Victor do this? Victor looked Karin square in the eyes and drove the nail deep into the webbing and through to table beneath. Karin screamed in pain and Victor smiled with the pleasure of having inflicted such pain on another human being. Victor watched and he saw a surge of defiance flow through Karin's body and she fixed him with a look from her intense blue eyes. The old Templar in her rose to the surface and she wasn't going to give Victor the satisfaction of hearing her wince. Victor saw what was happening. He grabbed her wrist and pulled on it. 'Scream, Templar! I want to hear you plead for me to stop! You are no Templar now. You are a spoilt woman caught in someone else's game – now beg me to stop!' In a mad moment all Karin could think of was to place his other hand on the table and goaded Victor with her eyes to do the same thing again. Victor stopped and stood tall. This was unexpected and threw Victor. He stepped back and nodded to his henchmen to release the grip on Karin. She stood as still as a statue, looking at the table. After a pause Victor laughed. 'Very good, Templar. Admirable, I must say. Your time will come and I promise you. I will hear you scream.' With that he threw the hammer at Karin's fingers and left the room leaving Karin still nailed to the table and shaking with pain and anger.

CHAPTER 26

On the plane, Finch had got his head down for a few hours. When he woke Kris was still out for the count and Finch had a chance to mull over what had happened. He pulled from his bag the velvet cloth containing the relic from the Ark that Varni had given to them. He unwrapped it slowly and took the piece in his hand. Was this really a piece of Noah's Ark? It just looked like a dry and unspectacular piece of wood. It didn't feel powerful or special and certainly didn't look it. Finch kept thinking back to how the dagger must have felt in the hands of Peter, how he went to Oman and how it seemed to beat with his own body. This didn't. So did that mean that all relics were mere objects with no power? Would the Grail – whatever it may be and if it existed – be the same? And if they found that the Grail was made by a person, given to another, be it human or extra-terrestrial, would that then mean that God really only existed in the minds of those who needed something or someone greater than themselves, but that it was all just fantasy? Finch couldn't bear to think of that. He wanted God to be God and that was it. Finch placed the wood back on the velvet and stared out of the window.

Kris woke and saw Finch lost in the clouds. 'Howdo! Wow, I needed that kip!' Kris yawned.

'Yep, me too. I wonder how Karin is?' Finch asked.

Kris shrugged. 'Yeah, poor bugger, not sure I would want to be in her shoes. Though I always looked good in high heels!' That last quip amused Kris. 'What do you reckon about that Ark?' Finch looked at it again. 'Ark – more like bark if you ask me. I can't believe I'm turning into such an old cynic. Maybe it is real. At the moment I don't care. I just want to get this over with. I'll figure the rest out later. It's funny, this could actually be authentic and all I want to do is forget about it.'

Kris smiled and stretched, 'You know, Jake – you think far too much. You are holding a piece of the Ark and if it isn't, then you're holding something which offers people hope and happiness. Enjoy it. The main thing we need to do is start ticking the relevant boxes so we can get back and help Karin.' Finch allowed himself to smile at Kris. There was something so grounded and pragmatic about him that gave Finch a great feeling of strength. He was glad he was with him. He stuck the velvet-wrapped Ark back in his satchel and helped himself to a drink from the fridge. It was going to be a long flight so a few 'sherbets' wouldn't do any harm.

The fasten seat belt sign blipped and the jet started its descent to Armenia. The pilot had informed Finch that they would be met by a chap at the airport with a visa, valid for one week and then they were on their own. The visa would make life a great deal easier as the Armenian authorities along with many eastern bloc countries, liked their red tape. The plane touched down. It was about four in the afternoon. They were met at Zvartnots International Airport by a member of the Omani Embassy, who no sooner had he handed the visa over to Finch, he disappeared. Oman obviously didn't want to be associated with anything in Armenia.

Having got through customs, the two men made their way into the capital city of Yerevan. The first thing they needed to do was to find a hotel for the night. Finch needed an internet café to find out where they were and where the cathedral was. He adhered to his seven Ps mantra and so a bit of knowledge about the Ark, Armenia and the cathedral would go a long way. Finally, he needed an ultraviolet light by which to read the inscription on the back of the Ark. The hotel they found was really nothing

163

special but it would do. It seemed clean and in an area that appeared safe. It had been a long trip and they had lots to accomplish. The last thing they needed was unprovoked trouble. Kris decided to go and source a small UV light from the local market while it was still open. Finch made his way to the local internet café to do a little research.

Varni was just settling down to eat when there was a discreet knock on the door. He thought it to be the wind and carried on, but again there was the slight tapping at his door. Varni made his way to the door and opened it. He was a quiet peaceful man and had no enemies and the only people who would disturb him were people who knew him. There on the other side of the door was a well-presented, tanned man in an open-neck shirt and jacket. The most noticeable thing about him was a scar that ran from his left eye down to the corner of his mouth. Varni looked at the man.

'Can I help you, my son?' The scarred man smiled and lit a cigarette.

'Yes, Father, I believe you can. May I come in please?'

Varni hesitated a while, for although the man was polite there was something a little sinister about him. 'Of course, but could I ask you to leave your cigarette outside? I have a bad chest and dislike the smell of tobacco.'

The man took a final drag and stubbed out the cigarette placing the butt in his pocket.

'Can I offer you some tea or water to drink?' Varni enquired.

'Water please.' The man walked around the small room scanning his arcs for anything of any use. 'It is a most unusual abode you have here, Father.'

Varni brought in the water and placed it on the table.

'Yes. It is simple. But it is home. How can I help you?' The man took a sip of water and looked Varni straight in the eyes. 'You had a visit from two gentlemen recently. Very blue eyes – you remember the men?' Varni nodded in agreement. The man continued, 'They came and asked questions of you, specific questions. I need to know what they said and what you told them. Please, Father. I have come a long way and it is most important you tell me the truth so I beg you, do not lie, for I tell you this, you may be a man of God, Father, but I am not. Now what was said?'

Varni took a sip of water. He knew the man was not playing games. He sat back and took a few moments to compose himself. Varni was God's true servant and was not scared of death. That being the case, he had no intention of meeting his Maker just yet. He decided to tell him the truth. It would be easier that way. Finch had time on his side, he may have even got the information required already and besides, Varni had been warned that this occurrence may follow, by his Omani contact, so he would tell the truth and inform Finch and hopefully end his part in the mystery.

'I told him that what he was looking for lay in Armenia at the Etchmiadzin Cathedral. There they would find the sacred piece of the Ark. Upon it is a clue to his next step which is likely to lead him to...' Varni hesitated, he was saying too much. There was the truth and there was giving up everything.

The man jumped in, 'Lead him to...?'

Varni took another sip of water. 'Lead them to Ethiopia.'

The man smiled and leant back in his chair removing a cigarette from his tatty packet. 'Well, well. Ethiopia. Good. What else?'

Varni looked surprised that the information given was not enough. 'Well, that's it. I gave them a little something. Insurance

165

if you like. A relic to help them achieve their goal and that was that.'

'Just like that eh? Very good, Father. I believe you, but you can never be too careful.' The man lit his cigarette and blew the smoke at Varni. 'You see though, sometimes there is always a little more, and the best way to ensure the truth is indeed the truth is to apply a little... pressure.' Varni stood up quickly.

'There is no need, no need at all. I swear to you. That is all that was said. Now please leave and go in peace.'

The man grabbed Varni by the throat and forced his face into the table. He tried to push away but the man was too strong. 'Now, old monk, is there nothing else you can remember?' Varni grimaced, his cries snuffled from his face being pushed into the table by the scarred man.

'I can tell you no more!' Varni pleaded.

'Well let us just make certain. My boss would be most displeased if he thought I was shirking my responsibilities.' The man removed his Zippo lighter from his pocket and struck the flint, igniting it. He then set it to Varni's ear. The heat from the flame blackened it swiftly and then it blistered and burnt, the smell was horrific. Varni screamed and pleaded with the man to stop; beseeching him, crying out that he had no more to tell. The ear was disfiguring like a wax candle. Eventually the man stopped and capped the flame. As calm as if nothing had happened. The man walked away from the table leaving Varni spread-eagled and distraught, sobbing in pain.

'Good, Father. It appears you were telling the truth all along. But I had to be sure, you understand.' Varni lay on the wooden table in agony. What was left of his right ear throbbed and hurt like nothing he had ever felt before. All was quiet. He heard the click of the lighter again as the man lit yet another cigarette and then it all went dark and the pain was no more. The man scanned

166

the room before leaving, but before he shut the door, he cast one more look at Varni, the gentle monk still and motionless on the table, lying in a pool of his own blood, his throat cut across his windpipe. The man had left nothing to chance. He shut the door and made for a telephone, to report his findings to Victor.

CHAPTER 27

Finch returned to the hotel room and saw Kris catnapping on the bed. He woke as Finch shut the door. 'Success?' asked Kris.

'Yep. Got some good stuff. I'll brief you over a beer and some grub if you like. How did you get on?' Kris pulled a small torch from his pocket that could flick between a white LED light and ultraviolet beam. 'Good work. Come on I'm starving.' Finch left the printed paperwork from the internet café, took his bag and headed out for some food, beer and a chat.

Finch and Kris found a tavern just round the corner from the hotel. Finch felt on edge. Kris on the other hand seemed to be unfazed by anything. 'So what did you find out about this place?' enquired Kris trying to get the waitress's attention.

'Well, we are about twenty kilometres from the cathedral so shouldn't take us too long to get there; plus, it's one of the main places to see on the tourist trail, so it shouldn't be a drama finding it either. I reckon if all goes well, we can be out of here by tomorrow afternoon. The difficulty will be getting into Ethiopia. We can either get a flight direct to Addis Ababa, but then we will have visa issues, though I am sure we can use a bit of 'dollar' action there. Or we can see if we can hitch a ride on a ship heading south. Then we have the time delays. I don't trust Victor, and Karin, in this life anyway, doesn't seem the most streetwise chick. Any delay could encourage Victor into doing something stupid.' The waitress came over and Kris wasted no time ordering beers and anything with chips. He always had a knack of looking like he hadn't heard anything or at least didn't care. But Kris saw and heard everything. It was a skill he had honed. The more than laissez-faire attitude was a front, but behind the veneer, he was as sharp as a blade and ruthless too.

'I think we should fly. We could be messing around for days trying to get to a port and then a tug down to Africa and then we still could be hit with the same problems. Let's get out of here and get into the country. We'll deal with any other crap when we get there.' Kris' assertion took Finch by surprise but he agreed with the principle. 'So once we get into this cathedral is it going to be plain sailing or what?'

Finch smiled. 'No. This is the cherry on the cake as far as the Armenian Church goes. All we need to do is sweet-talk this priest into letting us see the Relic. That would ordinarily be impossible but this extra piece of the jigsaw Varni has given us should ensure we get a good crack of the whip.' Finch tapped the satchel indicating the red velvet-wrapped relic they had themselves. He continued, 'The cathedral is the oldest state-built church in the world built around AD 300 and it was Armenia that became the first officially Christian country in the world. So, needless to say, they take their religion fairly seriously here.' The waitress returned with two large cold lagers and two plates of burger and chips. Kris smiled.

'Yes! Now this is what I have been waiting for.' Both men raised a toast and took a well-earned swig of beer. 'He's going to want to know what we are looking for. And if he sees you playing around with that UV torch, he will probably do the same. So how are we going to get him to leave us with this priceless artefact, so you can do your thing?' asked Kris.

'Hmmm. That's a good question and one we may have to play off the cuff.' Both men tucked into their food. Kris looked at Finch quizzically. 'I am guessing that UV torches weren't available a couple of thousand years ago, so how did these guys ever see what they had written?' Finch's eyes lit up at the chance of explaining some ancient engineering.

'Well, the ancients were always trying to invent codes and ways of hiding their secrets, whether it was Newton and his invisible ink or da Vinci with his back to front writing. They invented an ink that was invisible to the human eye but when sunlight was passed through a clear white crystal prism and a filtered lens placed in front of the light, refracting it and giving it colour, the natural UV light would filter through and illuminate the otherwise invisible writing. It was quite ingenious really.' Finch finished, expecting to hear gasps of awe from Kris, but instead he shrugged and tilted his head in acknowledgement as if it was the answer he expected anyway. No. Food and drink were the only really important things on Kris' mind at this present moment in time.

The next day the two men woke early and were in a taxi headed toward the cathedral. When they pulled up outside, Finch was surprised by its size and lack of the spectacular. He had seen a few pictures of the place on the internet but in real life it was fairly drab. He supposed he had been too spoilt with architectural masterpieces, which beheld splendours such as Salisbury Cathedral, Winchester and Westminster Abbey. This in comparison was rather mundane. They made their way to the entrance and from within could already hear the muted sounds of choral singing. As they entered, the air was thick with frankincense, a choir of boys occupied the far end and there were a handful of folk dotted around, all bent over deep in thought and prayer.

Although Finch considered the external façade of the building to be drab, the inside was wonderful. A large dome commanded the main vista – in the manner of a mini St. Paul's. There were breath taking friezes and paintings dating back centuries, and at the far end, an altar which spanned the breadth of the church. It was a magical place and Finch's soul began to shine once more and for the time being anyway, alleviated all the nagging doubts that had been dogging him since the start of this journey. They scanned the area for Father Dimoculous, the priest they were told to meet by Varni. Neither of them knew what he looked like or whether he was even there. They headed into the cathedral, lowering their heads to the altar in respect and looked for a side door to the private rooms. Kris found a large wooden door and went to push it open when a voice stopped them.

'May I help you?' The men swung round and saw a young priest dressed in black.

'We are looking for Father Dimoculous. It is very important that we see him,' Finch answered.

'I am sorry but Father Dimoculous is very busy and will not have any time to see you today, but if you give me your names, I will inform him of your visit.' The priest had now worked his way between the doorway and Finch.

'You don't understand. We must speak with Father Dimoculous. Now.' Finch urged once more, but the priest had been given strict instructions not to disturb him and was determined to carry out his orders. 'I am sorry, but Father Dimoculous is busy and—'

Kris interrupted. 'Look we need to see Father Dimoculous now. Not tomorrow, not next week but now, and if you don't go and get him now, we'll find him ourselves. Got it! Now go get Father Dimoculous - please!' The young priest looked like a rabbit caught in the headlights and didn't know what to do. Finch gave Kris a nod of appreciation for his direct approach to the situation. Kris stared intimidatingly at the priest.

'OK I will fetch him now. Please wait here.' The priest scuttled off through the door in a semi run.

'I am guessing that was slightly less cordial than what he is used to. Nevertheless effective.' Finch smiled.

171

A few moments later he returned with Father Dimoculous who also wore a black gown but sported a bushy black beard and thick seventies-styled glasses. He looked more like a lumberjack than a priest. Even so, he appeared visibly annoyed at having to present himself in front of these two foreigners, having ignored his more youthful apprentice. 'I am Father Dimoculous. What may I do for you?' Finch put his hand out to introduce himself, but the priest was cold, in no mood for pleasantries. Finch knew straight away that this was going to be awkward.

'We need to talk to you in private, Father, and appreciate that you are very busy, but we have come a long way and need to speak with you on a matter of the utmost urgency and will not be dissuaded.'

The priest looked at the two men realising that this was a matter he would have to deal with and scowled. 'Very well. I can give you ten minutes. No more. Follow me.' He left through the door, followed by Finch and Kris, with the young priest bringing up the rear. The four men entered Father Dimoculous' office.

'Sit, please. What is it that is of such urgency?' The priest demanded. Kris leaned in toward Finch and whispered, 'Come on Jake! Let's not mess about with this one - threaten him and crack on.'

Finch hushed Kris and whispered back, 'That will be plan B.' Finch continued, 'Father, we have come from Bermuda where we have spoken with a monk who goes by the name of Varni. Do you know him?'

The priest replied, 'Yes, I have heard of Varni and...'

'He told us that you were a good man of God and that you would help us in our mission. We need to... I mean, we would very much like to be able to see the relic that is housed here. From the Ark.'

172

Father Dimoculous was unmoved by the request, his face dead pan. 'Out of the question. I am the Guardian of the Ark. You are not the first people to want to see the relic; every Christian in the world wants to see the relic. There is no way. It is sacred. No, gentlemen. Absolutely not! Go in peace with God's blessing.' Father Dimoculous gestured for his young apprentice to show the men out, but they were not moving.

Finch continued, 'Father. We are not just anyone. We need to see the Ark. It is a matter of life and death and we intend to complete what we have started.'

Father Dimoculous leant forward. 'Do not think to threaten me, in this, God's house, in my own country. The relic is locked away and all I need do is make one call and you will never leave this city. You are a long way from home, gentlemen, I suggest you go back to where you have come from.' Finch kept the man's stare for a beat.

Kris interjected, 'You know, Father, for a man of God that sounded strangely like a threat? Which shows a stereotypical hypocrisy that is all too abundant in today's Christian establishments. Now, how about you stop being so damn awkward and you do what we ask?' Finch rolled his eyes in despair. This wasn't a time for the good cop, bad cop routine, though it was looking far more likely that plan B was going to be the only solution. Father Dimoculous went to pick up the phone receiver. Finch placed his hand on top to prevent him.

'Father, wait! We are not the enemy here. My friend is tired and anxious as am I. We are not your usual pilgrims; we need to see the object. We mean it no harm or disrespect. Merely to see it. I appreciate your resistance but maybe this will encourage you and maybe you will accept this as a gift offering, or a token of our goodwill in exchange for a brief look.' Finch removed the velvet wrapping from his bag and placed it on the table. He

173

carefully slid it over to the priest who was still bristling from the exchange with Kris.

'What is this? I do not take bribes. You disrespect me,' the priest said, sliding the package back to Finch, who calmly slid it back.

'It is no bribe. Please open it, you'll understand.' Father Dimoculous took the velvet wrapping and started to unbind its contents. When it was revealed, he held it and inspected it.

'Another relic or just a piece of wood picked up along the way,' he said dismissively.

'Father, do you really think we would travel halfway across the globe having met with Varni to waste your time? It is a missing part of your Ark relic. It is the same wood that was found underneath Bishop James' head when he woke from his dream many years ago. A gift from an angel,' Finch said quietly, looking for Father Dimoculous' reaction.

The priest looked at the wrapping with suspicion and trepidation. He knew that there was a piece missing from the original, but he thought it had been lost in time. He studied the wooden shard and he had a feeling that it could be authentic. He touched it delicately with his fingers and then picked it up with immense care and compassion, still wondering if it was real or if he was being duped. He placed it down on the velvet and said a silent prayer. Finch took the opportunity of taking it back.

'It is part of the Ark, and it is a present from us to you and to your church – just as long as I may inspect your piece right now.'

'How can you bargain with a divine gift; do you have no shame?' The priest's eyes were fired with rage.

'No,' Finch replied coldly. 'I need to see it. Do we have terms?' The priest knew he had no choice. He wasn't going to

174

allow a potential missing piece to disappear with these two vandals.

'We have terms. Come, let us go so you will leave this place,' the priest answered with venom. The three men made their way to a room at the back of the church and in front of them was a cabinet filled with artefacts and religious connotations of great importance to the Armenian Church: goblets, boxes, books. In the middle was what they were looking for. A gold plaque with two folding doors. These were open and in the middle was a gold cross with precious stones running along it's centre. This was resting on a wooden background. On the left hand side was a small sliver of wood. The Ark. The priest took the item and laid it on the table in front of them and stepped back.

'There it is. Treat it with the utmost respect, for God is watching.'

'Oh, He's watching, and it may surprise you to know that He is on our side,' replied Finch, eager to crack on.

Kris turned to the priest. 'Father, I will have to ask you to leave us alone with the relic for a moment. You must trust us, we are on the same side and mean it no harm, but we must inspect this without interruption or prying eyes.'

The priest stood firm. 'Who are you people, what are you really looking for? I will not leave you with it. It is my way or you can get out!'

Finch was about to explain when Kris took the helm once more in a somewhat less diplomatic way. 'Look, Father. I am not sure whether it was lost in translation, I'm not asking. If we wanted to steal it or destroy it, we would have done it by now – it's hardly Fort Knox in here, so if you don't mind, let us get on with what we need to do and you can have your other piece and we'll be out of your hair – got it?' Kris looked menacing and was bored pussy-footing around. The priest saw in his eyes he wasn't joking and could see the logic in what he was saying.

'You have five minutes,' Father Dimoculous said storming out of the room.

'Very impressive Kris. There may be a job for you at the Embassy yet.' Finch laughed. Kris just offered him the finger in return.

'Right, let's open this thing up,' Finch whispered. It wasn't hard. The rear casing was attached by three clasps of gold and could be opened without too much force. Finch took out the UV light and shone it on the back of the wood. In the top right-hand corner was once again the same phrase he had read in Egypt in Greek 'Θυμηθείτε – Ζωή αιώνιος για την καθαρή ψυχή του. Εμπιστοσύνη στο Λόρδο ο Θεός.' (REMEMBER – 'Life Eternal For The Pure Of Soul – Trust in The Lord God'). It must have some relevance but just what, was a mystery to him. Underneath that was a group of numbers: 77°47'34" δύση (West) and 1°56'00" νότος (South). Finch scanned the rest of the wood and at the bottom of the piece was a shape. It was a rectangle with nine parts to it and within these parts were obscure shapes. Again, this made no sense to either man. Finch took his phone out and took a photo. It wasn't a great shot but it would do. A final scan and Finch placed the wood back in the frame, clasped it tight and placed it back neatly on the table. Knowing full well that Father Dimoculous was wedged tight up against the door, Kris pulled it open violently, almost flooring the priest as he fell through.

'We are done, Father. You are most kind. Here is the gift I promised you.' Finch handed over the velvet wrap and offered a hand to shake in conclusion of business. Father Dimoculous took the wrap and kissed it tenderly and stared at Finch's hand with disdain.

'We are not on the same side. Now please leave this place of God and never come back.'

'Now, now Father. That really isn't a very Christian attitude. Aren't you supposed to welcome sinners and not judge? You stand there so pleased with your own sanctimony and yet your heart is cold, and if I had my way, I would cut it out and let you see it for yourself. You, Father, have forgotten what it actually means to do God's work here on earth. You have lost your way, or perhaps you never were blessed with being on the right path in the first place.' Kris spoke with passion and meant every word. Finch had to admire Kris. He was uncomplicated and was more of a Templar than all of them. Kris stared at the priest and shook his head. Then with a sigh he left. Finch wanted to leave on more amiable terms.

'One day, Father, you will understand the importance of why we are here, and whether you like it or not, we do God's work; we just use different methods. We are here to ensure your world continues to turn in the same way it has always done. Thank you, Father. I'm glad you can reunite the pieces of your Ark now.' Finch smiled at Father Dimoculous, but the priest's heart was cold, he had lost his way like so many other over pious men throughout the centuries and the last thing he wanted to give Finch was a smile.

The two men left and jumped into the nearest taxi and headed for the airport. 'Well, what an unpleasant man. Can we leave this place now?' Kris shouted.

Finch sighed. 'Yep, though I'm sure he doesn't think that highly of us either; he's just doing his job as Guardian.'

'Yeah well,' continued Kris, 'Why is it that most men in a robe we've ever met, Guillaume, is a jerk?'

The two men arrived at the airport and scanned the place for a ticket office. 'I'll get the tickets; you have a hunt for an internet café. I need to know what that sign and those numbers mean. Oh, and I'll have a coffee and cake – any cake. I'm starving!' instructed Finch.

After half an hour they met up. Finch had booked them on the twenty-one thirty-five flight to Addis Ababa, which gave them hours to kill in the airport. Kris had found an internet café of sorts, which meant Finch could try and make some sense of their findings.

'You know, there is such a thing as smart phones you know. then we wouldn't have to run about trying to find internet cafes.' Kris said puzzled at Finch's lack of technical awareness.

Finch laughed, 'I know, but where would be the fun in that. Besides, I see folk wedged to their phones, their faces constantly glued to the screen. They have no idea what they are missing by just looking up. It's a slippery slope and I don't want to get into the whole dependency thing.'

'Understandable Jake, but if you had your way, you'd be carrying around a dozen leather bound books, parchment and a quill!' Kris huffed.

Finch took his old phone out and looked at the photos and the numbers he had taken. They were definitely co-ordinates of some kind. He put them into a search engine and came up with the Amazonian province of Pastaza in Ecuador on the River Pastaza. The pictures on Google Earth showed an empty piece of land. No towns or villages nearby and no significant landmarks apart from the river. He looked at the phrase he found in Egypt and on the Ark and put that into a search engine to see if it gave any clues at all, but nothing emerged. Finally, he searched for anything that may sound like the description of the symbol found on the Ark with the other bits of information. Nothing really was definitive, yet the Ark of the Covenant and various hieroglyphics kept popping up. Finch went to meet up with Kris who was now on his third cup of coffee.

'Sorry, mate. Ate your cake. But if it's any consolation – it was totally minging. Any clues? And why Ethiopia?' asked Kris. Finch took a large gulp of coffee.

'I input the numbers which were, as I thought, a grid reference of sorts. It leads to part of a river in Ecuador; It's got something to do with the Library of Tayos that Varni spoke about. Nothing more really. As far as the phrase goes, that drew a blank as well. But the symbol. The Ark of the Covenant kept coming up in my searches, and Varni himself said we would be heading to Ethiopia. I suspected it initially but needed more information, but I'm pretty certain now that the symbol relates to a mark on the Ark of the Covenant, which by popular belief is said to be housed in the Ethiopian Orthodox Church in Axum, not far from the Eritrean border. The symbol is somewhere, I guess, on or in the Ark which we will need for Ecuador, I suppose. I thought that the Ark was destroyed in 586 BC when the Babylonians destroyed Jerusalem and Solomon's Temple where it was kept. Records since then have been sketchy. There was some who thought that when the city was ransacked, priests from the temple secretly moved the Ark through the underground tunnels running to the edge of the city and out towards the Red Sea. At the time, they had limited options and the Jews weren't very welcome in many places. They couldn't go back north because of the Babylonians, Egypt was too hostile, so the only solution was south towards Eretria and Ethiopia, so there is some method to this madness. The Ethiopians swear it is the Ark in its true form, but it's guarded very tightly and no one but a few high-ranking priests are allowed to see it, and anyone found taking a peek are disposed of fairly rapidly.'

179

'Then we're screwed,' Kris sighed.

'Hmmm. Yep, well you may have a point because I have no idea how we are going to get into Ethiopia and absolutely no idea how we can get near the Ark, let alone actually see it.' Finch sat back and drank his coffee, deep in thought. He thought he would tackle Ethiopia later. As for the Cave of Tayos, it was sitting heavy on his mind. It was thought lost and even mythical. Finch slumped back in his chair and stared at the computer screen. Was this all true? Were they being led to this pagan and once thought fictional place, because it was where the Grail originated? Were all the stories relating to Christ all formed from a real extra-terrestrial life force – was God real or perhaps, was 'God' a being from another planet who created everything and was not an omnipresent white bearded man living on a cloud? Finch sighed.

His mind was everywhere and he screwed his face up in thought.

'We need to make a call to Major Rami. I know they said we were on our own, but we need to get a visa for Ethiopia or it's going to be a very short trip.'

Finch went away and found a quiet place to make the call. He was sure that Oman would be prepared to help and was confident of a positive outcome. Meanwhile, Kris had read Finch's face. He knew that he could deal with the religious relics, such as the possibility of seeing The Ark and even the Grail, but confronting anything strange at the caves was playing on his mind.

Finch returned with a relieved smile, 'Rami will sort out a visa, though I think we are wearing our welcome a little thin in Oman.'

Kris smiled and looked at Finch intently. 'I can read you like a book Guillaume. You know we're going to end up at the caves, don't you?' Finch nodded and lowered his eyes. 'Don't waste your time thinking about it, Jake. We need you on your game for the mission ahead. Don't cloud your thoughts with things we don't know or don't understand. When it is time to confront whatever it is we need to confront, we'll try and answer as many questions as possible, together.' Finch smiled and nodded. He appreciated Kris' words and more so appreciated his empathy. The two men waited in silence, waited for their transport to Ethiopia.

CHAPTER 28

Victor paced up and down on the street outside the abandoned café. He rarely showed emotion or anxiety, but he was getting tetchy. He had been briefed about Finch's visit to Varni and his next step. Victor was in no doubt at all that Finch wouldn't risk his friend's life for anything. Finch knew that he would kill Karin in an instance if he tried anything. But Victor's patience was wearing thin.

Victor was bored. He wanted to be proactive, he wanted to get involved. He considered killing Karin now and getting closer to Finch until it was time to make his move. He had made the decision to find Finch after Ethiopia, which he knew he was heading for. He gestured for one of his henchmen to come over to where he was.

'I want to know the minute Finch leaves Ethiopia and I want to know where he is going. Do you understand?' The henchman acknowledged Victor's instruction and left swiftly.

Karin could hear the conversation and felt helpless. She had thought about escaping, but it was impossible; besides her hand was pretty useless after removing it from the table. The amount of hate brewing in her heart against Victor was clouding her judgment. He would pay for what he had done. Karin just had to bide her time, but for the time being, she knew that she was just lucky to be alive.

The flight from Armenia was a bumpy one and Finch and Kris were pleased to be on the ground. Once again waiting for them was a representative from the Omani Embassy, who, as before, gave them an envelope containing a couple of visiting visas. The man vanished into the melee that was Bole International Airport without a word. The place was heaving with people jostling and shouting. It was organised chaos. Finch and Kris slipped through immigration pretty much unnoticed. Finch purchased a map from a local store and a bottle of water, as the heat was stifling. He checked the map and looked at where Axum was. He hadn't thought to look prior to setting off and was shocked to see that it was nearly a thousand kilometres from Addis Ababa. About thirteen hours on good roads. But this was Africa and it could take them days. Finch packed away the map and turned to Kris.

'Right fella – we got a thousand clicks and no way of getting there. We need to find either a local airport or car. You head over to the market and see what info you can find on how to get north; I'll head over to the hotels and see what their advice is – you never know; we might get lucky.' Kris nodded and the two headed for their chosen destinations. Finch felt uncomfortable in Africa – particularly the north. He didn't trust many people but he particularly had a deep distrust of the people there. The only pro was that the best language was the currency of the dollar. It could get you anything you wanted and quickly. But it could also get you killed just as easily. No one would turn a blind eye to yet another body in the gutter or some back alley. It happened all the time, and $100 would last a family a month and would be worth killing for. Finch and Kris were streetwise enough and their Templar heritage stood them in good stead. They had a manner about them that instinctively said, 'Back off!'

Finch got to the Sheraton Hotel in Addis Ababa, which was as fabulous a hotel you would find anywhere in the world. The concierge gave Finch a cold, snooty look as he walked in looking just a little dishevelled. He hadn't shaved for days and he looked as if he had just been thrown out of a truck. He scanned the foyer

183

for anyone who may have the skinny on local knowledge. It was eventually too much for the concierge to handle and he sauntered up to Finch.

'Hello, sir, are you looking for someone or just passing through?'

Finch knew the concierge had to find out what this vagabond wanted and then to get him the hell out of his hotel. Finch knew the best way to quell the concierge's anxiety was to flash some cash. He unfurled a roll of US dollars from his pocket and flicked through the notes looking for a suitable amount to give the man in exchange for some reliable information.

As soon as he saw the money the concierge's eyes opened wide with delight and his posture softened to a more submissive pose.

'I was wondering if you could help me. I am not in the country long and want to go on a pilgrimage to the holy dwelling of the Ark of the Covenant in Axum. Tell me, what would be the best and most economical way of getting there?' Finch pulled a fifty-dollar note out in front of the man and tempted him with it. The concierge leaned in toward Finch.

'You are British. Yes?' he asked. Finch nodded. 'If you want my advice, there are many ways of getting up to Axum, all tourist traps and will cost you a fortune. But if you want to get there quickly and cheaply you need to speak with a man called Barnett. He owns his own twin propeller plane and runs trips all over Ethiopia for cash. He is a bit off the wall but he will get you there when you want and won't ask questions.'

Finch looked at him and smiled. 'Thank you. Where can I find this chap?' he asked.

The man pointed to an old green leather chesterfield chair in the corner of the bar and said, 'He will be here in forty-five minutes. Regular as clockwork. You can't miss him. Grumpy bugger.' Finch laughed and clapped the chap on his back and discreetly handed him the money.

Finch made his way into the market and sure enough found Kris encamped with a hookah in his mouth, cup of tea and a big grin on his face. 'Feeling at home, old chap?' Finch asked.

Kris laughed, 'Well it's a tough job but someone has to do it. Take a pew and have a tea.' Finch pulled up a chair and helped himself to a cup of tea and tried the hookah for himself. After a fit of spluttering and coughing, Finch briefed Kris.

'I went to the Sheraton and spoke to the concierge there. I bunged him a bit of cash and he told me there was some old eccentric English chap who frequents the Sheraton for afternoon tea and who has his own light aircraft. So, the plan is to hijack this chap this afternoon and persuade him to take us up to Axum. Save us a load of grief, particularly if he can hang about and take us back.'

'Do you think he will?' asked Kris.

Finch took another sip of tea. 'Not sure, but I'll put on my finest English accent and keep a wad of cash on the table. I'm sure that will persuade him.'

Over on the other side of the road was a burly-looking Arab in a poorly made suit and large mirrored sunglasses. He had been paying a little too much attention to Finch and Kris, which had not gone unnoticed. 'You get the feeling we're being watched, Jake?' Kris said.

Finch flicked his eyes subtly over the road at the man. 'Who? The extra from *Miami Vice* over there? Yeah – can't really miss him. Though I guess there's no point trying to be too secretive. It's not really too much of shock that Victor would have his beady eyes on us.' Kris nodded in agreement and continued chugging on his shisha pipe.

185

'Shall we acknowledge him?'

Finch smiled. 'No. Let's not spoil his fun. He looks the part; why ruin his day.'

The two men sat and enjoyed the tea and pipe and relaxed in the busy marketplace and watched the world go by. Eventually, Finch checked his watch. It was mid-afternoon and he decided to up sticks and head to the Sheraton. The pair entered the hotel and immediately the concierge clocked Finch. On doing so he tilted his head subtly over towards Barnett. Finch acknowledged the tip-off and wandered over towards the man.

'Mate. Why don't you go to the bar? If we both go over to him, he may smell a rat. Beside you look like a mugger.'

Kris was about to argue his case but caught a swift glimpse of himself in the foyer mirror and shrugged. 'Do you want anything?' he asked.

Finch asked for a beer and wandered over to where Barnett was reading the paper.

'Excuse me. Are you Mr Barnett?' Finch enquired politely. Barnett continued reading his paper and kept his eyes fixed on the print.

'Depends who wants to know, old chap.'

Finch continued. 'My name is Finch, I'm an archaeologist and don't have much time in this country and I wondered if I could hire you to take me to Axum this afternoon?' Barnett still kept his gaze fixed on the paper, though he was well aware of Finch's disposition.

'Archaeologist, eh? Dosser more like. Expensive camping, what! Couldn't possibly, old boy, certainly not today; gets dark quickly see. Can't trust the desert in the dark – just like the French, Ha!' Barnett seemed particularly pleased with his last comment. Finch smiled but time was of the essence and he needed to be more forward.

He placed a big hand on the paper and pushed it down with force making Barnett lose his grip. 'Mr Barnett. This is important. I am British and need to go to Axum as soon as possible. It is a matter of life and death… literally. I will pay handsomely. You have a plane and the ability to fly it and I need to be on it.'

Barnett looked up for the first time, folding his paper back into its original shape. 'Finch, hey? Where were you schooled, Finch?' he asked. The question took Finch aback for a while and he floundered a little.

'Malvern College. It's in Worcester.' Finch pulled Malvern out of the bag as he had a friend who was a former pupil and he went to watch the old boys play cricket there and was most taken with the place.

'Ah Malvern. I know it. Nice cricket pitch, small boundaries. St George keeps his eye closely on proceedings. Yes! I was an Harrovian myself. Dreadful place but taught me well. Full of the nouveau riche now, more's the pity. Anyhoo… so you needs a lift eh…. to Axum? What are you then – Indiana Jones and wanting the Ark eh?'

Finch grinned. 'Kind of, but not quite.'

Barnett leant forward and studied Finch's face. 'Hmmm. Interesting eyes you have, blue the likes I have never seen; bet the ladies flock to fall into them, eh?' He studied him again. 'Life and death, eh? Sounds to me like an adventure. The right battle for an Englishman; no French involved by any chance?'

Finch baulked and laughed. 'Funny you should say that, but yes and he's a real bastard!'

Barnett barked loudly. 'Glorious! Glorious! In that case, it must be done, but a few provisos. I don't carry drugs or guns and if you're on the run from the law, you can hop it. I like it here and don't want to be embroiled in some rubbish. You will pay me cash, negotiable of course, and you will settle my bar bill here. Modest, but admirable. And finally, we leave tomorrow at 0730 hours; the morning air is kinder on the aircraft. All understood?'

Finch nodded.

'Good – call me 'Badger'; everyone does. Not sure why… perhaps it's because I smell!' Barnett looked at Finch for his reaction to that last salvo.

Finch sniffed and said, 'Yes, very probably.'

'Ha! Good form! Great form!' Barnett shouted. Finch and Barnett haggled for a short time about costs, though the money wasn't hugely important to Barnett.

In the end Finch clapped his hands together. 'Until tomorrow then. I'll see you at the airstrip for seven thirty.'

Barnett smiled and raised his eyebrow. 'Perhaps. Now bugger orf!'

Finch headed toward Kris who had been a keen spectator at the bar, quietly sipping on a bourbon and ginger.

'Well? All good? We sorted?' Kris asked.

'Sorted. Seven thirty tomorrow. Mad as a fish but he's a good one. Not sure you'll like him though.'

Kris looked at Finch. 'What do mean by that? I get on with everyone.' Finch took a sip of his beer and smiled. 'Of course you do, Kris.'

Kris and Finch found a cheap hotel to bed down and woke early with a real feeling that they were making progress. The fact that they had managed to get a flight up to Axum rather than claw their way up through hostile and uncomfortable roads was a real boost.

They arrived at the airstrip just outside of the main city at 0700hrs. The airstrip was pretty rudimentary – just a small building and tower with a tarmacked runway. That was a surprise as they expected a grassy overgrown patch. There were a few planes dotted around and without any sign of Barnett, they couldn't get a handle on what they were going to be travelling in.

It was now 0715 and still no sign of Barnett. Kris was getting scratchy. He hadn't slept well due to the lack of air-con in the room and so he had tossed and turned without getting much quality sleep.

'Right! Where's this old sod! I knew it was all going too smoothly,' Kris growled. Finch fanned his hand at Kris' reaction.

'Easy, Kris – he did say 0730 and we have fifteen minutes; besides he's a bit of an eccentric, he probably won't turn up for hours. But he'll be here. Trust me.' Kris tutted and kicked at the gravel.

At 0725 the sound of an old motorbike swept through the morning air. There was 'Badger' sitting atop a vintage green Royal Enfield 1946 motorbike with sidecar. It was beautifully suited to Barnett's character. Old, but classic in its eccentricity. He was a robust man with cheeks that told of his love of fine wine, whisky and cigars. His thick white hair blew recklessly in the wind and his generous white moustache stretched across his face. Although his face was screwed up in a grimace, his eyes, which were hidden behind his old goggles, couldn't hide the cheeky boy that still lived behind the old façade.

'You aloo!' Badger cried. He aimed straight for the boys. 'Out of my way, boy!' he shouted at Kris. Finch had expected him to fly off the handle but instead he laughed out loud and could tell that he was going to like this mad old man. The bike spluttered to a halt and Barnett de-bussed. 'Ah, glad to see you keep good time, sir. It's good form. Now I take it this vagabond is part of your clan?'

'Yes,' Finch answered. 'I didn't mention it yesterday, but he is part of the trip as well. He's a good chap and watches my back.'

Badger walked up to Kris and looked him up and down. 'Hmmm! Schooled?' he asked Finch. He hadn't expected that question and decided to lie.

'Umm, Marlborough – though expelled for drinking.' After a pause Badger's face cracked and he clapped his hands together.

'Form! Great form!' With that he made his way around the back of the building beckoning the boys to follow him.

Kris walked up to Finch. 'Marlborough? Why?'

'Because he's old school. If I told him you went to Grange Hill you would have had to walk, OK? So put the chip away and play the game, all right? I think I may even start calling you Rupert!' Finch chuckled to himself.

'Rupert! I quite like it.' Kris mused.

The guys went round the corner and saw their air taxi for the first time.

There in all its finery was a C-46 twin prop plane in military green and a large RAF symbol on its flanks. 'Gentlemen, may I introduce you to Clarence, the finest gentleman in all of Africa.' Barnett introduced the plane proudly to the men. Both Finch and Kris looked at the plane and smiled. They both expected to be wedged into some tiny single prop tin can, but this was so very Barnett. They boarded the old plane. In the back were enough seats to take twenty or so people.

'Why don't you perch up here, chum?' Barnett called to Finch. 'You can put Billy Bunter in the boot.' He indicated pointing at Kris.

'Sure thing, Captain!' answered Finch, who was quite enjoying the whole experience.

'Ooh Captain – I like! Though always thought of myself as a Brigadier but Captain will do.' Barnett went through his pre-flight checks and bellowed at some poor lad who was clearing the chocks. Slowly though, the engines fired into life and growled as they warmed up. The plane turned and lined up on the runway.

'Hold on to your jewels, chaps, time to leave this sun blanched land and play with the clouds!' Barnett pulled on a pair of worn white flying gloves and pushed forward on the throttle and the plane thundered down the runway and up into the clear blue skies.

From above, the ground below was a barren and bleak featureless plain. There wasn't a moment that Finch didn't thank his lucky stars for being up in the air and not having to traipse across the ropey roads of Ethiopia. It was bothering him how he was going to get to see the Ark. The Ethiopian priests and the Guardian of the Ark in particular were well known for not allowing anyone to enter into the room containing the Ark. They were also renowned for being typically explosive in nature and any attempt to push them about could result in being mobbed and possibly even killed. Reasoning with them was hopeless. Should he wait until dark and sneak in, should he try and negotiate or bribe or silence the priests and get in and out quickly? Either way it was not going to be easy, but it was vital that they set eyes on the Ark and find what they were looking for. Apart from the job in hand, Finch was contemplating the impact of seeing the Ark, if indeed it was the real thing. It had

191

just crossed his mind about what he would do if it was just an old box and didn't contain anything which would help him in Central America. But what if it was the real deal? The actual Ark of the Covenant. The journey so far had been such a whirlwind of action and travel that he hadn't really had a chance to digest these finds. But the Ark of the Covenant. Built to house the Ten Commandments written by God and given to Moses. Held by the Jews for years and searched for centuries by men for various reasons, the last notable one being the Nazis to use as a weapon of war. To be able to touch that which he had sought and protected all those years ago and really feel the presence of God would be incredible and certainly help to re-affirm his beliefs, particularly if the next part of his journey proved to be a little controversial.

Finch was lost in his own thoughts when Barnett blasted over the intercom. 'Axum is about ten minutes away. So pick up your marbles. Don't let the school bully find 'em; or you'll never see 'em again!' Finch laughed; he had no idea what Barnett meant but he guessed it meant 'get ready 'cause we're almost there!'

Finch took the opportunity to ask Barnett the favour he needed. 'Badger, as I told you this is an adventure – a mission. We are going to the church that houses the Ark and will be about an hour. I'm not going to lie to you, the people there won't be best pleased with us and we'll need to get the hell out of Dodge pretty sharply. I don't suppose—'

Barnett interrupted Finch, 'I suppose you want me to keep the motor running outside the bank, eh... for the quick getaway?'

'I wouldn't quite put it like that, but yes please, if possible,' Finch answered as humbly as he could. There was silence.

'You're not going to nick it are you?' asked Barnett.

Finch sighed, 'No. No. Not at all – we need to take a look at it. That's all. They're just protective about it and won't take

192

kindly to a couple of white men going where only Holy men can go. Might cause an upset. You know?' Again there was silence.

'Do I get to wear a mask or bandana?' asked Barnett.

'No, just stay in the plane,' Finch replied.

'Shame,' Barnett said. 'I've got a bandana. Would feel like a Comanche, eh?'

Finch thought. 'Then you should wear it, just in case.'

Barnett exploded into a fit of giggles. 'Bloody great. The game's afoot! I will keep the old boy purring and await you and the ensuing dust cloud. But if you're caught, I'm orf. Roger!'

Finch nodded in agreement. 'Roger!'

The plane circled and straightened up on the runway and glided in effortlessly, though this time the airstrip was a grass track, but the old C-46 managed it with ease. Finch briefed Kris and as soon as they could, he opened the door, gave Barnett the thumbs-up and exited. He had asked Barnett during the flight where the church was and he had a good idea; now they had to make haste and get there.

CHAPTER 29

Axum housed about fifty thousand inhabitants and was, at one point from about 400 BC into the 10th century, a great naval and trading power that ruled the region, but was eventually destroyed in 960 by Gudit, an invading queen of the area, and it was even rumoured that the great Queen of Sheba lived in the town at one point. Nowadays, Axum was known for the Aksumite monuments. At 1,700 years old, the obelisks had become a symbol of the Ethiopian people's identity. The obelisk in Axum stands at twenty-four metres high and weighs a mighty 170 tonnes. It had been removed by the Italian army in 1937 but was returned to its rightful home in 2005. The structures are an imposing and wondrous sight and something Finch as an archaeologist longed to spend more time mulling over, while he was here next to them. But this was no busman's holiday. Finch had to stay focused and remember the task in hand.

The two men made their way carefully but briskly to where the Chapel of the Tablet was. Axum was used to seeing white faces and travellers, so they didn't stick out unusually. But once again, Finch felt as if they were being watched and scrutinised and he did his very best to try and melt into the background without drawing attention to themselves. The streets were bristling with activity and the market was in full flow and the sight of more tourists made them a magnet for market barterers.

Kris enjoyed the attention and would have liked to engage in a bit of banter, but he could see that Finch wanted to get this part of proceedings over with quickly. Both men were instinctively surveying the town for dead ends and escape routes, just in case they needed to get out of the area quickly. There was no way the local population would take kindly to a couple of

Western foreigners muscling into the holiest place in the whole of Ethiopia. So every scenario needed to be recced and prepared for. After getting through the hustle and bustle of the town, the two men found themselves on the other side where the roads were wider and clear of any marauding crowds, and about 500 metres down a poorly marked road they could see the Chapel of the Tablet, the resting place of the Ark of the Covenant.

As they approached, they could see the building clearly. Finch had expected to see armed guards patrolling with dogs and a heightened sense of security, but that was far from the truth. The church itself was a relatively plain square building with a small dome atop, holding an old iron ornamental cross. There was a large door to the side and the only security in place was a red eight-foot-high metal fence running round the perimeter of the building. That, coupled with a handful of Ethiopian monks wandering in and out, was the sum of all the security measures. All of which indicated to Finch that the likelihood of the building actually housing one the greatest artefacts in history was slim, to say the least. The two men walked up to the railings and peered through. The gates leading to the church weren't locked and there was only a short path running through a small garden to the great red doors of the building itself. With no time to lose Finch and Kris opened up the gates.

Kris looked at Finch. 'Jake. You gonna just walk in there and crack on or should we try and negotiate with the guardian? This is Ethiopia, they are likely to cut our heads off if we desecrate their holy land.' It wasn't like Kris to be cautious but he had a point. They were here now and Finch hadn't fully thought it through.

'Look, if we are out here and ask, they'll say no and we will never get to be within fifty feet of whatever is through that door, and if we try and sneak in, they will shoot first and ask questions later. We have to try and at least get our hands inside the biscuit

195

tin and then if caught, we can negotiate. Yes?' Kris nodded and the two of them ventured up the path to the doors.

There was not a soul in sight, neither monk nor member of the public. The doors were closed and Finch delicately turned the large handle and leant against it with his shoulder. To his relief the door creaked a little and it began to swing slowly open. Kris kept an ardent view around all his arcs and signalled to Finch to keep going. In front of them was an empty room with an altar cut into the wall housing a gold cross. The room was ornate, and covered with frescos and colour on plaster, which was looking chipped and a little tired. To the side of the altar though, was a doorway covered by a thin curtain. Finch made his way to it and silently pulled it aside. Behind that again was an empty smaller room, which led to an archway with draped fabric obscuring what lay beyond it. With every step Finch's heart got faster. He felt the chances of finding the real Ark in this dusty, uncared for place would be like finding the Crown Jewels in a musty old drawer in one's granddad's garage. Highly improbable! Kris followed closely, flicking his eyes back and forth, checking for any knife-wielding monks. Finch crossed the second room and pulled the drape back, revealing yet another larger, seemingly empty space save what looked like an old-fashioned dressing screen. Finch checked that the coast was clear and headed over to see what lay behind the screen. Kris stayed at the archway making sure that no one had come into the church while they were venturing forward. Finch crept lightly and poked his head around the screen.

Kris watched from the archway and saw Finch still as marble. He was motionless and had turned pale. 'Jake! Jake! You OK?' Kris whispered and thought Finch had been hit by something or someone and was about to collapse in a heap. Kris, fearing the worst, leapt forward to Finch's aid. He was just about

196

to grab hold of Finch when he saw what had made Finch stop in his tracks. There, in front of the two men, who stood agog with their mouths open, was a shiny gold box with two kneeling angels on top, their wings folded forward, shrouding the lid. Kris stood beside Finch and gasped. The two men looked at each other in utter amazement.

'Fuck,' Kris whispered.

'Exactly,' Finch answered. 'I can't believe my eyes. The Ark of the Covenant!' Finch gasped.

Kris looked at Finch. 'Is it real? I mean, is it THE Ark? It could be a fake, made to look real like cheap bracelets you could buy from the market. What I mean is, look at this place. It's a pit, in the middle of nowhere and this is the Ark...' Kris' voice tailed off.

Finch pushed his hand forward delicately and hesitated before he touched the relic. 'It could be,' Finch replied starting to breath heavily. 'It very well could be.' Finch suddenly woke from his reverie and took his phone out to take a picture, as much for proof's sake than to look at the markings in case they were interrupted. He flicked through his photos to check those from Armenia and found the markings on the back of the wood of the Armenian relic. The markings on the Ark resembled those found on the wood but they were not the same. Kris was dumbstruck. He remained rooted to the spot, staring at the gold container in front of him.

'Kris,' Finch called. 'Keep an eye out for anyone. I have to try and work this out. We are in a world of pain if anyone comes in. OK?'

Kris was mesmerised and ignored Finch.

'Kris!' Finch raised his voice. This appeared to shake Kris out of his trance and he headed toward the archway. Finch studied the photo and tried to skirt around the Ark looking for a match. He was looking for a small panel, a rectangle with nine parts to it and within these parts there were obscure shapes. Finch scoured the Ark as methodically as he could while keeping up a fair sense of haste. Finch searched and searched but there was no plaque resembling what he had photographed in Armenia. The only thing he could find was a small recess where something must have been. It was about the size of the plaque they were looking for but whatever was there had gone some time ago. Finch's heart sank.

Finch knelt beside the Ark and sighed.

'Any luck?' Kris whispered loudly. Finch shook his head and made his way toward Kris.

'Whatever we are looking for has gone. I'm sure of it,' Finch replied.

'Have you looked inside?' Kris enquired. Finch hadn't thought of that but hesitated and looked at Kris.

'No. And. I don't want to.'

'What!' said Kris. 'You have to.'

Finch looked back at the Ark. 'No. Some things shouldn't be looked at by just anyone. If that is the Ark and the Ten Commandments are inside, written by God and given to Moses, then who am I to see them now? It's not right.'

Kris looked at Finch for a beat. 'I'll do it!' Kris stormed off toward the box but stopped abruptly. He stared at it. 'It's incredible, isn't it?' He looked back at Finch. 'You're right, there is no way I can open this.'

Finch sighed with relief at Kris' decision. Now though, they were stuck. They obviously needed that piece of the puzzle and now had nowhere else to look and neither wanted to leave empty-handed. They also needed to get away quickly. They had been lucky not to be spotted thus far. Finch needed more time to think. 'We should go. Before anyone sees us. I need to think. Clear my head and think logically. We can come back later. Agreed?' Kris nodded and the two men back-tracked slowly and made their way to the entrance. They had got as far as the first drape when a tall dark Ethiopian priest flung back the curtain and saw Finch and Kris. Then chaos ensued.

The priest immediately began shouting and yelling at the top of his voice, waving his hands around and trying to strike Finch and Kris with his long wooden staff. Finch side-stepped the swipe while Kris handed off the crazed priest and made for the door, but by that stage, like a nest of ants, once the alarm was raised people seemed to spring from all corners, yelling and shouting and determined to apprehend the two white men who had broken their laws. Finch and Kris were in deep trouble. There was no way they could escape through the main doors as a group of about twenty men had barred it. They looked around desperately for a way out. Finch grabbed Kris and dragged him back into the room containing the Ark. The only way out was a window, which led into a side garden. A quick vault over the fence and they could get away. The last thing they needed though was to get cornered by a baying mob. In the frenzy they could get beaten, stabbed or stoned to death. Their only hope was the priests. No one would enter the sacred room of the Ark apart from the Guardians of the Ark. Finch and Kris stood in the room side by side. They felt confident in their abilities and although concerned for their safety, were not paralysed with fear. They would fight to their very last breath, if needs be. The curtain opened and in front stood the priest who had raised the alarm with four others. All had absolute hate-filled eyes and the room echoed with their shouts. Finch and Kris were wide-eyed, with adrenaline coursing through their veins; any attempt to harm them would lead to a swift counterassault. The lead priest was silent and looked at the men, looked at their eyes. After a moment he raised his staff, which had the effect of silencing the others. The man straightened himself and spoke to Finch in Oromigna, a local dialect. Finch stared back at him. Although fluent in many languages, he had never heard anything like this. The priest spoke again gesturing at Finch and Kris. But again, all Finch could do was indicate that he could not understand what was being said by pointing at his ears and shrugging his shoulders.

The priest stopped and looked at Finch hard and then spoke in broken English. 'You know it is forbidden for all to see the Ark. You have broken our laws. Why have you come?' The priest spoke clearly, firmly and calmly, but was clearly furious at what they had done. Finch raised his hands, palms up, toward the priest. He paused and thought about his opening salvo; it needed to be good.

'Great Guardian of the Ark,' Finch started. 'We have broken your laws and laid our eyes on the Ark, which in truth is marvellous, and we are truly sorry for what we have done, but we are here on a mission from God. A matter that will free or imprison all men. You, wise priest, are a Guardian of the Ark, and we are protectors of the souls of men and the word of God.' Finch paused to see if his words were having any effect whatsoever.

The priest looked at them quizzically. 'Your eyes? In all my years have I never seen eyes like that.' Finch pounced on this straight away.

'Yes. Yes. Our eyes are a sign that we are who we say we are, for only the purest warrior monks, as we are, can possess such a window into our souls.'

The priest walked slowly up to Finch and grasped his face in his hands, balancing his staff on his shoulder. He pulled

Finch's face close to his own and studied his eyes from different angles.

'Not all windows show the soul, but the imperfections of the glass,' the priest said releasing Finch's head from his grip. 'What did you want in here? To steal that which is not yours?'

Finch and Kris immediately shouted 'No' in unison. Finch wondered how he would explain this to the priest. 'Guardian, our friend is in mortal danger as are the souls of all man. We are warrior monks on a journey which has led us to seek and find great gifts from God which are showing us a path to our end goal. A goal which will help us understand our faith and go some way to banishing evil forever.' Finch spoke slowly and earnestly, trying to gain control of his breathing and attempting to connect with the priest. Instead, the priest asked again and this time prodded Finch in the chest with his staff.

'What are you doing in here?' His impatience was visible. Finch took a long, deep breath and glanced at Kris.

'We have come here from Armenia where we inspected the piece of Noah's Ark that the Armenian Church possesses. On the back of that shard there was a diagram of a plaque about six to nine inches in length which was part of the Ark, a piece we need to complete our quest.'

The priest listened to Finch and erupted. 'You are nothing more than tomb thieves, trying to steal the Ark for gold. You must be punished.' The priest gave a signal for the other priests to rush at Finch and Kris. Kris wasted no time and launched a right-handed punch which floored the first priest who came near; the second priest, who was more robust, bear-hugged him. A swift knee in the groin and he sank to his knees. Finch eluded the first of his guards with a strike across the eyes and a blow to the sternum. The second stopped in his tracks.

'We don't want any trouble, you must believe us,' shouted Finch.

'Screw this, Jake, let's grab this old bastard and use him as a shield,' Kris demanded. It sounded like the only real option but before they could grab him, he yelled out and the room was flooded with men, all furious, having been whipped up into a frenzy and all with the intention of killing Finch and Kris. There was nowhere to run or fight. Both men took educated swings at their first few assailants and succeeded, but eventually numbers overwhelmed them and they were overcome and driven to the floor. Kicks and punches rained down on them and they adopted foetal positions in an attempt to safeguard their heads. It seemed to go on forever until a horn sounded and the frenzy stopped. Finch and Kris were pulled up and held by the crowd, both of them sporting bloodied faces and bruised torsos. The main priest parted the horde of people like Moses through the Red Sea. He obviously held a great deal of power and commanded the greatest respect from them.

'You dare to enter into a place where only the blessed may come. You must now be judged.' He turned to the other priests and nodded, then returned his gaze to the two battered men. 'Your judgment is death,' the priest shouted and all but the four men holding Kris and Finch left the room, averting their eyes from where the Ark was housed.

The priest turned to speak with the other guardians and Finch knew this was his last chance. 'If you do this, you will be killing innocent messengers from God and will be judged accordingly and will be condemning mankind.' The priest half listened and gave a cursory glance back at Finch.

Finch continued. 'There was an inscription on the relic, which was the same as an inscription found in the Great Library of Alexandria that I discovered a few weeks ago in Greek which said, Θυμηθείτε – Ζωή αιώνιος για την καθαρή ψυχή του.

Εμπιστοσύνη στο Λόρδο ο Θεός.' 'Life Eternal For The Pure Of Soul – Trust in The Lord God.' The priest stopped in his tracks and slowly turned towards Finch. He repeated the saying again in both Greek and English once more. The priest stared at Finch and repeated the phrase in Hebrew. He stalked next to Finch.

'Those words have been passed down to the heads of the Guardians of the Ark for centuries and have not been uttered in as long a time. It is a key to help unlock questions I do not want answered.'

Kris looked totally confused, as did Finch who was trying his best to understand what the priest said. The words were effective and held a great sway over his intentions. He swished his arms and the men holding Finch and Kris released their hold immediately and were sent from the room.

'Only a handful of men in the world know of this,' The priest said looking shocked and saddened. He then turned to the four other guardians, who appeared as bewildered as Finch and ordered them all to leave as well.

Once the room was theirs, he turned to Finch and pulled apart his robes. On a chain hanging around his neck was a gold medallion, almost nine inches in length with the same inscription as seen on the back of the Armenian relic. It was what they were here to find. The priest looked at Finch.

'This is what you have come to find.' Finch, still winded from the mob attack, nodded.

'I do not intend to steal anything. My whole life has been about the protection of relics and artefacts such as these. But I must have that pendant. If I can, I will return it, you have my word. I must though have what hangs around your neck.' The priest pulled the chain from around his neck, kissed the gold pendant delicately and placed it in the hands of the wheezing Finch. 'If you can, I would like it back,' the priest said. 'But if you don't, I will understand God's will.' With that, and with tears in his eyes, he turned and left the chapel. He looked the most dignified man Finch had ever seen.

Kris straightened himself up. 'He was lucky, I was about to really lose my temper!' The two men laughed painfully. 'Now, Jake, do you think we can get the hell out of here?' They collected themselves and hoped that the priest would have instructed the waiting mob to leave them alone. They edged slowly out of the room, but before they left, Finch took one more look at the Ark. It was beautiful and every time he saw it, he knew God HAD to be real. He touched it gently and then left.

When they reached the large red doors of the building, they expected mayhem; instead, here was nothing. Not a soul. As empty as when they had entered the building not so long ago. It was eerie. Whatever, they weren't disappointed and weren't going to hang about to wait for another riot. They hobbled at a quick enough pace back through the town and to the waiting C-46 and Barnett, who had waited, as he promised he would.

Barnett already had the old plane running when Finch and Kris came round the corner. He had heard the fracas in town and suspected that something had gone wrong but decided to give them a couple of hours grace and then get out of there. The two men boarded the plane gingerly and were greeted by a hearty embrace from Barnett, which left both men wincing. Barnett closed the door and prepared the plane for take-off and within minutes they were airborne and heading back to Addis Ababa.

'Thought you was a gorna!' shouted Barnett. 'The locals were making a great old ding-dong and by the looks of you, it appears they taught you a few lessons. Ha!' Finch waved his hand in acknowledgement but had no wish to regurgitate what had happened. Finch and Kris slumped back in their chairs and caught each other's eye and began to chuckle to themselves at the close shave they had encountered.

Finch eventually fell into a deep sleep; he dreamed of being held at a post, it was dark and there were men everywhere, shouting, swearing and spitting. His hands were bound. The chainmail he wore was heavy and his tunic was dirty and covered in blood. There was confusion. Then he recognised a voice looming from the dark. It was Victor. He could hear him just about through the melee, condemning him. As he was doing so Finch was bound to the post and a procession of lit torches flickering in the thick black air came snaking toward him. He started to panic, trying free his arms, but he was tied fast. The flames came closer and were eerily beautiful. Then he could feel the heat of the fire around his face and the noise and intensity grew all around him. He could hear ungodly screams from his right-hand side and men laughing and jeering. Then he could see the light of the fire grow brighter and feel a searing pain. He was burning. He was attached to a stake and burning. He threw his head back in pain and saw the full image of Victor's face staring at him with hate-filled eyes. The plane hit a small air pocket and jolted Finch and he woke with a start, gasping and sweating. The recent adrenaline fuelled fight must have reignited those suppressed anxieties he had hidden for a time. Finch looked over at Kris who was still fast asleep. He took stock of the situation and calmed his breathing down and instantly his thoughts turned toward Victor and Karin. Victor was devoid of feeling and possessed no guilt and Finch wondered whether Karin was even still alive, though they had done nothing to provoke a response from Victor as he was sure that tabs were being kept on them both.

Finch took the golden medallion from around his neck and studied it closely. It was beautiful. It looked like gold but was strangely light. And not soft. The markings on the face made no sense at all, just symbols and pictures of weird faces. There was no rhyme or reason to them and the writing didn't resemble anything that he had seen before. On the back was a small nubbin. Big enough to hold on to. The rest looked like it had been sanded down with abrasive paper. What was this for? It was obviously important, but how? he wondered. Was this part of the treasure of the metal library? Was this some alien jewellery? Finch's mind was whirling, but he was too tired to make any sense of it. The first thing was to try and figure out how they were going to get to Ecuador. They had used up all their favours from Oman so they would have to do it alone. The best chance of a successful entry without drawing attention to themselves was to go by boat, but that would take weeks. They would have to fly and try and blag it at the other end. They just had to get to South America quickly. He had got some co-ordinates and had now got everything he was supposed to have retrieved. He had read about the cave and it was an enigma. Many people, if not most, didn't really believe in its existence anyway; after all, it had never been rediscovered again and verified since it was allegedly found in 1969. If he had learnt anything during this trip it was, never to make any assumptions. So far, he had opened doors he couldn't have even dreamt about and there was still more to come.

The plane touched down back in the capital and Finch and Kris disembarked.

'I don't know how to thank you, Badger,' Finch said shaking his hand warmly. 'Can I buy you a drink?' Barnett looked at Finch. 'No, old chap – think I'll have a cup of tea and schlarf. The mind is willing but the body – well – it's knackered!'

'Schlarf?' asked Finch.

'Sleep, me boy. I needs me sleep. I'll not ask what you've done. People like you always have enemies and if they come looking for me, best I know nothing eh?'

Finch nodded. 'Thanks, Badger – you're a star.'

Kris shook Barnett's hand. 'Thank you. Men like you make me want to go and be epically great.' Barnett rather liked that and smiled as the two men made their way back to their hotel room. 'Make me want to be epically great. Think I'll write that down. Ha!' Barnett chuckled to himself as he headed back to the plane to shut the old boy down for the night.

Once back at the hotel room, Finch put the plug in the bath and ran the water for a well-earned soak. 'What's the plan, Ke-mo sah-bee?' Kris asked.

'First things first. I'm going to rest my weary bones in a hot bath. Then we have to book the next flight to Ecuador. Then I need to find out everything I can about the caves at Tayos to give me some reading material on the plane. I have a feeling this is going be a nightmare!' Finch sighed.

'Can we eat? I could eat the arse out of a dead otter,' Kris shouted.

'Yes. You have the otter – I'll just settle for a burger and chips. Right. I may be a while,' Finch replied, shutting the bathroom door.

CHAPTER 30

The door to the room was flung open violently and Victor's usual entourage entered and stared at Karin. They were quickly followed by Victor, who was looking much less agitated than their last encounter. 'Karin. How are you? You're frowning,' Victor enquired sarcastically. Karin was still hurting physically and emotionally from the last torturous incident.

'Up yours, Victor,' Karin growled, walking over to the window.

Victor looked disgruntled at Karin's insult. 'Now, now, Karin. That sort of language will lead you to having your other hand nailed to the table. So a little less bile… you're not that important.' Karin's initial burst of bravado escaped her after hearing Victor's response. She knew that Victor didn't really need her so there wasn't any point in trying to get herself killed. 'Get your things together. We are leaving this horrible, sweaty place and going to Ecuador. My sources tell me that Mr Finch and the other one are playing by the rules and doing rather well. But it is time that our paths crossed once more and we would all be better placed to do it out there. Chop chop.' And with that, he left the room.

Two large men grabbed Karin by the arms and hauled her outside and into a waiting car. It was the first time she had been outside in some time and the change of atmosphere was much appreciated. The cars sped off to a waiting private jet which Victor had procured. It was luxurious. Karin climbed the steps to the plane and was bundled into a beige leather chair. Victor sat on the other side to her, strapped in. There was limited room so that only allowed for two of Victor's security to come along. As the doors shut and the plane began to taxi, Karin thought about overpowering Victor's men. But they were huge and Victor was quite handy as well. She'd end up being thrown out of a moving jet somewhere over the Atlantic. No. It was far better to ride this out. Her time would come and she would make them pay. In the meantime, a large glass of champagne was poured for Victor and Karin.

'Good health, Ms. Edwards. Here's to Finch's successful mission and our... hmm... piracy! Here's to the Templars, eh?'

Karin raised her glass sarcastically and took a huge sip of champagne. The bubbles tickled her nose. There was nothing to do for now but enjoy the ride.

CHAPTER 31

Finch and Kris had a busy but successful few hours. Finch had sourced some information on Tayos and had managed to get two of the last seats on a 747 out of Ethiopia bound for Florida and then on to Simon Bolivar International Airport in Ecuador. Finch knew that if they had to, they could pay their way into Ecuador. The dollar was king in South America as well and no one would make much fuss if a few hundred dollars exchanged hands. So, for now, they could relax. After the usual excruciatingly bad meal, both Finch and Kris enjoyed a few beers and the chance to chat and plan their next moves.

Finch piled up the paper he had printed out from the internet café and started to sort through the information he had gathered. It was intriguing. Kris was stuffing his face on nuts, crisps, beer and anything else he could ram in his mouth.

'How the hell do you stay so thin?' Finch asked, bewildered.

Kris just laughed. 'Easy. I have a bigger bumhole than my mouth!'

The lightness of the conversation was a welcome relief after the last few days. 'So, brief me up. What are we getting ourselves into now? Operation Certain Death? Eh?' Kris asked with a real sense of foreboding. Finch took a long swig of his beer and drained it.

'This place is amazing, if it exists. There was a priest some time ago, early in the 1900s, who kept accumulating amazing treasures. Gifts given to him as a thank you from the local people. He would accept them and stored them in a room and that was that. His name was Father Carlos Crespi. By all accounts he was an incredible man. He was adored by everyone who met him, was truly godly and as much of a saint as one could meet. One of these artefacts was known as the Crespi Plate, which strangely bears a great deal of resemblance to this medallion.' Finch pulled the gold chain from under his shirt and showed Kris. Finch continued, 'No one could work out what the inscriptions were; Samarian, Egyptian, Magyar. Magyar were the locals. As with everything else, because of the strangeness and quality of the items, more interest was starting to be drawn to the area and the artefacts. And like many unexplained finds some thought they were artefacts from the lost city of Atlantis.

Anyway, eventually a chap by the name of Stan Hall, a Scotsman, was intrigued by the story and decided to investigate. He met Father Crespi and saw his artefacts and even led an investigation down to where he thought the caves were, which included none other than Neil Armstrong of 'the moon' fame. But nothing was ever found. Hall eventually met up with a chap by the name of Juan Moricz, an Argentinian/Hungarian aristocrat who claims that in 1969 he stumbled upon the cave system and found the library. In fact, he swore an oath that he found it and met with the Ecuadorian president who gave him complete jurisdiction over the caves as long as he could produce photographic evidence. An author, a German, called Erich von Daniken, wrote a book on it and was taken to the cave system. He never actually saw the library but said all the passages formed perfect right angles and were smoothly polished. Anyway, long story short, von Daniken's book and sources were rubbished because Moricz could never actually take them to the library itself, just the cave systems and wouldn't tell how he found it. It works out that Moricz wasn't the discoverer of the cave at all, but a third man who was nameless.

Eventually Moricz had named the man who originally showed him the caves as Petronio Jaramillo. When Moricz died in 1991, Hall found Jaramillo and he opened up to him. The actual library wasn't in the Tayos caves system at all. Jaramillo had told Hall that he was seventeen years old in 1946, when he had entered the library. He had been shown it by his uncle who was on friendly terms with the local indigenous population known as the Shuar, and they had introduced him to the library as gratitude for all his kindness. Jaramillo entered the system again and said he saw the library and it held thousands of large metal books stacked on shelves, each with an average weight of about twenty kilograms, each page impressed on one side with ideographs, geometric designs and written inscriptions. He also said that there was a second library. This one consisted of crystal tablets. As well as that, he mentioned that there were human statues on plinths, metal bars of different shapes, sealed "doors" – possibly tombs, covered in a mixture of coloured semi-precious stones. There was a large sarcophagus, sculpted from a hard, translucent material, containing the gold-leafed skeleton of a large human being. Jaramillo told how he took down several books from the shelves to study them, but they were too heavy to replace, which fortunately meant they were too heavy to take away from the library (which was convenient). He told Hall that he wrote his initials in the book to prove he had been there, and when asked why he hadn't taken any photos as evidence he merely said that it would not prove anything and stated: "Other discoveries, such as the infamous Burrows Cave in the United States, prove that seeing actually isn't believing".

'So, Hall needed to know where it actually was but Jaramillo was tight lipped. He had mentioned that the access was an underwater entrance, or under the River Pastaza to be exact. Anyway, in 1998 everything hit a brick wall when Jaramillo was assassinated and the trail went dead. Ecuador was having internal problems and everything was shut down. Hall died a few years back and I think his daughter is still fanning the flames but there isn't much on that.'

Kris was still munching through his third bag of nuts. 'What about the Padre's treasures; can't that be studied?'

'The day after Father Crespi died every last bit of the treasures he was given vanished into thin air,' Finch replied.

'I'm getting the feeling that someone or something doesn't want the library to be found. Listen, Jake, let's just stay in Florida. Karin will live again and if the library is so hard to find Victor has no hope – what do you say?'

Finch laughed whilst brushing the crumbs of peanuts spat from Kris' lips off his shirt answered,' Yeah, why not! I could do with the break. Any chance of another beer?' Kris called the air hostess over.

'Incidentally, Jake – you tell a lousy story!' The two men laughed and relaxed and prepared themselves for the next part of their journey.

The plane touched down at Simon Bolivar International Airport. Both Finch and Kris were in no rush to get off the plane. They figured that if they went through customs last and if money had to change hands, then the quieter the better. The boys sat in the baggage reclaim area until the last bag had been collected and the hubbub had died down.

'Right. You ready?' asked Finch. Kris waved his passport at him in agreement. 'Look, let me do all the talking. If we need a story, we are two amateur archaeologists keen to visit the jungle to see if there was any proof of Iron Age man. We are at uni doing a thesis, yeah?' Again, Kris nodded.

'What's a thesis?' he grinned.

'Nice one,' Finch snapped. 'Game face on now, mate. This could be the quickest visit to Ecuador on record.'

213

Finch walked up to the desk. The man attending it was smart and steely-eyed. '*Pasaportes por favor señores,*' he asked. Finch's Spanish was good and he thought that this was a good way of making his appearance here more amenable.

'*Habla usted español?*' the man asked as opened up Finch's passport.

'*Si senor,*' Finch replied.

'*Cuál es su propósito para visitar Ecuador?*' (What is your purpose for visiting Ecuador?).

Finch decided to be overwhelmingly enthusiastic about why he was here and what he was doing so that he didn't look too shifty. Some guy throwing his arms around shouting about ancient civilisations in an empty hall might arouse less suspicion. Kris looked on in bewilderment. '*Estamos aquí para estudiar la existencia en su caso de las tribus indígenas en la selva. Somos estudiantes de Inglaterra y no puedo esperar a ver su hermosa selva. Tenemos ganas de escribir nuestra dissertaion sobre él y tal vez volver más tarde y, si encontramos algo tal vez conseguir fondos y...*' (We are here to study the existence, if any, of indigenous tribes within the jungle. We are students from England and can't wait to see your beautiful jungle. We are hoping to write our dissertation on it and maybe come back later and, if we find anything maybe get funding and...)

The customs officer held up his hand and hushed Finch. He obviously didn't understand what he was talking about and what's more didn't care. He looked at Kris and then back to Finch. He noticed that they both only had minimal baggage. Finch, his trusty satchel and small rucksack, and Kris a small rucksack also. '*Usted viaja la luz para una expedición, ¿dónde están sus maletas?*' (You are travelling light for an expedition, where are your bags?) Finch hadn't considered that but thought swiftly.

'*No señor esto es un reconocimiento a la teoría, además de nuestra aerolínea perdió su maleta en la Florida.*' (No, sir, this is a reconnaissance into the theory, plus our airline lost our suitcases in Florida.)

The officer wasn't convinced and left his station and went behind a two-way screen. Finch turned to Kris, 'Laugh as if I have just told you a joke and make a gesture.' Kris looked puzzled but then realised what Finch was doing. He started to laugh and make a wing gesture with his arms. That would hopefully show that the mood was light and they didn't have any concerns as they were plainly being observed.

A few minutes later, a large man with a thick black moustache, blue shirt and wide tie came out from around the screen. His weight was a contributing factor to the excessive sweat marks under his arms and Finch could smell him before he saw him. As he rounded the screen, he took a crumpled handkerchief from his pocket and wiped his brow which went high due to thinning hair and a receding hairline.

'Senor Finch, my name is Pedro Almeida. I am head of security here. I speak English. Could you both come with me please?' Finch and Kris followed him into a small room to the side where along with Escobar stood a formidable, uniformed guard.

'Mr Finch, could you empty your bags on the table please,' he ordered politely. Finch started to empty out the meagre contents of both bags and stood back. Almeida looked at the contents on the table and then at Finch. 'You travel light, huh? I know about your lost luggage, but even so…' Finch shrugged his shoulders. 'We have to be diligent here, Mr Finch. Many people come and try to traffic drugs and the like. You are no drug smuggler. I have been round long enough to know a mule when I see one and you have no cross on your back. So you are here for your studies?'

215

Finch steadied himself and tried to look as innocent as possible.

'Sir. We are here to study the tribes which may have lived here and...' He was cut off.

'Yes, I know all that, I could hear you. But I wonder, why a man who is clearly a post-grad as you are, no, how do you say, spring chicken, comes here to study and doesn't apply for a visa of any kind, work, digging, visitor and spends all his time in the luggage hall, but has no luggage? Strange, no?' Finch's tongue was trapped and he searched for the words to explain the head of security's accurate findings.

Just then Kris came forward. 'Hello, sir, my name is Kris, I am Finch's colleague. We are indeed post-grads, my background is... tobacco. I worked as a marketing manager for British American Tobacco for eight years. Mr Finch was translator for NATO in Brussels. We met on an amateur dig in Crete and the bug caught us. I quit my job and Finch his and just by chance ended up at the same university. My marriage broke up which devastated me and Finch was recovering from a bad accident. It is our rebirth, sir, our chance again. I didn't realise we needed a visiting visa and certainly not a work one. Our ignorance is not arrogance, sir. We have come to plan and test theories. Nothing more. It hasn't started on the best note, losing our bags, but this is where our lives are heading and as you pointed out we are no smugglers. So is there any way at all we can sort this out and offer our most humble apologies?'

Finch looked at Kris and was surprised and shocked by not only his eloquence but his sincerity and, he might add, the distinct lack of swearing. Almieda wiped his brow once more and picked up Finch's old notebook and threw it down. He was hot and bothered and tired of the day. He looked up at the guard and

216

sent him away. 'You know, a visa in an embassy will cost you three hundred dollars. Hmmm?' Finch and Kris nodded. 'Gentlemen, you understand, yes?' The penny suddenly dropped and Finch rushed for his wallet, which he had previously been prepared for. 'Yes. Yes, of course.' He removed six fifties from his wallet and held it out to Almieda. He smiled and his fat, sweaty fingers grabbed the money. He glanced at it and put it in his top breast pocket, tapping it for good measure. 'Thank you, gentlemen. Remember in future, to think about your trip. If you go outside the officer will stamp your passport for one week. Enjoy your visit to Ecuador and be careful of the snakes; they bite.' Almieda left and shouted an order at the customs officer as he did so. Finch and Kris collected their belongings, got their passports stamped and headed out of the airport.

'You know, Kris, that was bordering on the brilliant. Where the hell did that come from and how did you avoid swearing?'

Kris looked at Finch. 'I am capable of being more than just a dishevelled uncouth mess. I just like it that way!"

'A translator for NATO and marketing guru for BAT. Quality! Absolute quality.' Finch shook his head in amazement and grinned at their close shave. It was back on. The task now was to head into town and find out the best way of getting into the caves. They had struck it lucky in Ethiopia. So Finch hoped a bit of local knowledge may point them in the right direction.

Outside the airport stood a blacked-out Range Rover Sport. Behind the glass, which was lowered enough to allow the smoke from his Gitanes cigarette to be sucked out, was Victor. He watched as Kris and Finch stood outside discussing their next moves. Karin was in the back flanked by two of Victor's men.

'Well. We've come this far. You just going sit and watch them?' Karin quizzed Victor from behind. Victor ignored her at first. Then after another drag of his cigarette he answered slowly and deliberately.

'Shut your mouth, Ms. Edwards. When I need your advice, I will be sure to ask for it. I have no intention of laying my cards on the table this early. The longer he thinks he's alone, the more productive he will be. No. We'll bide our time and, in the meantime, I think I'll just watch – if, of course, that's all right with you.' Karin sat back and could tell from Victor's voice he wasn't in the mood for being wound up. One of the men from the back seat passed Victor a phone that had already been connected to the recipient at the other end. 'Don't lose them. Keep me informed of everything and as soon as they reach the river, tell me. You understand?' Victor tossed the phone into the back seat and buzzed the window up. 'I'm thirsty. From the frying pan into the fire, yes? It would be nice to visit a more temperate country. This heat starts to get into your bones after a while.' Victor gave the instruction to drive on and they left Finch and Kris to their own devices.

CHAPTER 32

Finch found a hotel in the centre of Quinto and immediately set about trying to source any information at all about how to get out to the grid reference they had acquired in Armenia. Finch told Kris to stay put in the hotel. He didn't want to raise too high a profile with two new white guys asking too many questions about the metal library's whereabouts. After hitting the streets for a good few hours, Finch rang the hotel and arranged to meet Kris at a bar in the central district.

'So how did you get on? Any leads?' Kris enquired. Finch had purchased a map from a local kiosk and laid it on the table along with a cold beer he had ordered for Kris' arrival.

'I took the grid references and fed them into a computer in the internet café and it came up with this location.' Finch produced a printed A4 piece of paper with a map printed on it. 'If you put this on to the bigger map, it places the entrance, supposedly, right about here.' Finch circled a bend in the River Pastaza about twenty kilometres from where the cave system of Tayos was last seen.

'I checked out the buses and they run every day to Riobamba which is about seventy kilometres from the caves at Tayos and fifty kilometres from the river. If we get down there, we can hire a vehicle and make our own way about. I'm not interested in the caves; we'll head straight for the grid reference; that will be our best chance.'

Kris acknowledged, 'Roger that, what can I do?'

'We need some underwater masks, waterproof torches, string, knives and some kind of breathing equipment. Can you handle that?' Again, Kris lifted his glass in accordance. 'The bus leaves at ten tomorrow. We have the rest of today and early tomorrow to get our stuff together. I've got a bit of admin to square away myself so will meet you back at the hotel tonight. If you run into any problems, leave a message at the hotel if you can. For some reason I think Victor is closer than he has been for some time.'

Finch and Kris parted company and Kris made his way into town to pick up provisions. That evening over a meal of steak and chips and a bottle of red wine from the fine reserves of Chile, the men pooled their resources. Finch tasted the full-bodied red wine and grinned with pleasure.

'Wow. Now that hits the spot,' Finch mused. Kris on the other hand quaffed his, explaining how a pint of Fosters would have sufficed. 'So how did you get on today? Did you get everything we'll need for the river?' Finch asked.

'Yep!' answered Kris smugly. 'I had a complete result. I bumped into some American businessman who is a mad keen diver and he gave me a heads up on the best places to find the gear we needed. I managed to pick up these 'spare air' pocket-sized regulators. They issue them to the helicopter pilots over here and I managed to get them at a surplus store for next to nothing. Managed to get all the other gear as well, plus was able to pick up a GPS device which will help. How about you?'

Finch was pleased with Kris' endeavours and was pleased that he was at his side. This was a monstrous task but would have been twice as hard to have to deal with alone. He was used to working in solitude but he liked the fact that his back was covered and he didn't have to bear this burden alone. Finch had been busy too.

'Yep, I've had a result too. I've managed to book us a place on a bus tomorrow morning heading down to Riobamba. From there we can source an old banger to get around in and won't cost us much at all. Just got to make sure it works. I've been doing some digging around on the net. As far as the library goes, all I know is that with the co-ordinates we've got, we are on the right track. The cave system at Tayos seems to be a red herring which is great for us as it means no one will suspect us of being up to anything. As far as any information on the library itself goes and what to expect, well you know as much as I do and what has been written by Hall. I just know that this medallion is the key to whatever we find down there. Whether any questions will be answered, who knows and how it will lead us to the Grail...' Finch took another sip of wine and scratched his head.

Kris looked at Finch. 'So suppose we find the library and get an inkling about where the Grail is. Do you know any info about that? And before you start, try and keep it brief, Jake, I know how you like your stories!' Finch flicked Kris a 'V' sign and pulled a face at the unfounded accusation.

'OK, so the Holy Grail is I suspect an actual vessel. I looked into where the experts feel that the Grail resides or at least has some relevance to. Some of the theories are bizarre. There are a couple of theories that place it in the USA and Canada. One thought is that it is in Maryland at a place called Accokeek where a nameless priest stowed away on a ship after fleeing England around the 1600s. He had some Templar ties and hid it somewhere, but no one knows where. Oak Island, Nova Scotia is another possibility. A 'Money Pit' was discovered by some kids in 1795. The Knights Templar again are said to have hidden the Grail there in the1300s along with chests of gold. Though I have no recollection of that! Apparently at least six people have died trying to excavate it which gives the story a more sinister edge. Not too sure about that one either. There is a way-out theory that the US government has it housed in Fort Knox. There is an urban myth that there is a room housing the Grail, the Ark of the Covenant, Noah's Ark satellite photos and the true Cross. I think we can rule that one out then, eh?

'Rosslyn Chapel in Scotland, of *'da Vinci Code'* fame is another possibility. Built by a Templar descendant and having lots of Grail and Templar symbology, but the owners won't let anyone inside the place. There are a couple of places in Spain; one is the Cathedral de Santa Maria de Valencia – this Grail is actually on display and been carbon dated from 300 BC to AD 100. The other is in Santa Maria de Montserrat, or Corbenic where Sir Galahad is said to have been born. It's nestled in the mountains and the Grail is said to be under the abbey. There is a peak called Sant Jeroni or Saint Jerome, who features in many Grail stories and is thought to have visited in about AD 300 and hidden it there. Then you have the Jerusalem connections – The Dome of the Rock is said to house it and this time it is more of a plate or bowl and is buried with Jesus in his tomb, but where that is, is still a mystery. Some think it's in the sewers. Miles of tunnels under Jerusalem. Some say it's in Italy, but it's mainly the Italians who say that, and finally there is Glastonbury Tor, which is supposed to be Avalon and hence bringing King Arthur into the frame. Templar and Arthurian legends go hand in hand.

Which leads me to the final place, which is Wales's Dinas Bran, an old castle in north Wales. This is quite an interesting concept, because Dinas Bran has always been said to be a model for the Grail Castle. But legend states that there is either a Silver Harp or the Holy Grail hidden under the castle and that only a boy with a white dog and a silver eye can recover it! That rules us out then. Interestingly enough the French for crow is Corbenic and the Welsh is Bran so that connects it to the place in France. The Arthurian legend is rife in Wales and Arthur's quest for the Grail is just as fantastic, so who knows?' Finch finished and sipped his drink.

Kris stared at Finch. 'Cheers, Guillaume! And that was the diluted story, eh? It's a good job I like you 'cause halfway through your soliloquy, I was about to drive a fork into your hand to get you to shut up!' Kris chuckled. 'By the way,' Kris added, 'I also tried a few regressions to see if it could offer up any clues, but strangely, there was nothing – it all just seems to be a big blank.'

Finch smiled. He hadn't thought of that taking that pathway, which in hindsight would have been an obvious thing to do. He was just glad Kris was watching his back.

All the while from the other side of the street, a silhouetted character watched from a hidden alleyway, inspecting their every move and reporting back to Victor. It wasn't worth thinking about what he would do if Jake and Kris got away from him, so he stood and watched and waited until the pair left for their hotel room.

CHAPTER 33

Finch and Kris rose early and after breakfast and coffee, boarded the bus for Riobamba. The trip was going to take them a good few hours as it was about 120 miles from Quito. Most coaches like this had been scrapped, but this one had slipped through the net. It was falling apart and was crammed to the rafters with bags, people and livestock. The smell was a mixture of diesel, cigarettes, sweat and animals and was enough to make you retch. Kris and Finch got comfortable near the back of the bus and Kris gave Finch one of those looks that said, 'what the hell?!'

Finch chuckled to himself and pulled his hat over his eyes and got ready for a bumpy sleep. Kris rolled a cigarette and stared at the man opposite from him, holding a goat that had urinated all over the floor. Kris picked his feet up to ensure none got on his shoes and lit up. This was going to be a long journey.

Eventually and after a few heart in the mouth moments, the bus pulled into Riobamba. Finch had pretty much slept the whole way, unlike Kris who had been on the edge of his seat for a great majority of the ride and had smoked more than he ever had before. As they came to a stop, Finch yawned and adjusted his cap and checked his surroundings. They hadn't really known what to expect from the town. Probably the result of watching too many Westerns but Finch certainly had expected to see a couple of run-down shops and an old gas station with a couple of homesteads and shacks to boot. Instead, they were confronted by an old Spanish colonial city with splendid architectural structures. Most impressive of all were the town hall and church buildings. As well as this, the whole town was dominated by the vista on the horizon of the Chimborazo Volcano, a snow-capped monster rising from the river valley. The city was a vitally important regional transport centre as well as being a major stop on the Pan-American Highway that runs through Ecuador. It was breath-taking. Finch immediately turned his attention to the job in hand and turned to Kris.

'Finding a car should be a breeze. So hopefully we can cancel the need for all those llamas!' They disembarked and immediately started their search for a car hire establishment. In no time at all, they found a middle of the road place which had on its forecourt a large white Toyota 4x4. It was perfect for what they needed and after hefty negotiation and being a few dollars lighter the pair had themselves a vehicle to start the quest for the metal library.

Finch turned to Kris, 'I don't know about you but I reckon we fill this bad boy up, pick up a couple of sleeping bags and food and make our way down there. It's about seventy kilometres, but there's no telling how long it'll take, and we can have a good recce tonight, get a feed and kip in the car if needs be, and start again at first light. By any luck we might be in and out pretty quickly, as long as it exists and we can find it.'

Kris nodded. 'Good plan, Stan. But I think trying to find the entrance – even with the co-ordinates, is going to be a mare.'

Finch and Kris set about gathering their extra provisions and rations and started on their way. Kris drove while Finch loaded up the GPS and followed the directions to the River Pastaza at 78° 13' W 3° 6' S.

'We are getting close,' Finch pointed out as they made their way up a dirt track overlooking the river. They had been hand railing the main artery for some miles now and been climbing so that the river now ran about seventy-five feet down a slight gradient. The scenery was outstanding and one couldn't help but be quite overwhelmed by the rugged beauty of the countryside. It was a great place to hide something that didn't want to be discovered, thought Finch, as this place was in the middle of nowhere with no real distinguishing features to draw people to the area. The only people they ever saw were the occasional river rafters getting their thrill out of a raging torrent of frothy white water. Up ahead was a passing lay-by on the track.

'Pull in there, Kris. We'll walk down to the river. The GPS says we are almost on the spot.' Kris pulled in and Finch put the absolute necessities in his rucksack so that they could travel light. The weather was clear and it was getting colder but being able to see clearly was definitely an advantage.

The river was wild and fast moving in the centre, but manageable on the fringes. At the point that Finch and Kris would enter the water, there was no shoreline. The river ran up against the side of the hill, allowing for a bit of depth to the water. Along the side of the hill were enormous boulders that had sat there for thousands of years and acted as a great platform for any able enough to fish or brave enough to dive in. Up ahead the river tapered slowly and ran down a rocky gorge, but here it was wide and smooth. Finch and Kris got to the water's edge and stood on a boulder overlooking the river.

'So how accurate is that thing?' Kris asked pointing to the GPS in Finch's hand.

'Pretty good, the only problem is that the co-ordinates it's given covers about two hundred square metres which means the entrance could be anywhere from here to that tree up there and ten metres down that way.' Finch waved his arms around trying his best to indicate where the boundaries were.

'Well, it looks promising. The water's deep enough to cover an entrance under the waterline and not too fast that you'd get swept downstream. It's a case of just trying to find it,' Kris surmised.

Finch crouched down on a rock. 'How long do those regulators give you?' he asked.

'About five minutes, if you breathe slowly. They are more of an emergency thing really for downed pilots trying to get free of the airframes after an emergency wet landing.'

'Well, it's not enough time for us to be able to get under the water and check out this bank. No, we'll have to think more laterally than that. Any ideas?'

Kris looked flummoxed and shook his head. Finch stared down the river and mused on how to tackle the problem. He squinted up at the sky and across at the other bank to see if there were any identifying structures to cast a clue over how to find the entrance, but there was nothing. Nothing at all.

'Now,' Finch started thinking aloud, 'down to our right the bank is too earthy, any entrance which was supposed to be kept open would either erode away, cave in or open up for all to see. Around here seems too rocky, that's not to say that there isn't a great opening underneath and up to our left the side of the hillside against the river is flat stone. Now supposing the entrance isn't an accident and was put there, the best place to site it would be up there. An easy point to remember, easy to cut into the wall and constantly under the surface of the water. That is, again, if the entrance was cut on purpose, otherwise I think we are going to need more than a week's visa!'

'Makes sense,' Kris replied. 'How deep do you think the water is?'

Finch shrugged. 'Only one way to find out. Wish I'd brought my swimmers.' Finch emptied his pockets and removed his shirt. 'Some rope would have been good.' Finch sighed.

Kris opened up the bag and tossed him a regulator. 'You'd better take this and this scuba mask. No rope, sorry.'

'That'll have to do. Wish me luck.'

Finch eased himself into the cool water and headed downstream trying to grab hold of the smooth rock wall as he went. The current on the sides of the river was almost non-existent so meant he didn't have to battle against the flow of the water. He adjusted the mask and felt around under the water for any sign of an opening. With none apparent, he took a deep breath and duck-dived under the surface.

Kris watched on, rolling a cigarette, only stopping occasionally to bite the skin around his nails.

Finch swam just under the surface and pressed his hands against the wall of the hillside. The visibility was about two to three feet and there was nothing but plain wall in front of him. He re-emerged on the surface and decided to see how far down the water went. He took another deep breath; duck-dived and kicked his legs hard creating a maelstrom at the surface. He swam hard and eventually got to the bottom, but he was right at the limits of his lung capacity and his ears were starting to pop. The water where he dived was about twenty-five feet deep. This was going to make things extremely tough. He scrambled up to the surface and took a big breath of fresh air.

'How deep is it?' Kris called from the bank.

Finch, trying to catch his breath answered, 'It's about twenty-five feet straight down. I'm just going to have to be methodical and work my way up about twenty metres that way and keep scouring up and down the wall and see what we come up with.' Kris gave a thumbs-up and Finch prepared to swim up the wall. Finch went on his first surface excursion up the wall scanning the few feet in front of him that the clarity of the water allowed. He swam along the wall and turned around and swam back. He popped his head up and shouted, 'Ah! Bollocks, no sign at all.' Finch persevered and dived down once again and again

228

and again. The sun was starting to disappear behind the hills on the far side of the bank and they were losing light, plus with the water flowing freely, Finch's extremities were starting to go numb and his teeth were chattering with cold. He needed to get out and warm up. He tried one more time.

Then suddenly he broke the surface of the water spluttering as he did. 'Kris! Kris! There's something down there about twenty odd feet on the floor of the river – an opening. I'm going down again.' And with that he was gone in a splash. Finch clawed his way down the face of the bank to where he could see a rectangular opening. He put his fingers on the underside of the opening and pulled himself down. He exhaled enough to lose his buoyancy and stood on the bottom of the riverbed. He looked up and there was a doorway. Simple but cut into the bank of the river with utter precision. Right angles, which even modern-day machinery couldn't achieve, and a finish to the sides that made the rock appear to shine like marble. Finch suddenly realised he needed to breathe and kicked hard off the bottom and ascended to the surface, fighting the temptation to breathe all the way up. As his head hit the air he gasped and took in a mighty breath of air.

'Yeeharrrr! Houston, we have found a doorway – and it's looking good.' Finch swam over to Kris on the rocks and Kris hauled him out. Finch was freezing and shaking uncontrollably, though his excitement was masking his possible hypothermia.

'It's there, Kris. In the wall. A doorway. A bloody doorway. We've done it.' They shook hands and Kris handed Finch his shirt.

'Mate, that's great. Let's get you warmed up in the car and tell me about it.' The pair headed up to the warmth and safety of their vehicle and Finch explained what he had seen. 'First thing tomorrow, we'll get down there and see what it's hiding.' Finch decided.

By now the light was fading fast and the two sat in the car with the heaters on full blast. They scrambled around for the bag of food and sat there eating some bread and cheese. 'Right – you have the back seat, Kris. I'll be OK in the front. Let's get an early one in and hit this at first light.' Kris crawled into the back and climbed into his sleeping bag. Finch did likewise in the front and they made the best of a bad situation and prepared for a crappy night's sleep in the 4x4.

CHAPTER 34

It was early morning. As the sun rose, its light and warmth dabbed the faces of Kris and Finch as they slept in the car. 'Argh – my back!' Finch groaned as he stretched in the front seat.

'You're getting old, Guillaume. I slept like a baby,' Kris said smugly.

Finch couldn't wait to get up and out, though Kris was slightly more reluctant. 'Right, let's see what there is down there.' Finch clapped his hands and removed everything of importance from his pockets and hid them under the seat. Kris did likewise. The two headed down to the river with all but a small rucksack containing a torch, regulators and knife.

'Can you remember where the opening was?' Kris enquired looking at the cold water without relish of the thought that he would soon be submerged in it.

Finch pointed downriver. 'Yep. It's just down there. I orientated myself with a landmark on the bank so will know where it is when we get down there.' Kris wasn't convinced but shrugged his shoulders.

'Right – let's get this over with.' Finch removed the torch and regulators, throwing one to Kris and both men checked the serviceability of them. Finch placed his hand on the medallion hanging around his neck to check it was still there. Then without a word both men eased their way into the flowing South American water.

The cold took their breath away and it was a while before their bodies adjusted to the temperature of the water. They put on their scuba masks and swam down to where Finch had remembered where the line of the portal was. 'Right. It's below us, about twenty-odd feet. Follow me. I have no idea how far it runs underwater so hold your breath first and use the regulator when you need to use it. OK?' Kris nodded and both men took a deep breath and duck-dived under the water.

The water offered about two feet of clarity but Finch's torch cut through the water admirably illuminating the doorway cut into the wall. Buoyancy was a problem and both men struggled to keep themselves submerged.

The doorway was incredible. Cut into the rock, it was a perfect rectangle and its corners were sharp and accurate. The sides and edges were flat and smooth. Finch pulled himself under the lintel of the door so that he was now inside the doorway. He was getting short of breath so pulled out the regulator and took a short gasp of air. He swam down inside of the doorway and checked Kris was there. He, like Finch, had become short of breath and so had used his regulator as well. As he looked down the corridor, the sides and ceiling were as they had been described and showed the highest level of construction, which the doorway had promised. Finch and Kris kicked on through the watery corridor. It appeared to be endless, though the poor visibility didn't help much. Both Finch and Kris were trying not to use too much energy and kept their breathing slow. They only had one attempt at this as they didn't have time to go and get more underwater breathing equipment. They were doing this on a shoestring and it could prove to be their undoing.

They had got about fifty metres into the passage when up ahead Finch could see that the floor was gently but noticeably sloping upward. As it did so, the two could stand on the bottom and walk up it. As they did the water receded and the pair poked their heads up out of the water into the passageway which was now full of air and not water. Finch, waist deep in what was left of the river, removed his regulator and took a speculative breath.

The air was stale, but it was breathable. Kris followed suit and the two of them walked out of the water and along the passageway. Finch shone his torch down and could see that the passageway still remained as cleanly cut as it was in the water. They walked up about another fifty metres when the passageway opened up into a large space. Off to the left-hand side was a room. Finch entered it carefully. He had been into enough caves and forgotten rooms of history to know that most of the men that had left the rooms had not wanted anyone else to find it and hence had left little surprises for the intruders along the way. He shone his torch and to his amazement he saw what Petronio Jaramillo was correct in what he had said he had seen, and if that was not proof enough, there, on the floor were four books that had been looked at. Finch opened one up and there on the front page were the initials 'PJ' in bold black letters. He had been here and been telling the truth. Finch felt a great deal of sadness at the thought that no one except Hall had believed Jaramillo and that he must have been some swimmer with bags of courage to swim down that passageway alone not knowing how far it went on for.

The room was enormous and was partitioned, creating smaller rooms. The walls had been made into natural shelving and housed thousands upon thousands of metal books. It was a metal unlike anything Finch had seen before. On the wall were flame torches. 'Kris. Do you have your lighter on you?' Kris patted his trousers but they were empty, having tipped out its contents in the car.

'Sorry mate.' Kris replied. Finch was scanning the floor and spotted a couple of flints, that had been purposefully placed within reach of the torches. He immediately grabbed them and struck them together next to the dry torch heads. After a few attempts a spark flew from the stone and ignited the torch without too much trouble. The other torches were ignited. As they were lit, the true splendour of the library was unearthed and shone with an eerie glow. Finch picked up a book at random and

233

studied it. It was heavy, at least twenty pounds. He placed it on the floor and looked through the pages which were lightly pressed metal, each one stamped on one side with ideographs, geometric designs and inscriptions. But they made no sense. There was no theme and nothing which could be related to anything. At least with hieroglyphics or wall paintings from Egypt you could make an educated guess at what was being said, but this was just gobbledygook. Nevertheless, they were mesmerising. The metal seemed to hum. Some were silvery and some golden to look at and each contained an intangible power that eluded Finch for words.

While Finch looked through the metal books, Kris had ventured back to the main opening and had a look at the room to the left. There he lit up more torches and saw a second library, but this time, again as described by Jaramillo, this one contained books of hard, polished, rectangular, translucent plates, each with parallel, encrusted channels, laid on gold-leafed trestles. These were even more incredible than the metal books, and their purpose even more bewildering. There were thousands of them as well.

Kris called Finch through. When he got there, he stared at them in awe. 'What are these? And where did they come from?' Finch asked rhetorically.

Kris shook his head. 'Have you ever seen anything like this before, from any of your digs or research?'

Finch looked dumbstruck. 'Never. I mean this is literally… out of this world.' The two men explored the books and then ventured past the main opening and into a further room. This one was as big as the other two rooms but contained hundreds of zoomorphic and human statues and heavy plinths. They displayed various examples of species from the animal kingdom and also humans in varying positions and portrayals of emotions. It was as beautiful as it was bizarre. Leading off that room was

234

another void filled with strange 'metal' bars of different shapes. Metal which again had no earthly explanation, some of them were metals that Finch could not give a name to, together with heaps of precious gemstones and alluvial gold – was this the mythical El Dorado? Finch thought to himself. Off that room, past the gold and precious metals was a smaller room. Smaller it might have been, but in the middle, on a stone plinth was a sarcophagus made of a translucent material almost like Perspex but harder and heavier. Inside could be seen a large gold-leafed human skeleton. It was magnificent.

'Human,' Kris spoke, breaking the silence of the lost tomb. Finch stared at it.

'Maybe. But it is huge.'

In the room containing the sarcophagus, there were at least 12 sets of sealed doors set into the wall and spanning the room. Each was shut tight but had precious jewels adorned over the doors in various patterns. Finch pushed his shoulder against one of the doors while Kris, on seeing Finch attempt to move one, tried his best to pry a door open using his fingers. Neither had any impact and the doors remained shut tight. At the far end of the room was a recess and a further obvious doorway; this one though was clear of any stones or ornamentation, but nevertheless just as tightly shut as the rest. Finch again pushed against this door, but it had no effect.

They exited the room and made their way back to the large opening from the initial passageway. They carried on up looking for anything else, any other clue as to why they were here, anything that could point them in the right way to the Grail. As they carried on up the passageway which continued in the same ilk as the rest of the chambers, they were getting to the end of the cave system. There was no other way in or out. This place was designed for only a few ever to find it. Finch turned round and made his way back to the library of metal.

'We surely can't have to look through every one of these books in the hope we will find a similar page to the medallion we found in Ethiopia,' Finch said frustratedly. 'It would take us years.'

Kris sat back on his haunches. 'Think about it, Jake. Look at this place. It wasn't designed to be found, not by us anyway and we have a key to open a door. We just have to find a lock. Now whoever had come up with this, would have made it easy to find the lock because without the key it would be impossible anyway. So I reckon the lock is staring us in the face.' It made sense.

Finch looked into the darkness. The books were not the key to finding the Grail. He left the room and made his way into the sarcophagus chamber. 'It must be in here. It 's the main chamber and those doors are locked and where there's a locked door there has to be a key to open it.'

Both men scoured the room, looking for any recess or clue that would help them at all. Kris leant on the sarcophagus and whispered sarcastically, 'Give us a clue, Arnold?' As he did so he realised that the top of the sarcophagus wasn't flat but contained a very slight impression about the width of one of the metal books opened up.

'Hey, Guillaume! Look at this!' Jake shot over to Kris and he showed him what he had just found. 'Maybe we need to put a book in this recess and somehow it will open up a door?' Kris wondered.

Finch agreed. 'Maybe. We just have to try a couple of hundreds of thousands of books – you feeling strong?'

'Guillaume!' Kris said. 'Think. It wants to be found. Use the medallion. There is an energy to this place. Energy, magnetism, whatever, maybe it will show you a path?'

Finch turned and headed for the metal library and once there, removed the medallion from his neck and held it on the chain at arm's length. Almost instantly the metal plaque started to hum softly and move like a magnet toward Finch's left and a long line of books on the upper shelf. The closer he got the hum increased and the pull on the medallion grew stronger. He carried on down the line until the medallion pulled forward and stuck to one particular book. Finch replaced the medallion around his neck and removed the cumbersome book and brought it into the chamber. He opened the book and every metallic gold page was blank and perfectly smooth except the two middle pages, one of which was silver and the other gold.

He placed the book in the recess above the face of the skeleton in the sarcophagus and almost instantly there was a rumble and the see-through casket began to radiate a white light. At the same time various 'clunks' sounded from the sealed vaults and escaping air hissed as the vacuumed seals broke. The doors depressed into the space and pulled to the side through a clever mechanical device. The vaults all revealed an incredible artefact of some sort in gold or other metal. The energy within the chamber was unbelievable. Finch entered the first vault which housed a sword on a plinth resting upright. The weapon was exquisite. Its handle was blue and the hand guard gold. The blade itself was of the finest unblemished metal. Finch couldn't help but pick up the sword. He did so with trepidation in case the doors shut tight, but there was nothing. The sword in his hand was wonderfully balanced and unnaturally light for a sword that big. He waved it about and just caught the edge of the plinth with the blade. The stone was sliced off and when Finch looked at the blade there wasn't the slightest mark. He inspected the face of the blade and engraved at the top was '*Caledfwlch*'.

Finch gasped. Kris could see Finch had hit on something. 'What's up?'

'Caledfwlch,' Finch said. 'It can't be. Caledfwlch was Welsh which combines the words *'caled'* meaning battle or hard, and *'bwlch'* which means breach or gap.' Kris looked unimpressed and shrugged. Finch looked at him and continued, 'This was Latinised by Geoffrey of Monmouth years ago to *'Caliburnus'* – This is *'Excalibur'*!

The silence was broken by Kris. 'Shut up!'

Finch gawked at the sword and placed it back carefully. He backed out of the chamber and looked at the other recesses. One had a large sledgehammer; one was empty but was easily large enough to house the Ark of the Covenant. Each void held an artefact from various myths and legends of history – one contained what Finch thought was the mythical Book of Thoth, a collection of Egyptian texts told to have been written by the God Thoth himself and is said to contain two spells, one of which allows the reader to understand the speech of animals, and one of which allows the reader to perceive the gods themselves. In another the Cintamani Stone, better known as The Philosophers' Stone, a stone that could turn base metals into gold. In another, a ring which was the Seal of Solomon, said to have the power to command demons, and possessed by King Solomon. The Armour of Achilles, made by Hephaestus and said to be unpierceable. There was the hammer of Thor, and a few other objects about which Finch had no idea what they were.

Finch, realising that he hadn't seen the Holy Grail, noticed that the main vault was still shut tight. They both frantically hunted around for any way of opening it up. In front of the door on the floor there emerged a small black plaque with similar markings to that of the medallion. There was also a large space missing, perfectly big enough for the medallion to rest. Finch wasted no time and removed the medallion from the chain and placed it in the slot. Immediately, it had the same effect as on the main door. It hissed as the air escaped and opened up. But what it presented wasn't what they had expected. There in the centre of the room was a translucent plinth with a crystal in the centre, upright and about the size of a mobile phone. Finch looked around the room for anything else but the room was empty. He checked the crystal for pressure pads and the like and bent down to eye level to inspect it. Kris shone his torch in and caught Finch's eyes next to the gem.

'Wow, the crystal is the same colour as your eyes, Guillaume. It's extraordinary.'

Finch got up and grabbed the torch. 'You have a look.' As Kris bent down Finch shone the torch at Kris' eyes and indeed they were the same colour. A blue that was pure and intense. Finch shone the torch around the chamber to see if there was anything else to guide them but it was empty.

Finch looked at the gem intensely. He was loathed to touch it in case it may be harbouring a pressure pad or switch triggering all types of unpleasantness should it be touched.

'What do you think?' asked Kris.

Finch shook his head and rubbed his chin fervently. 'Not sure, old chum. I am not sure. There are no clues and we're a long way from everything if anything goes pear-shaped.' Finch stalked the gem on the plinth like a lion would its prey, trying to see things from a different angle. He stopped and leant with his back against the wall of the chamber.

'You know, Kris. This has been a hell of a journey. I have seen and done some incredible things in my life and unearthed some marvellous objects, but if you had told me what we are about to uncover a few months ago, I would have laughed and thought you were mad. I can't believe that it wasn't that long ago that we discovered the Great Library of Alexandria and yet that pales into insignificance against our last discoveries. Maybe though, just maybe, we were destined to find this. It was meant

239

to be. That through the regressions of who we are, we were supposed to be here now, and our eyes are proof of who we are, who we have always been. That our souls belong here.'

Kris agreed. 'I am there with you, Guillaume, but how does that help us now?'

Finch stepped forward in front of the crystal. 'Maybe this time we are the key. We are interlocked with whatever this crystal possesses and only we can unlock it.'

Kris shrugged, not really understanding where Finch was coming from. Finch beckoned Kris closer.

'Just copy me, but don't actually move the object, OK?' Finch placed his first finger on top of the crystal and then Kris followed doing the same. At first there was nothing but then the whole room shone in a blue light; it was blinding. Finch and Kris looked at each other in wonderment and the colour of their eyes seemed to be amplified tenfold. The crystal was feeding off their energies and illuminating the chamber. The light became so intense that both men closed their eyes to shield them against the glow. As they did so, visions started to flow through their minds of places they had visited on the journey so far. Ethiopia and the Ark, Armenia, Oman and the Library, then visions from way back formed. Templar visions. White jupons with the red cross clearly visible, chainmail and swords. Victor was there and the anguish of fire. Then came flashes of where the Grail had been. Visions of Jesus, Jerusalem, castles and boats, deserts and fighting and endless travels. The visions were quick and disjointed, blurry and confusing. Then a vision slowed down and there on an exposed hillside were thirteen standing stones none higher than half a metre tall arranged in a horseshoe shape. There was a truncated end, rather like the portal on some elongated burial mound and a stone of seemingly more significance. The place was Wales. Unmistakably, but neither one knew how they knew; then flashed a vision of Arthur Pendragon, dead, being

240

laid to rest and finally a gold glow emanating from the ground. Then all went white, burning white and a face appeared which could not be seen properly, lots of colours and noise, along with great peace and understanding and then it was gone. As quickly as the visions had erupted, they finished, along with the intense glow from the crystal, which had now become opaque blue once more. Finch and Kris stepped back from the crystal and looked at each other, mouths open in amazement.

'Bloody hell!' Kris stuttered.

'Yep,' Finch replied, gobsmacked.

Kris fell back against the wall. 'What did you make of that?'

Finch shook his head and looked uncomfortable. 'We should go,' he said quickly.

He checked the room for anything and left the chamber. He retrieved the medallion from the floor and as he did so the door leapt into life and started to close, sealing the room in darkness once again. He then checked the other chambers and gave them all one final mournful look and removed the book from on top of the sarcophagus. As he did so there was a collective groan and each doorway crunched and sealed once again. Finch stood and watched and felt immensely sad. Such treasures, potentially never to be seen again.

His heart lurched. 'Come on, mate,' Finch said as he rushed to replace the book from the empty space on the shelf. They had got what they had come for and now it was time to leave this place of mystery and unanswered questions. The men did their best to extinguish the torches and headed for the cold water in the passageway. Finch had been pretty silent and Kris watched him. Finch did a final check of all his gear and prepared to go.

'Guillaume,' Kris called in the darkness. 'Guillaume. Wait. Are you OK? These gifts – artefacts – they are not going anywhere. We can come back and explore properly?'

Finch stared down at the water. 'Yes, maybe we can – perhaps, but do you not see, Kris? We were meant to find this. Throughout the centuries we have been coming back, for this time now. We are Templars, Kris, and part of that has been our faith. Our faith in God, Jesus Christ and all that He represents. Good, decency and right. A belief in an omnipresent being and a real man who God sent here on earth. Our lives have been all about upholding this belief and we have died for it and killed for it, yet now, from all that we have been through and what just happened in there, you can't hide what we just experienced. All this, Kris. All this. The passageways, the artefacts, Arthur, the myths and legends, even the Ark and the Grail, all real! All REAL, but all made by some kind of beings – extra-terrestrial beings that have been visiting this place for millions of years and supplying the earth with wondrous gifts, but above it all – it's not GOD. How can that be? Everything we have ever been, has all stood for nothing...'

Finch's voice trailed off but the utter despair was clear to hear; he was a broken man. Kris stood and watched Finch crumble in front of him. It was an answer to a question that Finch had avoided wanting to know for the entire journey. Eventually Kris walked over to his friend.

'Guillaume. I have known you for hundreds of years and you are without doubt the most virtuous man I have ever known and my only regret in this life and the past is that I am not more like you. But you are wrong here, Guillaume, or are missing the point of it all. We have lived and, as you pointed out, died by a code which had shaped us for years. We are proud, strong warriors of Christ. To me it makes no difference that ET has had his hand in all of this and to be honest Kermit the Frog could be to blame; it would make no difference. You see, whoever these people are, they believe in giving mankind the benefit of the doubt and whenever we have let them down, they hid the things which we didn't deserve and could do most harm. They

242

entrusted the most important things to men who were the most righteous and virtuous of all. Whether it was King Arthur, Achilles or more importantly, Jesus Christ. His impact on the world is still felt every day on millions of people, giving hope and light even when there is none. He might have been human, but does that make him any less divine? So, if anyone can control mankind and embrace us, offer hope and ensure the right men do the right jobs, surely, they are wondrous and that is what God is? I would love to think God was a grey-haired old man who looked like Father Christmas, surrounded by beams of golden light, but maybe, Guillaume, just maybe, God is the maker of all of this whatever or whomever they may be. We have not lost any faith or been told some incredible truth; it just isn't what we thought it was. Wood is still wood whatever shape the tree may take. It doesn't change us or what we stand for. We are defined by our actions, deed and thoughts. We have been right or we wouldn't be here now. At least now we know without doubt Jesus lived and that there is a God.' Kris grabbed Finch's shoulder and squeezed. Finch appreciated Kris' thought, but he was going to need time to digest all that had been said and done. 'Come on, Guillaume – I'm hungry,' Kris said entering the water and attaching his regulator. Finch did the same and with one final look back waded into the water and his light left the cave for good.

CHAPTER 35

Finch and Kris emerged from the cave and swam up to the surface of the river. The air smelt so fresh and clean and both were relieved to be out of the claustrophobic and dark caves and back into the light and clear air of the outside world. They got out of the water and shivered from the cold.

'Come on, old boy, I'll buy you a beer and some chips,' Finch whispered to Kris. He had appreciated what he had said in the cave but would need time to get his head around things. The two men made their way back to the vehicle and shook themselves off the best they could. Both just wanted to be back on the road and being blasted by the car's heating system. Finch got into the driver's seat and checked the medallion was still around his neck. The plan was to get back to Quito as soon as possible and get a flight home. He hadn't heard anything from Victor but supposed that he would contact them when he needed answers.

Just at that thought, Finch felt a surge of pain scream through his body. He stiffened immediately and then the lights went out. Finch and Kris had been zapped with a taser and knocked unconscious by a man in the back seat. The door of the car opened and there stood Victor, unruffled and elegant.

'Hello, Guillaume, it's good to see you again.' Victor turned to his goons. 'Get him in the car and take him to the house.' He headed back to his own car and got in. Beside him was a jaded looking Karin. 'Fear not, Ms Edwards. They are just stunned. It would not do any good to kill them, not yet anyway. It looks like they have been good boys. Now we need to find out what they know. But all in good time, all in good time.'

Finch came round on the floor in a basement room. It was dirty, cold and dark. The only light offered was from a slit of a window near the ceiling which appeared to be at ground level outside. He pulled himself up on to all fours and rubbed the back of his head. He felt dreadful and could just about remember speaking to Kris and getting in the car and then it all went black. He looked up and around the room and saw Kris slumped in the corner. He was still out cold. Finch shuffled over and gave his foot a firm shake and then slapped his legs hard.

'Oi! Kris – wake up,' Finch whispered as loudly as he could. Kris started to stir and opened his eyes slowly.

'Jake? What the… Where are we?' he muttered groggily.

'In a world of shit, it looks like.' Finch grunted leaning himself up against the wall. 'It must have been Victor. I don't know what he did, but it knocked the stuffing out of me.' Finch suddenly grabbed his chest searching for the medallion, but it had gone. 'Bugger!' Finch cursed. 'He's taken the medallion.'

Kris shifted a little. 'Well, he obviously needs us to help him, otherwise we'd both be dead now. What are you going to tell him about the cave?'

'The truth,' replied Finch. 'Look, he has Karin. He knows we won't risk her life. He also knows that we've done all that he has asked us to do. I'll tell him what I know and then we'll find the Grail. Then, well, we'll have to play it by ear.' Kris looked at Finch.

'Sounds simple. We can't let him take the Grail, Jake. Whatever it takes. Victor can't be allowed to use whatever the Grail is for his own ends.' Finch nodded and rubbed the back of his neck again. After a bit Kris spoke. 'Tell me, Guillaume. What do you expect the Grail to be?'

Finch smiled to himself. 'Who would have thought we would be talking so confidently at finding the Holy Grail? But it

245

just seems like one of the many labours of Heracles. I think the Grail is what many have said it was in the past – a cup. Goblet. Made of metal and indeed the chalice used by Christ at the Last Supper. The Grail is a cup made by some living entity of an unknown material. Gosh! I mean, in the last few months we have seen the Great Library of Alexandria, the Ark of the Covenant, a Piece of Noah's Ark, witnessed a library made from metal, and seen artefacts from myth and history which exist. Excalibur! Now I feel slightly blasé. They are just things along the way to the Grail. It is said that Joseph of Aramathea guards the Grail and it has been sought since the time of Christ. It is said that whoever drinks from the Grail will drink in the elixir of life and become immortal. But with immortality comes a great burden. Once immortal only the sword from Joseph of Aramathea can end the life, but he who drinks from the Grail can rid a man of his soul for eternity and hence cleanse the world forever. The Grail cannot and should not be owned and was used by the most pure man to have ever walked this earth.'

Kris listened to that last sentence intently and smiled at Finch's passion. As the two men thought about the Holy Grail the door swung open violently and five large men entered the room. This time Finch and Kris saw what was coming. The men cornered Finch and Kris, one of the men drew a large cattle prod out from his jacket and poked Kris hard in the ribs, delivering a large volt to his body. Then he turned it on Finch. He tried to protest but it was over quickly enough. Both men succumbed swiftly to the electricity and slumped on the ground. The burly men lifted them and dragged them outside.

When Finch re-emerged from his involuntary sleep, he found himself bound to an old dentist's chair. He had been stripped naked and felt vulnerable. There was no chance of escape. He was tied fast and his mouth covered to prevent him making any sound. He looked for Kris. When he saw him, he could see that he had been plastic cuffed to a bar and hung there limply. He, though, was clothed. The room was lit with two fluorescent tubes which would have been ample anywhere else but in that room, emanated an eerie half-light which gave the room an ominous sense of doom.

A further ten minutes passed and then the door creaked open and in walked the five men who had taken them earlier. One man walked straight over to Kris and poured a bucket of water over his head, arousing him instantly. Kris gasped in shock and spluttered phlegmy water from his mouth and nose. The same man then walked over to Finch, grabbed his chin and yanked his head up to look at him. When he could see Finch was awake, he backhanded Finch across his cheek just for good measure. The force of the hit rocked Finch and any grogginess he may have had left him, along with the spittle that flew out of his mouth as the hand whipped across his face. The men took up positions in the room and waited. Seconds later, in walked Karin being escorted by another one of Victor's heavies. She was taken to a chair in the corner and cuffed to it securely. She looked worn out and pale and Finch could see her hand which was bandaged and assumed it must have been Victors doing. Karin and Finch caught each other's gaze and Karin winked at Finch and forced a smile. All Finch could do was to wink back. Finally, in walked Victor. He looked unruffled as usual and sauntered into the gloomy room without a care in the world. He moved a chair to stand in front of Finch and removed his black jacket and placed it carefully on the back of it. He then removed a cigarette from its packet and lit it, taking a deep drag of the nicotine and tar. 'Hello, Guillaume. Nice to see you again,' Victor said, smirking as he did so.

Finch attempted to talk but it was nothing but muffled nonsense. Victor jerked his head to one of the guards and he removed the gag that was preventing Finch from speaking. 'Thank you. Always a pleasure to see you too, Victor,' Finch replied and almost sounded sincere. Victor placed the chair more central to Finch and sat down deliberately in front of him and crossed his legs. 'You have been very busy, Guillaume, and may I say most successful in your quest. I am very happy indeed and I can tell you that I am not the only one. Ms Edwards here is most relieved by your endeavours as well. Though she had a slight accident with her hand. Very careless.' Finch looked at Karin and she stared at the back of Victor's head with spite and malicious intent. Finch didn't want to let this drop.

'A little uncalled for, Victor, bearing in mind we abided by all the rules, wouldn't you say?'

Victor took another long drag of his cigarette and looked at Finch out of the corner of his eye. 'No,' he replied glibly, 'I wouldn't. Ms Edwards was rather inappropriate and I lost my temper and she needed to be placed firmly back in her box. So, I merely meted out a small punishment for her insubordination. If I have learnt one thing, Guillaume...' Victor leant forward so that his cheek was next to Finch's, '...you Templars are a law unto yourself, always have been, and just occasionally you need pulling down a peg or two!' He sat back and stared at Finch and then turned his attention to Kris. He looked to his guard. 'Give him a chair! We are not animals.' The guard did as he was instructed and sat Kris on a chair, allowing some of the blood to fill his arms once again.

Victor now switched his attention to Finch once more and moved to the business of the day. 'So sorry about the manner of your abduction, Guillaume, but I hate faffing about and just needed you here. You have done well and this trinket is most interesting and probably quite important as you still had it on you when we got to you.' Victor took the medallion from his pocket, that Finch had around his neck and held it up in front of him. 'It is most strange. I have never seen anything like it in my life, but I take it you know its importance and use. That is one of the reasons why you are still alive. The reason I have you here is so you can fill in the gaps and we can end this folly and I can have the Holy Grail. So what did you find in the caves and where can I find it? And I want the truth, Guillaume.' Finch straightened his back and looked Victor in the eyes.

'Do you want the long version or the condensed one?'

'Just tell me what I need to know,' Victor replied curtly.

'The cave was the resting place of the metal library. It was a place whispered about but rarely believed. In fact, the whole world believes that the Library exists in Tayos but they are far from the truth. It contains thousands of books all made out of either pressed metal or some sort of translucent crystal. There were also vaults which could be opened by the medallion you hold, which was given to me by the Guardians of the Ark in Ethiopia. Everyone we met so far has led us to this place. The priest in Armenia, Varni, etcetera—'

Victor interrupted. 'Yes Varni, he was indeed most helpful and most loyal.' Victor paused and looked for Finch's expression. 'He will be very much missed. Very sad.' Finch glared at Victor.

'You bastard. Why did you have to do that? He was no threat!' Victor shrugged his shoulders and enjoyed the fact that he had hit a nerve.

'Continue,' Victor ordered. Finch took a moment and carried on.

'The vaults in the cave opened and inside held treasures from the dawn of time. Treasures which place myth and legend into the realms of reality.'

'Such as...?' Victor asked.

'King Arthur's sword, Excalibur, the Book of Thoth, the Philosopher's Stone, the Ring Seal of Solomon, the Armour of Achilles, a hammer, a box and other objects. It also contained a

249

crystal that when touched revealed the path of the Grail through the years and its final resting place now.'

Victor leaned forward. 'Which is where?' he said, over-emphasising the 'w' on where. Finch paused for a moment. He didn't want to reveal what he had seen and for a moment even considered lying. But what good would it have done? He wasn't in a position to do anything and he knew what Victor was capable of. He sighed and with a heavy heart told Victor.

'The Grail lies in Wales. It is hidden in what is thought to be King Arthur's burial mound or Bedd Arthur in the Preseli Mountains.'

Victor sat back in his chair and folded his arms. 'The Holy Grail. The Chalice of Christ. The most sought-after relic the world has ever known is in... Wales? Why? Why Wales do you suppose?'

'The Arthurian legend is rife with Grail stories. I always thought it was a myth, but obviously it was taken to Wales and King Arthur had something to do with it. The Preseli Mountains have long been the subject of mystery. The great blue stones of Stonehenge originate from there and are said to be magical. There are also hundreds of UFO sightings around that area; maybe it is all linked, perhaps it is an area of activity. Whatever it is, it is the vision I foresaw and it is where I believe it to be. It was so vivid. I don't see how it could be wrong.'

Victor lit another cigarette and looked thoughtful. 'It is true, Guillaume, you have done well and there is no reason why you would lie to me; but, Guillaume, I have to be sure. You have always been a strong and devious bastard and you may be hiding a few truths. Truths which could be vital and so, I need to be sure.'

Finch's face changed and he suddenly realized what Victor had in mind. Victor, although he got others to do his dirty work was well versed in the art of torture and killing. He was good. Victor stood and rolled up his sleeves. One of the guards pushed a table over to him on which stood an array of instruments with the sole purpose of inflicting pain.

'I am telling the truth, Victor. You know this! Why would I lie? Why now!!' Finch pleaded desperately.

'This may be true, Guillaume, but we need to be sure. A man will always reveal his true soul under unfathomable pain. It is also a great art to be able to inflict such pain and create a suitable threshold for a man to talk without killing him or rendering him useless. An art, I modestly admit to being quite adept at.' Finch kept protesting vigorously but it fell on deaf ears. Victor turned to him and placed a finger to his lips and hushed him into silence. 'In the past, I would just sit in and watch people get tortured. It was interesting how quickly some men gave their innermost secrets and loyalties away and in the same respect it was even more interesting that occasionally there would be the men who would keep quiet throughout the most horrendous sessions. The Templars back in the day were like that. It didn't matter what we did, your loyalty and strength of character in the face of searing pain was, I have to admit, admirable. And even as you cooked attached to the stake, very few cried out in pain as the fire blistered and charred the skin and the hair crackled in the heat. But we are a long time away from those days, so let us see.'

Finch's feet were up on the seat, the soles facing Victor. Victor took a cane from the table and whipped around striking Finch on the soles of his feet with the bamboo. The pain shot through Finch like a volt of electricity and he had never appreciated how much a whip across the soles of the feet would hurt.

'Now, Guillaume, does that jog your memory of what you found?'

251

Finch took a breath. 'I told you everything there is to tell. This is pointless.'

Victor took another swipe and the blow was as painful as the first. Finch gritted his teeth and stared at Victor. Victor delivered a further few blows to Finch's feet, leaving them raw and swollen and, with every hit, Finch's resolve became stronger. Kris and Karin looked on. Frustrated at their inability to help their friend, their combined hatred of Victor growing.

Victor put the cane back on the table and then took out a couple of strange devices. Finch could see straight away what they were. Victor attached the first to Finch's thumb and the other to his head. The two were screws, designed to put pressure on the chosen parts of the body and eventually, if required, crush them. It was never Victor's intention to kill Finch; he still needed him, but he disliked him and all he stood for and he just wanted to enjoy the moment of power over him and see him wince. He knew that Finch was telling the truth. He had no real interest in the artefacts and follies of the cave, he just wanted the Grail. In the meantime, he wanted to hurt 'Les Templars'. The thumbscrew was in place and the head clamp was put on Finch's head. Victor looked straight into Finch's eyes as he ratcheted up the notches on the screw. At first the pressure was bearable and that's all it felt like, a pressure, no real pain. The head clamp though was different. From the first turn he could feel the screw bore into his skull and there was instant discomfort.

'Now, Guillaume. What else did you want to tell me? Anything pertaining to the Grail? Are you sure it is in Wales, hmm?' Finch didn't want to give him the satisfaction of answering and stared back at him in silence. 'OK.' Victor hummed, and with that turned the screw on his thumb and his head once more. Now the pressure in his thumb had turned to discomfort and the pain in his head was relentless. Victor could see that it was Finch's head that was hurting so he turned the screws again. Now Finch couldn't help but growl in pain and as he did so a smile grew across Victor's face. He ignored the thumbscrew for the moment and concentrated all his efforts on Finch's head.

'Before I crush your head, Guillaume, are you sure you have not forgotten anything?' Finch was silent and sweating with the pain. Then Kris shouted out.

'Tell him about the metal, about the fact the Grail is made of extra-terrestrial metal, that it could all be rubbish.' Finch shot a look round at Kris for opening his mouth, but for Kris, it was the only way he could help his friend.

Victor looked at Kris. 'What?'

Kris dropped his head in shame, realizing now he should not have said anything.

'Speak!' Victor sang out while turning the screws again on Finch's head causing an instant reaction.

Kris took a breath. 'The metal we found could not have been made by humans, the workmanship and the language are not of this world. The metal that made the Ark and the Grail and a hundred other artefacts is made from... I don't know what but is not divine.'

'Are you saying aliens made everything? Why not God? Your assumption, Templar, is that an alien came down and delivered mankind great gifts and left. I disagree; I think God made them and left man to get on with it. Really, Templar, I thought you had more faith.' Victor stood face to face with Finch. 'And this is why Guillaume looks so lost, for he thinks God does not exist and, in his place, an alien race of intellect and aloofness? You make me sick, Templar, I could have worked this out for myself. I can read too. And with all your piousness you see some proof of something else and throw away your years of dedication. And I thought I was supposed to be unworthy.

253

Whatever. That Grail holds immense power and soon it will be mine to do with what I wish.' He turned the screw again leading Finch to cry out in pain. 'You know there was a time, Guillaume, that you wouldn't have made a sound. How things have changed.' Victor removed the vices and looked at Finch. 'I wonder?' he said to himself. 'Is it still the fire you dread most, hmm?' Victor took his lighter out of his pocket and ignited a flame. He moved slowly and deliberately over to Finch and wafted the flame in front of his face, close enough to feel the heat. Finch recoiled as much as his position would allow him. 'Ah yes, Guillaume, you still fear it. Can you recall the pain, growing from your legs as they burnt, the smell of your own skin as it crisped from the heat, watching me as I watched you go up in the choking acrid smoke? Yes, Guillaume, you can't hide it, you still fear the fire, as you all do. It will always be your real weakness. It's pathetic!' Victor closed the lighter and Finch's pulse began to slow.

Victor suddenly straightened and put his jacket back on. 'We must get to Wales quickly. We still have a great deal of work to do. Meet me at the airport,' Victor said to the main guard. 'And I almost forgot.' He nodded to the same guard who stepped forward and produced a Glock handgun from the holster strapped to his chest. He cocked it and handed it to Victor.

Finch looked at Victor and didn't know what to expect. Surely he wasn't going to kill him; he still needed him, he had said so himself. 'Now I have you and we are once more together, I feel that two is company but three is definitely a crowd and there is someone who has been an irritant for some time now and has become surplus to requirements. So with that in mind, I think we should say goodbye to Karin.' Finch looked up at Karin and saw the look in her eyes. He instantly remembered Khalifa and how Victor hadn't given killing him a second thought. Victor wasted no time and as he walked out of the room, he raised the gun to Karin's head and was about to pull the trigger when Finch yelled out.

'Wait! Victor. The only reason we were able to access the information from the crystal in the cave was because Kris and I were the conduits for the crystal to work. It somehow used us as a means to work. It was the same colour as our eyes and it used whatever power we have to illuminate and show us the way. Now I can't be sure but, it seems reckless to have come this far only to find that there was a reason why Renaud, I mean Karin is here. That she or all of us would be needed to open up whatever doors are still in place to find the Grail? Would a moments vengeance be worth having to wait yet another lifetime to get what you want?' Finch implored Victor and sounded desperate, but what he said made perfect sense.

Victor stopped and thought about what had been said. This trip had been one of coincidence and destiny, and it would be irritating to say the least if all the Templars were needed. Victor released the trigger and threw the weapon back to the guard. 'You are a lucky lady Ms Edwards. Let us hope that you will be required.' Victor left the room shouting, 'We leave in two hours.'

Finch and Kris stared at Karin, who in turn was shaking uncontrollably. They all knew how close she was to being shot and if it wasn't for Finch's clever intervention there was no doubting that Victor would have killed her. The room was silent. The guards untied both men and Karin, dressed Finch and marched them out and on to the airport at Quito, preparing them for the onward journey. All three were still numb, but Finch knew that there was no way in hell he was going to let Victor possess the Grail and before this mission was over, Victor was going to have to die.

CHAPTER 36

Victor's private jet was ready and on the runway at Quito airport. Finch, Kris and Karin, two of Victor's men and Victor boarded the plane and it rumbled down the tarmac, destined for the United Kingdom. The atmosphere was tense. Finch, Kris and Karin sat silently while Victor stared intently at Finch, trying to figure out what he was thinking. After a while Victor took the lead and broke the silence. 'Why are you so angry, Guillaume?' Finch looked at Victor with his piercing blue eyes and said nothing. 'You despise me. You think me heartless, but it is all a game until the prize is won, and we are so close now, that I will not allow anything to get in my way. And then the game will be over. You think you saved Karin's life. Well maybe you did and perhaps my dislike for that woman almost got the better of me. It would have been a schoolboy error to kill her when she still may be of use. Why take the risk? Be under no illusion though, I would happily kill you all in the blink of an eye if it meant getting what I want if not indeed for the sheer sport of it. Do you understand me, Guillaume?' Finch looked at Victor with an empty gaze. For now, he would play Victor's game, until it mattered. He turned to Kris and they exchanged a look of reassurance that they both understood and settled into the flight, preparing themselves for the mission ahead.

Finch was tired both physically and mentally. His feet were swollen and pulsing with pain and his head showed the scars of the screws. It pounded and occasionally the wounds would weep. Finch dabbed the blood away and tried to ignore his discomfort. He didn't want to give Victor any satisfaction of knowing that he was suffering.

The plane touched down at Cardiff International Airport. It felt good to be back on home soil after such a fraught trip. Victor had everything planned. Once through customs and immigration a car was waiting and a hotel had been booked near Cardigan, a small town that overlooked the great sweeping bay of the same name on the West Wales coast. This meant that it would only be a short drive of about twenty-odd miles to Bedd Arthur and the final part of the quest. It was late and dark and all were weary after the trip.

The Castel Malgwyn Arms Hotel was an apt place to finish. An old Georgian manor converted into a hotel and consisted of wood panelled walls, leather-bound books and large open fires surrounded by comfortable brown leather chairs. It gave Finch a warm comforting feeling of coming home and he needed it. His feet were still in bits from his earlier encounter with Victor and his entire body was in need of a good rest and a decent night's sleep. Victor's party entered the hotel and collected the keys to their rooms. Victor turned to Finch.

'I have allowed a room for each of you. Needless to say that there will be eyes on you at all times, but I think escape at this point in the game would be a pointless exercise. I will see you at breakfast and may tomorrow be the greatest day of all our lives. *Adieu.*' Victor had a quick conflab with his head guard and disappeared upstairs.

Finch, Kris and Karin were tired, ragged and smelly but before heading off to their rooms, they decided to go to the bar and order a large whisky to enjoy beside the fire. It was a strange feeling. They felt beaten and empty and were now under house arrest. Running away at this point was useless. And besides he wanted to see the Grail and more importantly needed to get it before Victor - the game indeed needed to be concluded.

The three sat in the chairs beside the fire. Finch took a deep breath, inhaling the deep aromas of his peaty Scotch whisky. 'To

257

Khalifa. May we see him again soon.' Finch said raising his glass in a toast.

When at last the ice had melted and the tumbler was empty, Finch turned to Kris and Karin.

'Well – this may be our last night. Tomorrow will be the most important of our lives and perhaps the last of this one. We may finally achieve our aim of finding, touching and protecting the Grail. It has been an honour to stand beside you all once more. I am just sorry we didn't all meet this time around sooner.'

Kris aimed his reply more at Finch. 'It's certainly been an adventure, Guillaume de Beaujeu.' Karin looked at the two men. 'I know I have only just joined this party, but whatever happens, I wouldn't change it for anything. Thank you for finding me and taking me on this journey. I just want you to know that whoever I was or will be in the future, tomorrow I will do all I can to help you save the Grail and kill that son of a bitch!' With that Karin placed her glass down and made her way upstairs. Finch followed, limping his way up to bed while Kris sat watching the flames dance in the fire.

The morning couldn't come too soon. Finch had slept deeply and almost forgot where he was. He opened the curtains and the day was bright and clear with the first rays of the sun warming his face through the window. It was the first time he was able to see the view from his window that overlooked lush farmland accommodating sheep and dairy herds. The call of a pheasant drew his eyes to the nearby river which was releasing a fine mist as it made its way to the coast. It was an idyllic area. In the distance he could make out some higher ground. The Preseli Mountains.

By the time he got down to breakfast Victor, Karin and Kris were at the table already. 'Ah, good morning, Guillaume. I trust you slept as well as I did? And I see that you don't appear to be limping as much, which indicates that your feet are feeling better.' Victor said that last bit with a smile, trying to mask his amusement behind his coffee cup. Finch decided to ignore him and instead turned to Kris as he took his seat.

'How's the breakfast?' Kris, who had devoured the contents of his plate and was trying to peel the glaze from the crockery in an attempt to get the very last drop of egg from it, looked up.

'First class, Jake, or as the locals say, half tidy!' Finch smiled and ordered a full Welsh breakfast with coffee.

'Morning Karin. How are you?' Jake asked.

Karin, like Kris was surprising upbeat. 'Good. I slept like a log and was able to wash my hair. Makes a girl happy!'

Victor looked at Finch. 'It is a truly beautiful place. You can see why the legend of King Arthur reverberates so abundantly around here – very... magical. Today will be a good day. We even have a clear sky. The omens are good.' He didn't care for an answer or any acknowledgement from anyone; he was just making a point. He wiped his mouth and stood. 'Be ready to leave in half an hour. It should give you enough time to eat; we have an important and busy day ahead of us today.' He leaned close to Finch's ear and whispered, 'For today, Guillaume, I become King!' Finch's spine straightened and he baulked at the thought.

When Victor and his cronies had left, Kris turned to Finch. 'How are we going to play this today, Jake? You tell me what to do and I'm there.'

Finch pulled Karin's chair closer and he leant in toward the table. 'We can't do much, we have to go with the flow. The first thing is to actually find the Grail; I mean we still don't actually know if it is really there. If not, we will have to act fast as Victor will kill us all. Just stay alert.'

259

'Whether we find it or not,' Karin interrupted,' Victor will kill us all anyway.'

Finch smiled. 'Highly probable, we just need to get our hands on it before Victor – at least then we will have something to bargain with and then perhaps use it against him. I'll just keep working on the rest.' Finch helped himself to some coffee and looked out the window for some divine intervention, but all that came was his breakfast.

The large black Range Rover was running as they left the hotel and Kris, Karin and Finch were ushered quickly inside. Victor, who was sitting in the front seat turned to Finch.

'OK, Mr Archaeologist, over to you. I have the key.' Victor produced the gold-looking medallion from his pocket. 'And you have the skills, so where to?' Victor threw Finch a folded map of the area and he unfurled it and got his bearings.

'It's about fourteen miles. Head towards the B4332. Then you want the A478 south.' The driver nodded and headed off. The car was silent. Everyone scanned the horizons at the breath-taking scenery and thought about what lay ahead.

After a while and a few alterations to Finch's navigation. the car pulled up in a purpose-built car park for visitors wishing to visit the site. They got out and made their way up the rough trodden pathway to the stones. It was still a wonderfully clear day and the air was still. It was almost a ten-minute walk to the stones and when they got up there, the view was incredible. Looking at the stones from the north-east, directly at the more prominent stone was a large rocky outcrop. Apart from that, it was just a rugged grassland. Victor's party stood on the site and surveyed the area.

'Well then, Guillaume,' Victor said looking at Finch.

Finch stared at the stones and stood in the centre. He took his cap off and ruffled his hair. To be honest he didn't know where to start. His mind was a blank. He turned to Kris and gave him a look which said, 'Any thoughts?' Kris made a face and shrugged his shoulders. Then Finch remembered the medallion. It was invaluable before and could help once again.

'I need the medallion you have, Victor.' Victor thought about this but then took it from his pocket and gave it to one of his guards to hand over to Finch. Finch took it in his hand and looked intently at the front of the plaque, trying to find any clues that would help him now. It didn't matter how much he inspected the relic as there were no signs at all to indicate where to look or what to do. He looked up at the sun and held the medallion up by the chain so that it hung loosely. As he did so the artefact started to swing to and fro. It was behaving in an odd way. No wind or unintentional movements of Finch's hand could have forced it to behave in that way. He held it at arm's length and let it continue to dance in the Welsh morning air.

Eventually the movement slowed until the whole pendant was slanted to the south as if being manipulated by an invisible thread. Finch looked at the direction it was pointing. He had expected the pendant to point to the head stone but it wasn't. It was pointing towards Carn Meyn or the Rock of Stones. It was a rocky outcrop overlooking Bedd Arthur and one of the main sources of the bluestones that are so prevalent at Stonehenge.

Finch whispered to himself, 'Of course; what better place, to be watched over by King Arthur up on a mound of bluestones and a place which no one would think about excavating.' Without saying a word, he followed the tug of the pendant and headed toward the outcrop. The others watched him and followed slowly. The closer he got to the stones the more intense was the pull from the chain. He hastened his pace until he was standing alongside the stones. The stones were enormous. They were at all different angles apart from four that stood apart and vertical and one that looked like a lintel of one of Stonehenge's stones that now rested on the ground. There didn't seem to be any particular pattern. The chain was almost being held horizontal to the ground. Finch placed the medallion on the ground to see if it would be attracted like a magnet toward the Grail, but it was still.

Finch picked up the medallion and thought until his head pounded. He had remembered something about the village of Maenclochog, which roughly translated meant 'noisy - stones' and was close by. Maybe that had something to do with it. Maybe the resonance of the rocks could help? He took a rock and struck it hard against the stones and there was a definite ringing sound. He hammered a few more times and the same thing happened. He tried it on the standing stones and the sound grew louder, like the sound you get when a wet finger is rubbed gently against the rim of a fine wine glass. Finally, he tried the fallen flat lintel stone and it was louder still. Finch knelt beside it and struck it again. He needed a steadier platform, so he placed the medallion down on the stone to enable him to ground himself more substantially. As soon as the medallion touched the rock the sound amplified many times over and it sung out over the valley and made one's bones rattle inside the body with the sonic bursts emanating from the stone. Victor, who was visibly getting irritated before this discovery, became more interested and walked toward Finch. He knew he was onto something and he didn't want to be too far away when anything of any importance occurred.

The hum from the stone was jaw shuddering. Finch stood and watched and as he did so the rocks in front of him began to crack and hiss. The resonance amplified by the medallion had triggered something deep within the stones and they began to move. Like an intricate jigsaw, rocks rose and fell and moved sideways and out until right in the centre of the outcrop there was now revealed a small opening with steps leading down into the heart of the stones and the Preseli Mountains.

Finch picked up the medallion and placed it back around his neck and made his way toward the entrance that had just been revealed. 'Guillaume! Not so fast, I think I should be beside you.' Victor held out his hand and the guard placed a large Maglite torch in it. Victor in turn threw it to Finch. 'Here. You'll need this.' Finch caught the torch and shone it down the shaft. 'Kris, you come with me. Karin, you stay up top. Is that alright with you?' he asked Victor sarcastically. Victor ushered him forward with a hand gesture and both men made to enter. Victor turned to one of his security men. 'Stay here. If the door closes, get help. If you see either of these two emerge before me, shoot them and the girl.' The guard acknowledged Victor and made a deliberate gesture of showing Kris and Finch his Glock pistol from under his jacket. With that, Finch, Victor, Kris and Victor's two armed guards entered the doorway slowly. As they descended the steps Finch shone his light to illuminate the way, aided by the lights the two other guards carried.

'Touch nothing – it may set a trap off,' Finch called back and turned to ensure everyone understood. Victor looked pensive; Kris watched Finch intensely and was just waiting for a chance to clean up Victor and his guards, who both looked terrified.

The steps curved round slightly to the right and descended for about thirty feet and led to an open stone chamber. At the far end, was a stone ledge about three feet off the ground built into the wall. On the ledge was a long shield adorned with a faded red cross on the front and a long sword, still as hard and bright as the day it was forged. No web or animal had dared to touch it, no rust or algae had blemished it. On the wall were torches. Finch indicated to Kris to light them up and the room was now filled with a flickering yellow glow. In the middle of the ledge was a small stone container made from the same blue stone that Finch had struck earlier. Finch approached the sword and picked it up by its handle. It was perfectly balanced, light as a feather

263

and sharp as a razor blade. The pommel on the handle had a cross emblazed on it and round the cross was written – 'TESTIS SUM AGNI' (''I am a witness to the Lamb''). Finch churned his mind and the name of William de la More, Grand Templar Master in 1304 sprang to mind. It was written that William had been given the weaponry of Joseph of Arimathea and it was this that encouraged him into the Order of the Knights Templar. This was the weapon. He must have protected the Grail until he died. The others, apart from Kris, looked suitably unimpressed and for a moment Finch had forgotten about the stone box in front of him. That was until Victor prompted him. 'Guillaume. It is a wonderful sword, but it is not why we are here!'

Finch placed the sword back with great respect and then squatted before the box. He inspected all four sides and checked for potential pressure plates and trap doors. The others were on tiptoes behind him, craning their necks to try and glimpse what was inside. Gently, Finch grasped the lid and applied enough upward force to move it. It shifted without too much effort and slowly he removed it completely. He placed it down on the ledge and peered into the box. Inside was a brown hessian cloth wrapped around an object. It was loose and brittle and as Finch moved the fabric it fell apart. He didn't know what to expect, but as the hessian dissolved away to dust, there in front of Finch was a shining chalice. He could only see part of it, but it shone out, bathing Finch's face in a haze of gold. Finch reached inside the box and lifted the goblet up, pulling the remaining cloth aside. Finch gasped and swallowed hard and as he did so he was overwhelmed with the spirit of God. This was confusing as he had been trying to convince himself that this was just an object made by flesh and blood and not divine. But seeing the Grail, this chalice used by Jesus at the Last Supper, the relic that so many had searched and had died for, a relic that Finch had shaped his lives immortal over and over, was now in his hand and it was magnificent. It wasn't heavy and was made of the same gold-like material as the Ark and the medallion; it was inlaid with four blue sapphires around its base and unlike all the other artefacts it was as smooth and flawless as anything he had ever seen. Finch cradled the Grail in his hands and tears welled in his eyes. Kris, glimpsing the relic, fell to his knees and was overcome with emotion.

Victor stared at the Grail. His eyes blazing with greed and lust. 'Is that the Grail?' he asked, his voice breaking. There was no answer. 'Guillaume! Is that the Grail of Christ?'

Finch looked up at him through his watery eyes and whispered that it was. Victor stepped forward and held out his hands.

'Give it to me. Now!' Victor demanded. Finch wanted to make a run for it but it would have been pointless. With every sinew of his being he didn't want to give Victor the Grail, but what choice did he have, and it would not profit anyone if he and Kris died now. Kris' teeth grated together and his eyes flared with hate toward Victor. Finch flashed a look at him begging him not to be foolish. Finch stood and handed it to Victor who snatched it without a thought.

'You know it is not divine. It was made like so many other mystical relics by a race we do not know and do not understand, thousands of years ago. Yes, Jesus Christ may have used it, but it is just a cup. All that we have believed in for so long means... nothing.' Finch was trying to throw Victor off the scent. Victor stared at the Grail; his face illuminated by the gold glow.

'If that is so, Guillaume, if that is what you really believe, why do you look to weep? Who cares who made it, and who is to say, Guillaume, that God Himself isn't an entity we don't understand, that may be of flesh and bone but capable of amazing things. What I know, is that Christ existed and He used this and with it comes unfathomable power for eternity and if you didn't believe that, then your Templar heart wouldn't be so empty now. And now that power is mine. It has been my destiny and now I have fulfilled it.' Victor nodded to his security guard and he gave Victor a bottle of water that he had brought along. Victor unscrewed that top and discarded the lid and filled up the chalice with water. 'The water of eternal life, Guillaume. Do you know I have killed you so often, but tonight I will do so for the last time. Though in truth, nothing will be as satisfying as watching you burn at that stake all those years ago. I saw the anguish and the terror on your face and I laughed as you died.' Victor whispered in Finch's ear, 'You have wanted vengeance ever since, as it haunts you to this day. But I have won, Guillaume, and I will watch you burn once more. For when I drink this and become immortal, the souls I kill cannot be reborn. You will die, Guillaume, forever. Tonight, the line of regression ends and you will all die.'

Victor held the Grail in both hands and placed his lips on the edge of the cup. As he tipped the chalice Kris shouted out. 'I wouldn't do that if I were you, Victor.' Victor stopped and turned to Kris. He was about to ignore him, but there was something in the tone of his voice, which made him hesitate.

'Why would that be?' he asked. Kris stepped forward.

'You are about to drink from a cup which is beyond Holy. What do you think will happen to someone with a soul as black as yours? It is well documented that lesser men have tried to drink from the chalice and have evaporated into dust as their soul was not worthy of such a prize. And your soul is as dark as they come. So, go ahead and do us all a favour, and vanish!'

Victor stopped. He was no fool and knew the stories and he had seen enough strange things in the world not to be so quick as to disregard such urban myths. He lowered the chalice from his mouth and his expression changed. He didn't want to give anyone else the ability to gain eternal life but he knew that if the stories were right, it could possibly kill him.

As he went through the scenario in his mind, Kris who had stepped forward to deliver his speech so eloquently earlier was now close to the sword that Finch had held. He had said how beautifully made it was and Kris was a warrior monk. His skills were instilled into his very fibre. The two guards were armed but their weapons were holstered. Victor never felt the need for weapons as he had protection and was more than capable of looking after himself.

Victor mulled over his quandary.

It was now or never for Kris as Finch was still distraught at handing over the Grail to Victor. Kris grabbed the sword and whipped around in a furious whirlwind. It was wonderfully weighted and easily maneuvered and in his hand, it was deadly. The sword ripped through the first guard's throat without breaking momentum at all. The guard recoiled back holding his neck as blood pulsed out of the gaping wound. The rear guard instinctively went for his gun, but Kris had performed a figure of eight movement and had planted the sword deep into the man's neck and down on to his chest. His blood loss ensured he was dead before he hit the floor.

The speed of Kris' actions meant no shots were fired and so no one was any the wiser above ground and Karin would be safe. Kris swung the sword round and placed the point at Victor's throat. Finch jumped forward and prised the Grail from Victor's hands and protected it in his arms, wiping away the blood smears that had splashed on to it with his cuff. There was silence.

'We must kill him, Jake, but we must do it for eternity. Let us send his soul to Hell, so that there is no coming back.'

Finch and Kris looked at each other; they knew it was the right course of action. Victor laughed out loud.

'You cannot kill me. And even if you do, you will never stop me. I will return. You are just prolonging the inevitable. You don't really think you can destroy my soul.' His anger had now started to build up. 'You think you can destroy me, Templars. I have always been stronger than you and I will rise again. How dare you!'

Kris shot a look at Finch and crunched the pommel of the sword into Victor's face, knocking him clean unconscious. The action had eased the pressure of the situation and meant they could now think with clearer heads.

Finch held the cup in front of them. 'I'll drink from it. Then I'll kill Victor and his soul forever.'

Finch was just about to take a drink when Kris placed the sword on top of the cup to prevent him from doing so. Finch looked shocked and thought Kris had gone power hungry as well, but a look into his eyes told Finch that Kris had better intentions. 'Guillaume. You can't drink it. I have never doubted your soul, but recently, since our visit to the cave, you have been in turmoil about what to believe. I have never doubted, Guillaume, and my soul is pure. I have lived my life for this moment; I will be safe. I should take this burden.'

Finch knew that what he said made perfect sense. 'But with it comes immortality and great responsibility; this isn't a burden you should take lightly,' Finch whispered.

Kris smiled at Finch. 'Do you trust me, Guillaume?' asked Kris. Finch smiled back and placed a hand on Kris' shoulder.

'Always.'

'Then trust me now,' replied Kris. 'No man has the right to live forever and no man would want to. I have been alone for many hundreds of years and never let anyone get close to me. My quest is mine alone, I don't want to do this for eternity and I am not adept enough to carry a burden that Christ would have carried.'

268

'But Christ wasn't immortal!' interjected Finch.

'He lives even now. Maybe not in the flesh but in everything else. I must drink the water. I must kill Victor and then, my friend, I must kill myself.'

Finch stared at Kris in horror. 'What do you mean kill yourself? That's crazy. It's not an option Kris!' Finch shouted.

'It is our destiny. We are dealing with things that only one man has ever managed to deal with and he was killed by man. We have found the Grail. But to prevent any evil laying claim to God's power and extinguishing His light we must close the circle. It is for you, Guillaume, to leave your own trail, so that once again we can be the guardians of the faith, Warrior Monks. And meet in a future life and follow the trail you have left, so we may still be the protectors and custodians of Christ's relics.'

Without a further word spoken, Kris took the Grail from Finch and finished the water. His arms went limp and hung by his sides and then he lifted his head and opened his eyes. They were glowing. He seemed to radiate a tangible light. He handed the chalice back to Finch.

'It is incredible. I feel Him; with every cell in my body, I feel complete. He exists, Guillaume. And whatever gave form to this Grail and gave it to Christ is a wondrous being, he is a god. He is God.' Finch knew that Kris was telling the truth, he could also tell that he was re-affirming to Finch that his faith should never have been in question. The two men embraced and laughed through their tears.

Finch placed the Grail back in the box gently. As he did so there was a large bang and Finch whipped round to see Kris looking at him in a strange way and then dropped to his knees. Behind him on the floor was Victor holding one of the guard's Glock pistols. He was leaning up against the wall, nursing a bloodied nose and a deep gash to his chin. Finch immediately went to the aid of Kris but Victor stopped him. At the same time the guard who was topside rushed in, gun at the ready. Victor held his arm out to be hauled up and the guard did so, holstering his own firearm. Kris was bent over, holding his stomach and blood weeping through his shirt, the sword, resting on the ground beside him.

'It is never over, Guillaume, until I say it is. Now get the Grail and give it to me,' Victor ordered. Finch turned and lifted the Grail and handed it to Victor. Victor looked inside the Grail to see it was empty. 'You threw away the water!' Victor shouted. Finch nodded staring at the floor. 'Get more water!' he screamed at the guard who promptly sprinted up the steps to the car. 'You think you can beat me now, TEMPLAR. And you dare to strike me! Know this, Templar, that as the blood drains from your pathetic body you will watch me drain this cup and be witness to a new age for mankind. I was Pope — I was the instrument of God's will here on earth, therefore my faith is unquestionable. I have nothing to fear! You look surprised Templar – Oh yes, I have faith, we just choose to manipulate it in different ways. You will see what my power will accomplish as I send you to the void. So, stay alive just a little longer.' Victor stepped back as he heard the rushing footsteps of his guard with a bottle of water. He kept the weapon and his gaze on Finch and held the Grail out as the guard filled it up. He was fixed on Finch. What he didn't see was the strength returning to Kris and his hand grip the handle of the sword.

With the chalice filled once more Finch took a step back. As Victor raised the goblet to his lips, Kris tilted the sword's tip up and into the groin of the guard from his kneeling position behind him. The guard screamed in agony as the point of the blade went through his crotch and deep into his abdomen. Finch saw his chance and lunged for Victor. Victor was in two minds whether to drink the water or shoot the weapon. That moment of indecision was all Finch needed and two hands against one was no match and the gun was eased out of Victor's hand and now Finch had control. He aimed the Glock at Victor as Kris returned the Grail to the box and then removed all the other weapons from the guards who were either dead or dying.

'But I shot you? How are you still alive?' Victor asked and then it dawned on him. 'The water – you drank the water. It saved you?' He looked amazed and incredulous.

'God is on our side, Victor. You lose. It is over,' Finch said.

Victor laughed. 'It is never over. The game will begin again, Guillaume, and we shall all play once more.'

'No more!' Kris shouted. 'No more. Tonight, Clement, you shall sleep in the shadows to return no more upon this earth. May God have mercy on your rotten soul.' Then Kris raised the sword and held it to Victor's heart, placed his hands on the pommel and drove it deep.

The blow was good and true and death came swiftly. Victor slumped down against the wall and as Kris withdrew the sword, Victor's empty eyes watched as the blood flowed out of his wound and down his shirt. Finch and Kris looked on. They were united in their hate against Victor and they looked on as the fire in his soul slowly extinguished. This time the white tunnel didn't appear, just darkness, and recognising this, his eyes filled with a split-second of horror. A look that sent a chill down the spines of Finch and Kris. Finch knew Victor's Soul had gone. His body was now an empty vessel. Victor was now dead. All that remained of that once malignant and terrifying beast was a vacuous carcass, hollow and devoid of any spark of life.

Finch looked at Kris. 'It's over. We've won.' Kris knelt down and wiped the sword's blade clean on Victor's jacket and stood.

'Almost, Guillaume. It is now time for me to bid you farewell, my friend. I don't want to live for eternity and I have enjoyed our adventure, but man is not supposed to harness such power. I don't want it. Keep the secret safe, Guillaume. Use your imagination and skills to leave a trail so that if we are called to protect these relics again, we can. We have done what we were born to do, and what we have always given our lives to – protecting the Holy Grail and upholding God's will.'

Finch looked at Kris. He knew he was right, but he had enjoyed being Guillaume de Beaujeu once again and remembering what it was like to have a reason for being. He also didn't want to lose his friend. He had got used to Kris and his odd ways, but he knew he was loyal and earnest and as was proved, pure in thought and deed. Finch struggled to get any words out. Kris could see how hard it was for him.

'Guillaume. Don't be sad. We will meet again. I will find you and we will remember. And no doubt you will be as awkward a bugger to convince as ever. We have an intangible thread which will always connect us and we will laugh again. You, me and Renaud. Say goodbye to Karin from me.'

Finch embraced Kris and tried to control his emotions. As he did, he whispered in his ear, 'Non nobis, Domine, non nobis, sed nomini tuo da gloriam! Obviam ibimus denuo (Not unto us, O Lord, not unto us, but unto your name grant glory! – We will meet again).'

They parted and Kris shook his hand and smiled. 'Now go and leave me to do this here. I am not alone. I am in the presence of Christ and could not think of a better place to die.' Finch smiled and turned to the Grail.

From his notebook he tore a piece of paper and scribbled on it. 'Guillaume de Beaujeu, Thomas Bérard, Renaud de Vichiers. Knights Templar. Always.' He slipped it under the stone box away from sight. He pulled the Grail out and kissed it tenderly, placed it back inside. He then turned to Kris and as he made his way out grabbed his shoulder and squeezed. There was nothing more to say. Finch slowly trudged up the stairs of the chamber and left Kris to die.

Finch exited the dark of the chamber and his eyes adjusted to the light. He saw the keys to the Land Rover and stooped to pick them up on the way out. The hillside was bare and the wind had picked up a little. He looked across at the tomb of King Arthur and wondered what he would have made of all of this. Suddenly Karin shouted from the car. The guard had plastic-cuffed her to the steering wheel, preventing her escape as he ran to the aid of Victor. Finch made his way to the vehicle and as he retreated from the opening with the medallion around his neck, the stones began to creak and wrench and slowly formed the original structure, once again concealing the secret beneath it to be hidden from man for as many years again.

He looked round and whispered to himself, 'Goodbye, Kris.' And with that he made his way back to the Land Rover and to explain to Karin all that had just occurred.

CHAPTER 37

Finch and Karin went back to the hotel and spoke for hours about the morning's events and the past few days. It was a cathartic moment each needed. Later that afternoon they parted company. Karin went back to London and Finch to his cottage in Wales. He needed time alone and took the chance to make a detailed account of the past few weeks. It had been so long, coupled with the discovery of the Holy Grail, that he had almost forgotten about the Great Library of Alexandria he unearthed in Oman. He needed to take stock of his own emotions. Losing Kris and finding Karin. He had re-awoken fears and images from the past and needed to know how to deal with the knowledge he now possessed. He had to ponder on what he was going to tell the Sultan; after all, he was going to contact him at some point. Should he tell him the truth? The Sultan had been more than helpful, and in fact the whole mission would have been impossible without his assistance. That said, there was still something Finch distrusted about him. Not necessarily him per se but anyone with the knowledge of the Grail directly. It was a mystery which had to remain just that. A mystery. So, he decided that he would tell the Sultan that the Grail's path went cold. That the caves in Tayos were a red herring and that Victor was killed by Kris in Ecuador, which put an end to the quest. That's all he needed to know.

In time, the Sultan contacted him and met with Finch in London. The Sultan was informed by Finch of the demise of Femi and Varni. But as far as Finch was concerned did not disbelieve his story and he wished him well on his way, giving him an Omani khanjar dagger made of solid gold as a gift and a thank you for his efforts. He was a good ally.

Finch also had to decide what to do with the medallion and how best to leave a trail that would allow him and other Templars to retrace their steps should they be called to protect the Grail once again. He was caught in two minds. If he kept the medallion, he would be responsible for it. It would be a huge burden, and when he died what would become of it? Lost in time. He was never going to return to the caves or the Grail, so why did he need it? He would have liked to spend years looking through the Library, the Ark of the Covenant and the metal caves and then maybe visit the Grail. But that would arouse suspicion and then the secret would be out. He couldn't tell anyone. Man would want ownership and then the troubles would begin. So, it all needed to remain hidden.

He didn't want it. He decided that it should be returned to the Guardians of the Ark. They had looked after it for an eternity and had only the best interests of the relics in mind. So, he would return it from where it came. Maybe he thought that in doing so, the guardians would be aware of who and what he stood for, and so perhaps in later years they would be willing to help the Templars once more if they came for assistance, and thus a trail would be left. Finch struck while his iron was hot and booked a flight to Ethiopia and reserved a room in the Sheraton. He then sent a text message, 'Hey Karin. I don't suppose you fancy a trip?' This was still a Templar mission and he wanted some company. Besides Karin was as involved as he was. Now he just wanted to get some fresh air and clear his head.

As he shut the door to the cottage, he kept expecting to see Kris and his heart sank when he realised that Kris was dead. Finch walked down to the beach and up the path leading to the sandy cliffs overlooking the bay. It was a beautiful day. There were a few large clouds dappled across the sky and the sun battled its way to poke through. The wind was firm but warm and it rinsed through Finch like a cleanser. He sat on the edge of the cliff and stared out to sea watching the waves dance on the water's surface. On the far horizon the clouds were thicker and where the sun shone through them, looked like God's fingers caressing the ocean delicately. The world was alive. The birds sang a loud tune and busied themselves with their daily routine. People walked along the sand. Animals foraged, the sun bathed the earth and sea and the wind blew all loitering fears and worries from the air. The smell of the sea and countryside filled Finch's nose and head. He felt alive.

Seeing the world now as it was and thinking back to all that he had experienced, Finch knew that there was a God. He didn't care how or what He looked like, but he knew that something out there was looking after us all and creating a man like Jesus and calling Him His son, he knew that it would increase hope, love and comfort. Finch felt proud and happy that his soul was complete once more. He was a warrior monk, a Templar, a Knight of the Faith and his work was done, for the moment. Now, he just needed a holiday. His phone pinged and broke his reverie. It was Karin replying to his text, 'Always. Where we going boss?'

He smiled and texted back, 'Ethiopia, for a start!'

Finch and Karin travelled to Addis Ababa and then on to Axum. He managed to liaise with Badger once again, to his delight and chartered his old plane. When they reached the chapel, the guardian who had given him the medallion recognised him instantly and the welcome he received this time was rather more cordial than the Western bar brawl last time. He invited them both into the side room of the church and stood inspecting Finch and Karin. Finch sighed a big sigh and smiled at the guardian. In a mark of respect, he bowed his head in acknowledgement of the guardian's position as protector of the secret of the Ark. The man returned the bow and with one look acknowledged that Finch had come in peace. He removed the medallion from his neck and placed it reverently into the waiting palm of the priest.

'Thank you,' Finch said clasping his hand around the priest's. The priest looked at the gold necklace and returned it to his neck.

'No. Thank you for returning this to me and for doing what needed to be done.' He leant forward and kissed Finch three times on the cheek.

'May I ask you one thing before I go?' Finch asked. The priest nodded suspiciously. 'I come from a long line of Warrior Monks, Templars, Protectors of the Faith. We are the same. One day I will die, but one day when needed, I will return and may need your help once more. We all carry this scar.' Finch pulled up his sleeve to reveal the mark he had on his arm. It was the Templar cross. He continued, 'Some may have eyes of blue like mine, these are our marks. I returned the necklace to you as you are the guardians and have been for hundreds of years, but our paths may cross again, and I need you to pass on our meeting throughout the generations of guardians to come so that if that day comes, you will be ready.'

The priest bowed his head to Finch and with a soft grin said, 'It will be done.' The two men embraced and Finch and Karin made their way out of the chapel.

Waiting for Finch at the runway was Badger. 'You and the fine filly done, old chap? No marauding hordes baying for the blood of an Englishman this time?'

Finch laughed. 'Not this time, old boy. Come on, if we make it back before sunset, I'll buy you any drink you want.'

'You'll regret saying that old bean, I have impeccable taste — and it don't come cheap. Ha!'

'And - OLD CHAP - less of the filly if you don't mind or she may very well geld you!' Karin said pointing at the characterful man.

'Right you are, Me Lady - that tells me! I likes to be put back in my box now and then - let us be orfl!' Badger shouted.

They climbed aboard the old plane and thundered into the Ethiopian sky toward Addis Ababa.

Finch left Ethiopian soil feeling light, as if a weight had been physically removed from his shoulders and his soul.

'It sounds like it was quite an adventure the last time you were here,' Karin shouted over the noise of the engines.

'More like a bum clenching white knuckle ride if you ask me', Finch replied, recalling how close he and Kris had come to being soundly beaten.

'So, what now?' Karen asked.

'France. It is the best way to close this loop.'

The plane landed in Toulouse. He was Guillaume de Beaujeu of Rocamador. He had decided to hire a car, take a short break and explore the region to see if it answered any questions and see if it jolted any memories within Karin's mind. Besides, he liked the wine and cheese and it all aided with the rest and recuperation he wanted. He had never been before and when he got there, he was astounded by its grandeur. After a good night's rest Finch and Karin climbed the steps to the top of the cliff and overlooked the view offered to him down the valley; it was marvellous and they could feel their soul's pulsing. They both felt incredibly at peace with themselves. They spent the rest of the day exploring all Rocamador had to offer; it was fascinating. The town rose in stages up the side of a sheer cliff face on the right bank of the Alzou that runs between rocky walls 400 feet in height. Flights of steps ascend from the lower town to the churches. One of the buildings was a pilgrimage church of Notre Dame, rebuilt in its present configuration from 1479, containing the cult image of a wooden Black Madonna reputed to have been carved by Saint Amator himself. The ancient subterranean church of St Amadour extends beneath St Sauveur and contains relics of the saint. On the summit of the cliff, stands the château built in the Middle Ages to defend the sanctuaries. A few shops and hotels make up the rest of the town and tourists flock from all over the world to visit. Throughout the years English kings have plundered the town and Richard the Lionheart stayed there after the Crusades. More importantly it is steeped in Templar legend.

It was late afternoon and Finch and Karin headed for the small 12th century church of St Michael. It was bijou but covered with wonderful, covered frescos.

Finch sat quietly and said a prayer for Khalifa and Kris in the atmosphere of the old chapel. They proceeded further into the underground Chapel where, hidden deep within one of the paintings, was a coat of arms. A shield in quarters. Two quarters housing the Templar red cross and two, a rampant black lion with an upturned crown around its neck. Finch took a picture of it and looked around the walls for more clues. On the back of one of the pillars near the base, carved in the stone, were three letters: 'GDB'. Guillaume de Beaujeu. He called Karin over. 'Check this out.'

Karin knelt down and saw the initials. 'That's you. So long ago.'

Finch smiled and traced his fingers over the inscription. He straightened and removed an envelope that he had placed in a sealed plastic bag and wrapped it in a cloth, from his pocket. It recorded who he was and named the Sultan, Ethiopia, Ecuador and Tayos and Guillaume de Beaujeu. The few details would be enough to pique an interest but not enough to give too much away to the uninitiated. He decided to hide the cloth package in the chapel as it would be a place that he would seek, given the right information. It was all a little bit hopeful but what else could he do? He had no idea that all this would have happened to him in this life, so who was to say what would be the course of events in the next.

'What's that?' asked Karin.

'Just leaving a trail of breadcrumbs. I just hope I am clever enough next time round to know what the hell I am talking about,' he said shaking what he had in his hand at Karin.

They entered the chapel and he hid the cloth behind a loose stone high in the wall behind the pillar. It was well concealed and was as good a place as any, and if it was found, wouldn't make any sense to anyone.

He just wished Kris could have been a part of it but was pleased that he was able to share it with Karin. She was indeed Finch's soul mate. In Karin he had found a friend who was loyal, funny, intelligent and brave and he knew that this experience had changed her and together they were set for a few more adventures before their time was up.

There was just one last thing Finch needed to do. He sat at the table in his hotel room and removed some writing paper and a fountain pen from his bag. He was going to take some time to himself and take a holiday. It would be fair to say that he was quite taken with Oman and while he was there, just maybe he could take another quick peek at the library he found. Well, it was worth a try.

'To His Royal Highness, the Sultan of Oman...